# PURSUIT OF LOVE

Reaching out, he stroked the ends of her hair with his fingers. "Was it worth it?"

"What?" she said, trying to concentrate on the conversation as his hands moved from her hair to massage her neck.

"Our careers," he said quietly. "Was it worth destroying what we had? Our friendship? Our support? Our closeness? Our love?"

She scooted to the other end of the couch, out of his touch. Her body was crying out for him and she didn't think she had the power to resist. "That's such an unfair question."

Xavier moved closer to her, prodding her to cradle herself in his arms. She gave in and rested her head against his chest. "Allow me to answer first. It wasn't worth it for me to hold on to the anger I felt toward you. It wasn't worth it to see how I hurt you last month. It wasn't worth the time we've wasted being apart. It's not worth it to continue to be apart."

Before Danielle could figure out what was happening, he leaned forward and placed a soft kiss on her lips.

# Doreen Rainey

*Pursuit of Love*

**BET Publications, LLC**
http://www.bet.com
http://www.arabesquebooks.com

ARABESQUE BOOKS are published by

BET Publications, LLC
c/o BET BOOKS
One BET Plaza
1900 W Place NE
Washington, DC 20018-1211

All Kensington Titles, Imprints, and Distributed Lines are available at special quantity discounts for bulk purchases for sales promotions, premiums, fund-raising, and educational or institutional use. Special book excerpts or customized printings can also be created to fit specific needs. For details, write or phone the office of the Kensington special sales manager: Kensington Publishing Corp., 850 Third Avenue, New York, NY 10022, attn: Special Sales Department, Phone: 1-800-221-2647.

First Printing: July 2005

10 9 8 7 6 5 4 3 2 1

Printed in the United States of America

*This book is dedicated to my husband, Reginald. You continue to offer unwavering support, and I couldn't imagine living this life without you.*

# Chapter One

Her lips parted slightly as she exhaled a slow, sensuous sigh. Desperately trying to curtail the scream that threatened to escape, she lightly bit down on her bottom lip. If the golden touch of his hands could be bottled and sold, there was no doubt in her mind that she stood to make a small fortune. The power of his touch had the ability to make her forget her own name.

As he gently massaged her breasts, her nipples stretched the thin silk material of her white, lacy negligee. The warming sensation of pure satisfaction slowly trickled from the top of her head, down her spinal cord, through her legs, to finally settle on the heels of her feet. But as magically as his hands performed, they only accounted for half her pleasure.

Nothing could compare to his magnificent, amazing tongue. That one body part could easily be declared a lethal weapon. She was not sure where he had learned such remarkable techniques, but men around the world could learn a thing or two from him. Starting with small, circular motions around her ears, he whispered words of love and affection as he continued down her neck. Between his tongue and the touch of his hand, it was possible that this was the day that she would be driven insane.

Licking, sucking, and gently pinching, he continued his methodical assault, moving lower and lower. His descent remained unhurried and focused, sending her into a spiral of anticipated uncontrollable pleasure. When the magic tongue circled her navel, the tickling sensation made her fully arch her back, not wanting to miss the slice of heaven he was giving to her.

As he continued his teasing plunge, the expectation of what was to come nearly drove her body wild in ways she'd never deemed possible. Her palms were sweaty, her legs became rubber, and her breathing was so erratic she found herself gulping for air. Finally, the warmth of his breath caressed her most private part and she stopped breathing altogether. Eager for the gratification only he could provide, she clenched the covers on each side of her and closed her eyes to accept every ounce of pure bliss he so freely gave. Just when she couldn't take another second, he stuck out his tongue and . . .


Danielle Olivia Kennedy sat straight up and her eyes popped wide open. Glancing from left to right, she frantically touched each side of her. Nothing. No one. The empty space in the bed confirmed it. She was alone. The darkened room was eerily silent except for the dramatic heaves in her chest as she tried to catch her breath.

Placing her hand across her heart, she felt it pounding at triple speed. Small beads of sweat formed on her brow and she focused on slowing down her breathing and reducing her heart rate. Once she regained some semblance of control, she shifted uncomfortably in her bed, realizing there were other moist areas of her body besides the sweat on her forehead.

Hugging herself, she didn't need to close her eyes for the image of him to come into focus. She easily recalled everything about him. The face. The body. The hands. The tongue.

Usually, her dreams faded from memory when a new day dawned. But tonight, every single, minute detail remained vividly clear. With the emotional, sensual feelings that the dream evoked, the longing and need it conjured up should have carried over into her waking hours. Instead, she felt nothing but annoyance and agitation.

Throwing the covers back, she stomped across the room, not bothering to put on a robe over her silk shorts and camisole top. Sliding her feet into her slippers, she fussed and cursed under her breath. *What is wrong with me? He's only been back in my life for two weeks. Two weeks! How could he have crept into my subconscious? Invaded my dreams? Taken over my nights?*

Softening her steps once she started down the hallway, she tiptoed down the flight of stairs to avoid waking her sister, who was sleeping just a few short feet away. Using her hands as a guide in the dark, she reached the first floor, turned the corner, and headed toward the back of the house. Passing the living room, dining room, and a home office, she stepped onto the tiled floor and flipped the light switch in the kitchen.

Adjusting her vision to the bright, glaring light, she rubbed her temples to massage away the beginning of a headache. Opening the cabinet above the sink, she reached for a glass and filled it with water from the cooler in the corner. Hoping to quench her thirst, she took less than a minute to empty the glass. Quickly refilling, she started gulping down water again. Feeling as if she'd run a marathon, she poured herself a third glass of water and wondered if anything besides him could extinguish the flames burning inside her.

"What's wrong, Danielle? What are you doing up?" Tanya said. "It's almost three o'clock in the morning."

Surprised by the sound, Danielle jumped, spilling some of the water down her nightshirt. "Damn," she said, grabbing a few paper towels and dabbing the front of her top. "Sorry, sis, did I wake you?"

Tightening the belt on her robe, Tanya Kennedy stood in the doorway, watching her baby sister dab the water as if her life depended on it. She'd been sound asleep when she heard noises in the kitchen; the fact that the burglar alarm did not go off meant it could only be Danielle. "Don't worry about me. The better question is, what's going on with you?"

Finishing the rest of her water, Danielle set the glass in the sink. "I couldn't sleep."

Opening the refrigerator, Tanya grabbed some grapes and took a seat in one of the chairs surrounding the wooden table. "That much is obvious. The question is why."

Danielle tossed the soaked paper towels in the trash and shrugged. How could she explain that erotic dreams had driven her out of her own bed?

"Nervous about tomorrow?" Tanya asked, when Danielle didn't say anything.

*Nervous.* That one word couldn't even begin to describe the emotions she was feeling in anticipation of her upcoming lunch appointment. Fear. Panic. Dread. Scared beyond belief. What happened later on that day would have a lasting effect on the rest of her life.

Whatever the result, she just hoped she could accept it. The bottom line was that she'd done all she could. Given it everything she had. The outcome was completely out of her hands. But tomorrow's event wasn't what drove her from her bed in the middle of the night.

Hazel eyes. Smooth almond skin. Strong arms. Muscular legs. Killer abs. Amazing hands. Fantastic tongue. That's what sent her running into the kitchen hoping to find something that would cool her body. That was a fact she wasn't ready to admit to anyone—even her sister. If

Tanya thought that her appointment tomorrow was the reason, then so be it. "I guess so."

Pulling several grapes off the stem, Tanya popped a couple in her mouth. "Try not to worry. You said yourself you nailed the screen test. They'd be foolish not to want you."

"Well, in case you didn't know, the industry is made up of fools," Danielle said, breaking off a bunch for herself.

Removing the scarf on her head that was beginning to come undone, Tanya set it to the side and her cinnamon hair began to unwrap, resting loosely on her shoulder. "And when did you become so cynical? If I remember correctly, you never doubted yourself—or your ability to get what you wanted."

Danielle agreed 100 percent. Over the years, she'd had to fight hard for everything she wanted. The problem was that she also fought *everybody* to get it. Taking a seat on the opposite side of the table, she said, "We've seen how far that got me."

The sarcastic comment didn't need an explanation and Tanya hoped to reassure her sister and give her a vote of confidence. "That was a long time ago."

"Some people never forget," Danielle answered quietly.

Studying her sister's expression, Tanya couldn't believe that Danielle actually questioned whether she could achieve her goal. The realization threw her off. This was the fist time Tanya recalled Danielle worrying about her ability to handle a situation. Danielle *always* got what she wanted. "I'm sure things will work out."

Rising, Danielle threw the empty grape stems in the trash and headed back to her room. Stopping just short of the door, she turned back to face her sister. "I hope you're right. Because if they don't, I have nothing left."

Tanya watched her sister disappear down the hallway. When Danielle had arrived almost two weeks ago, Tanya never doubted whether she would get this role. Danielle had experienced a rough time lately, but Tanya had never known her baby sister not to bounce back. She had an innate ability to fight to make things go her way. Sometimes the attitude that came along with that personality trait turned people off, but surely she could recover from that.

But listening to her now, Tanya started to have second thoughts. If things didn't work out for her sister, was she going to be able to handle it?

Sliding back under the covers, Danielle glanced at the clock on the nightstand. Almost four A.M. Punching her pillow, she lay down and forced her eyes shut, willing her body to fall asleep. Since she had arrived at her sister's house, her nights had followed the same pattern: dreaming of him. Based on experience with the Dream, it would be at least another hour before her body returned to normal. That was how much time she needed for the tingling, warm, erotic sensation to filter its way out of her body.

As she straddled his body, her brown eyes stared down at him, full of passion and power. The flickering lights from the candles scattered throughout the room reflected off her glistening body, eliciting a shimmer from her bronze skin. The sweet aroma of vanilla wafted through the air, mixed with the natural scent that distinctly belonged to her. Her dark brown hair, barely grazing the tips of her shoulders, was pushed back off her face and a little sweat moistened her skin, giving her a sexy glow.

Her eyes hypnotized him as they stared at his, filled with longing and adoration. With her riding him to a rhythm created just for the two of them, their bodies melded together like the perfect pieces of a puzzle. Her fingers, expertly massaging his chest, sent ripples of raw, sensuous pleasure throughout his entire being.

His heart raced at breakneck speed as she breathlessly whispered words of endearment. Accustomed to being in a position of power, he was rendered powerless by her ability to give him exactly what he needed . . . craved . . . desired. Her perfect face, her amazing body, and her captivating expression of pleasure blended together to send him into a state of euphoria. Just when he thought he couldn't take it any longer, his body constricted and he screamed her name in all-consuming satisfaction.


The screech of the alarm invaded his mind and Xavier Johnston practically jumped out of the bed, tangling himself in the covers. Several seconds passed as he frantically glanced around the room, trying to get his bearings. Then it hit him. He'd been dreaming—again. Pounding the button to shut off the maddening buzz from the alarm, he flopped back down on the pillows, running his hands across his face. He felt his heartbeat at every pulse point on his body; his blood pressure had to be pushing the limits.

"This has got to stop," he said to the empty room. His breathing, labored and deep, sounded as if he'd just run a race. Lifting the sheet, he peeked underneath. The hardness staring back at him made it quite obvious how real the dream seemed to be.

Throwing back the covers, he grabbed his sweats off the back of the chair and his sneakers from the closet. Hopefully, he could work off some of the tension that had built up inside of him. Tension that hadn't been there until she walked back into his life—just two short weeks ago.

An hour later, Xavier stood in the center of the double-sized shower stall, allowing the water to pelt his body with optimum pressure from the six shower heads positioned at various parts of his body. The three-mile run, which was designed to help him relax and push her out of his system, failed miserably. Glancing down, he realized he was no better off now than he was when he had snapped out of the dream. Her legs. Her breasts. Her beautiful face. The alluring eyes. They were like snapshots that kept replaying over and over again.

Closing his eyes, he determined to concentrate on other things. If he could just focus on something else, he could get her completely out of his mind. It shouldn't be too hard. There was a long list of topics that he could focus his attention on. The slew of business meetings he had this week. The dinner he had planned with his brother tomorrow night. Taxes that he needed to file. A visit to the dentist he needed to schedule. Anything was better than thinking about her. This was exactly what he needed to put her out of his mind. Out of his dreams. Opening his eyes, he gazed downward and cursed. It just wasn't working.

Every night he closed his eyes, and every night she showed up, making it impossible to sleep through the night. Every time he crawled under the covers, it only took a few minutes for her to make her appearance. How could it keep happening?

Seven hours. That's how much time he'd spent in her presence the past two weeks. That didn't even equal a full workday. But it was just enough to set his entire being off balance. His mind wandered during meetings throughout the day, causing his colleagues to have to repeat themselves. At night, his body betrayed him. His behavior mirrored an inexperienced teenager consumed by a lack of self-control. The entire situation seemed ridiculous. At thirty-two years old, he was far removed from his high school days.

Searching his mind, he tried to recall the last time a

woman had affected him this way. Was he fifteen? Seventeen? Nineteen? Suddenly, the woman's face came to him—and that released another slew of expletives. It was the last time he was with her—two years ago.

Moving so that he was fully under the spray of the water, he turned the knobs to change the temperature to ice-cold. This physical and mental reaction to her was the last thing he wanted. He didn't need another round with her. She was arrogant, egotistical, conceited, bigheaded, overconfident, full of herself, vain, smug, snobbish and an all-around pain in his derriere. She defined complicated. Epitomized complex. Characterized difficult. And the last thing he needed at this point in his life was a complicated, complex, difficult person. A professional relationship with her was barely conceivable. But a personal relationship? That would be like shooting himself in the foot.

Turning off the water, he stepped out of the shower with renewed confidence in his ability to get her out of his thoughts. He had no intention of developing anything with her on a personal level. He'd been there, done that, and he had no desire to experience that again. Moving his eyes downward one more time, he sighed in frustration. Now if he could only convince his body.


Danielle stood at the entrance of the restaurant, saying a final prayer. As it was unseasonably warm for late February in Washington, D.C., she took advantage of the bright sunshine, carrying her cashmere coat instead of wearing it. Just before entering, she briefly closed her eyes, utilizing a technique she had learned many years ago. Visualization.

Every time she went after something big, she'd go through this process. And nothing was bigger than this.

By constantly seeing herself already where she wanted to be, she'd hope to influence the Higher Power to work things out to her advantage.

After several seconds, the picture in her mind became abundantly clear. A nondescript building in the northeast section of the city. Fifty thousand square feet of space, fully equipped to handle the production of television shows. Outfitted with the latest technology to produce top-notch quality programming, the soundstage was perfect to play host to *The Fashion Design House*, a half-hour weekly show that focused on fashion, designers, and the goings-on in the world of haute couture.

The set, designed to give viewers an insider feel for the fashion world, had enough space for a runway to showcase the upcoming season, a comfortable conversation pit with oversized furniture to interview special in-studio guests, and bleacher-style seating for a small studio audience. It would be the hottest new show on All Entertainment, the cable channel that reached more than twenty million homes.

Opening her eyes, Danielle released a slow breath. Landing the job as host would be a major coup for her. Not only was it a fantastic opportunity, it would signal the resurrection of her very dormant career. This role would put her name back in the game and her face back in the spotlight.

Unfortunately, making her dream job a reality was ten times easier said than done. If it was all about qualifications, Danielle would be a shoo-in. Style? She had it. Fashion sense? No doubt about it. Talent? Unparalleled. Beauty? Without question. The ability to carry this show to the top of the ratings chart? Easy. After all, Danielle Olivia, as she was known years ago, had been a highly sought-after fashion model for more than ten years. If she understood anything in this world, it was fashion.

Starting her career at age sixteen, Danielle never lost her confidence, her stride, or her looks. Now almost thirty—old by industry standards—she could still model a new line of clothes down the runway with the best of them.

In her prime, Danielle had commanded upward of twenty-five thousand a show for strutting her stuff for Chanel, Gucci, Prada, Dolce & Gabbana, Phat Farm, and Sean John. During fashion weeks in New York and Paris, Danielle would model for several high-end designers, making close to seven figures for runway work alone. With all that income, one would think she would be living on easy street. But life has a funny way of slapping you in the face, especially when spending habits outpace income.

Exotic vacations, homes in Paris, New York, and Los Angeles, and more clothes than she could ever wear became absolute necessities for Danielle. Diamond jewelry, hosting expensive parties, and enjoying nights on the town continuously cut into her finances. It was nothing for her to hit the VIP room of the hottest club in the city she was in, spending five figures in one night. Not to mention the seven cars, the furs, and her ever-present entourage. Years ago, she had found it next to impossible to travel without her hairstylist, manicurist, masseuse, and seamstress. She was a bankruptcy waiting to happen. But money was only half of Danielle's problems.

With her reputation as a control freak and pompous diva, Danielle had more personality conflicts than anyone in the business. Toward the end of her career, it was a challenge to come up with a handful of names of people who actually enjoyed working with her. As word of her temperamental ways made the rounds, the jobs started to dry up way before her time. Temper tantrums. Demeaning treatment of others. Demanding ways. They were witnessed by everyone within twenty feet of her. Photographers, designers, other models, and the press. Bets were starting to be placed on how long it would take before she became obnoxious on her latest assignment. The last few years she worked, she'd even been banned from a few designers' shows. As beautiful as she was, her backstage antics just weren't worth the cost to the designers.

Michelle Ford, her agent since she started modeling, tried over and over again to convince Danielle to chill out if she wanted to continue building a solid career. Michelle had been in the business a long time and had seen many models come and go. If Danielle wasn't careful, she would disappear from the scene and no one would care.

Claiming to be a know-it-all, Danielle refused to heed her advice. Believing the fashion industry should be glad to have her, she didn't see the need to change her behavior. Danielle couldn't imagine that a time would come when she would not be in high demand. When someone would tell her no. That moment arrived sooner than anyone expected.

Danielle's agent reached a point where she couldn't even call in favors to get her client work. And the fallout from that was major for Danielle. Not only did it destroy her modeling career, it did irreparable damage to her reputation. What should have been a smooth transition from the runway to a career in television or the movies suddenly became impossible for Michelle to maneuver. No one would touch what had, at one time, been the cornerstone of her client list.

With her finances depleting fast and jobs becoming few and far between, Danielle slipped into denial. Ignoring what was happening to her career, and trusting her business manager to always keep her account balances in the black, Danielle kept living as if everything would be okay.

Refusing to acknowledge the shambles her life was becoming, Danielle's wake-up moment came only after she started receiving phone calls from creditors. Needing to hold on to her lifestyle, she made one final desperate move to get her finances back in order. But when that backfired, she had no choice but to face reality. The career she had built, the lifestyle she'd become accustomed to, it was all over. And there was very little she could do about it.

Panic-stricken, depressed, alone, and broke, she ultimately swallowed her pride a year ago and moved back home with her parents—in Dankerville, Georgia. As the line goes, "It was the best of times; it was the worst of times." The worst because her modeling career tanked. The best because it gave Danielle much-needed time to take a closer look at herself.

Living in the country, she found the hustle and bustle of the city a distant memory. With nothing but time, Danielle was able to fully evaluate her life—where she'd been, what she'd done, and why she'd done it. The soul searching had been difficult—but worth it. She emerged from her hiatus stronger and more committed to her career than ever. With her newfound hope, she embarked on a journey to rebuild her reputation and repair and restore the personal relationships she'd damaged along the way.

Some had said that she had no choice but to change her ways—and that might be true. But the change in her was genuine. Her biggest challenge lay in convincing everyone else.

That's why landing this job was so important. To say that her entire comeback hinged on this one show would be an understatement. Michelle did a lot of fast talking and called in several markers to get the audition. Refusing to take this opportunity lightly, Danielle spent every waking moment preparing for her audition. Her voice, intonations, looks, posture, facial expressions, and hand gestures had all been practiced to create the image the TV executives were looking for.

There had been no immediate feedback on her performance. She'd read twice, prepared two videotaped interviews, and had several conversations with the producer, director, and writers. None of the key people gave any indication about her performance, either way, but she believed she'd nailed every part of the process.

If the decision were based on talent alone, Danielle had little doubt that the part would be hers. Unfortunately, that was not the case with her. There was another major issue that plagued the final decision. One problem. One wild card. One unknown. One thing she couldn't control. It had the power to destroy her chances in one fell swoop. She called it the X-factor.

Pulling her compact out of her purse, she held the mirror into the light, making a quick final check of her face. Having been styled by some of the best makeup artists in the world, Danielle recalled every trick of the trade. She could highlight, contour, line, and blend like a professional.

Her brown hair, streaked with highlights, had been pulled back in a clip. With it resting just above her shoulders, she'd decided to give her hair a break from the tracks and extensions that had become a staple in her life at the height of her career. It looked, and felt, healthy and shiny.

Her honey-beige skin, high cheekbones, and brown eyes stared back. This face had graced the cover of *Vogue* five times, *Glamour* seven times, and the *Sports Illustrated* swimsuit issue once. In all, she'd gotten covers forty-four times over the years. It was a career most models only dreamed of.

Snapping the compact shut, she squared her shoulders, giving herself one final pep talk. *You got this, girl. You are the perfect choice for this job. This show was made for you.* Without further hesitation, she stepped through the doors of the restaurant, ready for whatever came her way. That included the major unknown. The X-factor. Xavier Johnston.

# Chapter Two

Xavier sat in the far corner table, near the back of the restaurant. From the moment she walked in, he couldn't take his eyes off her. With her height, attitude, and sense of presence, she commanded attention when she walked into any room. Today was no different. Without looking around he would wager a bet that several men gave a look of appreciation. The womens' expressions would range from admiration to curiosity to jealousy.

As she checked in with the hostess, Xavier thought her olive-green wool pantsuit was a perfect selection for the weather and for her. She could make the most ordinary clothes look extraordinary. The hostess pointed his way and when she turned, her eyes locked with his. Flashing a confident smile, she made her way to him.

A flash of her body straddled over him swept through his mind, and he quickly thought about his taxes. The last thing he would allow her to do was turn him into one of the men unable to get past her gorgeous face and that stunning body. Getting his mind back on the purpose of the meeting, he began to regain a sense of control. The only time he would spend with her revolved around business—and he had every intention of keeping it that way.

As the executive producer of *The Fashion Design House*, he'd actively participated in the search for its host.

Auditioning fourteen well-known women in the fashion industry, he thought it quite obvious from the first reading who the front-runners were going to be. The fact that Danielle was one of them had him firmly situated between a rock and a hard place.

When it came to Danielle Olivia Kennedy, there were countless examples that he personally knew of, and from people in the business, about her shenanigans. Designers. Photographers. Crew members. The list went on and on. Danielle had driven just about everyone she came in contact with crazy. She'd even had the audacity to almost ruin one of the live fashion shows he directed on network television. People in the business had long memories. They never forgot. And neither did Xavier.

The gift of burning bridges came as naturally to Danielle as a three-foot putt for Tiger Woods. That's why people associated with this show were surprised when Michelle managed to wrangle an audition for Danielle. No one connected with this project thought enough of her to want to work with her, and some even questioned Xavier's decision to allow her to get this far in the process. What people didn't know was that he'd waited years for this opportunity. This situation was the perfect chance to shell out the ultimate revenge. He intended to pay her back for all she'd done. There was only one flaw with his plan. Danielle Kennedy was a showstopper.

Once the lights came on and the cameras started to roll, no one could argue that she was a natural. The minute the director gave her the cue, she commanded the stage and captured her audience. Her presence consumed the space. Her speech was impeccable. Her facial expressions on point. Her ability to own the segment could not be denied. Danielle was, by far, a solid candidate for the job.

At five feet ten, with a million-dollar smile and a perfect

body to match the perfect face, she left no mystery as to why the camera lens loved her so much. Unfortunately, the camera was the only remaining thing in this business that did. How receptive would fashion industry insiders be to appearing on the show if she was the host? Would they grant interviews? Let her into their showrooms, their homes, their lives? Or would it be a case where old grudges would rule? If that was true, then the show would be doomed to failure.

Difficult wouldn't begin to describe how people felt about Danielle. And how could Xavier blame them? He understood exactly where they were coming from, for he was one of them. One who found it difficult to forgive and next to impossible to forget.

Watching her follow the hostess to the table, Xavier felt that the time to make a final decision was running out. All the players had weighed in with their opinions, leaving it up to him to not only make the final choice, but to deliver the news. With production scheduled to begin in two months, he ran the risk of losing advertisers and sponsors if he didn't name the face of *The Fashion Design House*.

As she made her final approach, he straightened his back and leaned forward. The moment of truth had arrived. And nobody was more ready for this than Xavier.

"Michelle said you wanted to see me." Standing directly in front of him, she offered no pleasantries. As soon as the words were out, she regretted them. Not the best way to start off a meeting with the one person who had the power to give her a job. She didn't mean for the words to come out so harsh, but coming face-to-face with Xavier Johnston caused her to be on edge. Not just because he held the future of her career in the palm of his hand, but because he'd been the man who invaded her dreams.

Even with him sitting down, she was drawn to his

almond-colored complexion, deep-set eyes, full lips, and slight dimples she knew to be visible only when he laughed. When they first met, she'd thought him to be the most handsome man she'd ever come across—and that hadn't changed.

Xavier smiled but didn't balk at the borderline-professional greeting. A cheerful hello wouldn't have fit her personality—or their relationship. While she could be cordial at times, when it came to the two of them, politeness wasn't at the forefront for either of them. And since this meeting was about business, that suited him just fine. They'd already taken a stab at a personal relationship, and the phrase "complete disaster" didn't do it justice.

In the beginning, their courtship had been extraordinary. Clicking on every level, both had a drive for success and a passion for enjoying the ride. As their feelings for each other developed, he found it challenging to reconcile the Danielle Olivia that walked the runways with the Danielle Kennedy that shared his life. A photographer would rant and rave about her behavior at a shoot, yet she'd come home to him and be the sweetest, kindest person, one he'd grown to care deeply about.

As things began to unravel between them, their careers blossomed. In the end, he was too driven and she was too selfish. Together, they were like oil and water. The final straw had come almost two years ago when she put one of his productions—a fashion show airing live on network television—in jeopardy by arguing with a French designer, threatening not to go back onstage if she didn't get what she wanted. The fact that they were going back on the air in one minute didn't faze her.

Xavier's request for her to just do what the designer wanted in order to keep the show moving went unheeded by her. She didn't care who or what they put onstage—but it wouldn't be her if she didn't get her way. The fact that she would treat him with as little respect as she treated others pierced his heart with more pain than he'd ever experienced. That day, he walked away from her and put a wall around his heart.

Now, as she laid her coat across the back of the chair, the scent of her perfume floated through the air, and Xavier understood the reason for his sleepless nights. The woman could stop traffic dead in its tracks during rush hour. An image of her naked body burst in his head, revealing every physical attribute that he knew to be true. The birthmark on her arm. The tattoo of a small butterfly on the small of her back. Those were what made his dreams so real—too real.

Clearing his throat, he fought where his thoughts were taking him, choosing instead to focus on the purpose of this meeting. "Have a seat."

"A gentleman would pull the chair back for me." The challenging words were only said to get a rise out of him.

At her abrupt tone, Xavier's lips curved into an unconscious smile and he silently thanked her. That funky attitude she possessed immediately pushed the erotic dreams out of his mind, reminding him that in the real world, he couldn't stand her. She always had to be the one in control—even when it wasn't necessary. "Must you always be this difficult?"

Pulling the chair back herself, Danielle tried to relax, giving a small tentative smile. She hadn't meant to be so rude, but all she could see was what his mouth had done to her in her dreams. Annoyed that she couldn't put the vision out of her mind, she reacted the only way she knew how. Rudely. Taking a deep breath, she looked around for the waitress. Anything to avoid looking at him. She didn't think she could handle that at this point. He looked too good and flashes of her dreams made their way into her mind. Regaining her composure and confidence on the outside, she finally focused her attention on him and the words he spoke.

"How are you enjoying your stay in D.C.? I understand you've been staying with your sister the last few weeks." The statement sounded innocent enough, but it was just a setup for his next words. "I didn't think you'd ever get her to speak to you again, let alone let you stay in her home. Didn't you ruin that relationship, too?"

The sarcasm in his voiced screamed for Danielle to give him a piece of her mind, but she desperately needed this job. So instead of telling him off, she motioned for the waitress and ordered a club soda with lime. Placing the napkin in her lap, she ignored his last words. "You requested my presence for a business meeting, so here I am. Why don't we stick with that topic?"

Xavier didn't know if her avoidance of the topic of her living quarters had more to do with her relationship with her sister or the fact that she wasn't interested in discussing anything personal with him. Having never met her sister, he'd heard through the gossip mill that they had a big falling-out a few years ago and many thought they'd never recover from it. The fact that she was letting Danielle stay with her could be a sign that the relationship was on the mend. Had her sister found a way to forgive Danielle for all the wrong she'd done?

"I arrived a few minutes early and took the liberty of ordering for you," Xavier said, explaining why there were no menus. "Grilled chicken over romaine lettuce. No cheese, and dressing on the side."

Danielle tried to hide her surprise that he remembered. Taking that as a good sign, she tried to relax and drop her guard—just a little. If she had to place a wager, she'd put her money on him ordering some kind of grilled chicken sandwich with pasta salad instead of fries. "Thank you."

"I don't believe it," Xavier said, adding sugar to his iced tea. "Have I ever heard you speak those two words in all the time I've known you?"

The mocking tone in his voice sent Danielle's blood pressure rising, eliminating any chance that they could be civil to each other. But sparring with him wouldn't help matters. This was his show. His meeting. He held all the cards. Without responding, she patiently waited for him to get to the point of this meeting, which was whether she had a job or not.

Judging from his malicious remarks, it couldn't be good news. For the first time since this process had started, Danielle felt in danger of not getting the part. Wiping her palms across her pants to dry the sweat, she felt her heart flutter and her confidence start to waver. All the bad blood between them didn't matter. Getting the best of him with tasteless digs was no longer important to her. When she decided to pursue her career again, there was no doubt that she'd have several helpings of humble pie. If she was serious about this job, there was no better time to start than the present. Taking a deep breath, she said, "Michelle said that you had made a decision about who would host the show."

Xavier raised a brow. The words were spoken so softly he almost didn't hear her. Was that humility? Taking note of the change in her body language, he observed the slight rocking back and forth, her fingers tapping quietly against the side of her purse, and the diminishing of the self-assured smile she had exhibited only moments ago. Motions so minute that someone who didn't know her might miss them—but not Xavier. He knew her too well. Everything about her said "anxious" and "concerned."

Shaking off the feelings of compassion that began to

creep up, he remembered his plan and moved back to the task at hand. "We have."

Xavier didn't say anything further and Danielle could barely sit still in her seat. In the past, she was always the one with the power. The demand for her services was so high she could name who, what, when, where, and how. She could get away with just about anything—and usually did. That was no longer the case.

Her star, which had shone so bright, had greatly dimmed over the years. She was now at his mercy. Judging by the limited information he was willingly giving her, he obviously planned to milk this moment for all it was worth. "Decisions like this typically come through my agent. Why didn't you call her? Why the special meeting with just the two of us?" she asked.

Xavier leaned forward, taking a sip of his tea. The stall tactic had accomplished its goal. While her smile still held firm, he could tell she was fuming on the inside. She was not used to having no control over a situation.

With a slight smirk, he paused a few seconds before speaking. "I thought it would be best if you got the information from me."

Danielle swallowed deeply, but worked to maintain an expression of indifference, ignoring the flip-flop in her stomach. Not only was not knowing driving her insane, but the way he wore that dark blue button-down shirt across his broad chest was also causing her anxiety. She never had to worry about attracting good-looking men—she'd dated plenty of them. But there was something intangible about Xavier that never ceased to draw out the most fundamental womanly parts of her. That was what had drawn her to him all those years ago.

It was no secret that she and Xavier had had a very public, professional falling-out that had led to their breakup. Everyone, including Danielle, said that the blame rested clearly on her shoulders. They both claimed that they would move on with their lives with no hard feelings. But that agreement, so easily made, was near impossible to carry out.

Xavier hadn't been forgiving at all. As a matter of fact, he'd been just the opposite. In retaliation, he'd been instrumental in keeping her out of work for the past couple of years, practically blackballing her from fashion shows, the big screen, and the small screen.

The fact that she had made the short list for hosting this television show astonished her. She'd literally dropped the phone when her agent presented her with this opportunity. Michelle, always a straight shooter, pulled no punches when she gave Danielle the lowdown on the new series and everyone associated with it. Xavier had initially voiced his opinion, saying that he wanted to keep Danielle as far away from this project as possible. But out of the blue, he changed his mind, giving Michelle the news less than a week before the auditions started.

Danielle didn't fool herself into thinking that Xavier would be objective about her and what she could bring to this show. She only hoped to impress him enough that he would be able to see past their personal differences and recognize what a great contribution she could make to the series. As she listened to him today, something inside said her opportunity was slipping away. "I know that things have been messed up between us. But I hope you won't let that influence your decision. I would be a great asset to this show. I know I could do a great job. All I need is a chance."

The heartfelt words were spoken with such emotion and depth that Xavier's heart started to soften. He almost believed her sincerity. Almost.

"I don't have to tell you how impossible people think it is to work with you," Xavier started. "Nor do I need to

share with you that most of the guests we want to profile
on the show have had run-ins with you somewhere along
the line."

Sitting back in her chair, Danielle shook her head in
disgust. "Is there a point to your monologue or not?"
Immediately berating herself for letting him get to her,
she just couldn't find the value in rehashing her past.
Unfortunately, he always brought out the worst in her.
Deciding to apologize for her rudeness, she started to
speak again when he cut her off.

"See, Danielle, that's the problem," he said, just as the
waiter placed their food in front of them. Her salad, and
his plain grilled chicken sandwich with orzo and vegetable
pasta salad, went untouched by both of them. "That's why
no one wants to work with you. That sharp tone and smart
mouth have always been your downfall. Here you stand,
the first opportunity you've had in years to prove to the
world that you're not the rich, spoiled, supermodel diva
who alienated just about everyone in the industry, and
you still have an attitude—a chip on your shoulder. That's
why you and I don't get along."

"It hasn't always been that way between us." In fact,
Danielle recalled a time when they'd gotten along quite
well. However, business ultimately became the most important thing—especially to her. What had started out as
a promising relationship turned into a struggle for
power, and they ended up loathing each other.

Looking back, she wondered, if she had done things
differently, what would have come of her and Xavier?
But there was no use in worrying about that spilled milk.
That ship had sailed years ago. There wasn't an option
to go back and change the past to give them a future.
Even if she could, Xavier wouldn't want to.

Every opportunity that had come her way in the past two
years was shut down by him. He'd used his influence to her

detriment with designers, casting agents, producers, and directors. Danielle didn't consider it a stretch that he was the number-one factor in her not having worked since she'd moved to Georgia. This led to the question that had been on her mind since she'd arrived in D.C. Why was he giving her a chance to audition for this job?

Xavier chose to ignore her comment about their personal relationship. "I want you to know, Danielle, that this decision was not mine alone. I solicited input from a variety of sources to be sure that the person selected would have the support and respect of the production staff, as well as satisfy our audience."

Danielle remained silent, trying to decipher where the conversation was headed.

Casually taking a bite of his food, Xavier seemed to be in no hurry. "My director, Stanley Dyson, had the pleasure of working with you in St. Barts when he directed the television special for the *Sports Illustrated* swimsuit issue. I'm sure you remember that shoot. You held up production for four hours because they didn't have the proper brand of bottled water on the set. Can you guess what his answer was when asked about you hosting?"

Danielle sat stoic, her expression unreadable. She'd officially landed in hell. Before she got the answer about the job, which she now assumed would be no, Xavier was going to make her sit through a laundry list of her past sins and the people she'd alienated along the way.

"Our head writer," Xavier continued between bites of food, "Dana Hanes, contributed to the pilot of *Along Came You*. Do you remember her?"

When she didn't respond, he shrugged at her obvious loss of memory and decided to answer for her. "She's the one you demanded script changes from on an almost daily basis during the taping of the show." Pausing for effect, he said, "Of course, it didn't get picked up by the networks. Something about an out-of-control ex-model that had been cast in the lead."

Staring at him with unwavering eyes, she felt it was useless to dispute any of his claims. Everything he said was true. To say she personified all of the negative characteristics associated with the word *diva* would be an understatement. She'd created more turmoil and developed a list of enemies that would prevent anyone from coming back into the business. Xavier seemed intent on reminding her of every last one of them.

"I'm sure you remember Selena Morino. She was the head stylist every year you did the Dolce and Gabbana shows. She hated you then, and when I spoke with her two days ago to finalize her contract for styling the host of this show, she still hated you."

When she arrived this morning, Danielle had prepared arguments to try to change his mind if his answer had been no. But on hearing him now, it became abundantly clear that there was nothing she could say. As a matter of fact, he'd probably made his decision before the auditions began. This was just his way of exacting his final revenge. At least now she understood why he changed his mind and allowed her to audition.

The last time they worked together, it had been she who'd held all the cards—the upper hand. Danielle knew it. Xavier knew it. The crew who worked on that television special knew it. She'd embarrassed him that day in front of all of them. This was his payback.

"You remember Bob Samper, don't you? He—"

"He was owner of the catering company I had fired when I worked as a correspondent for *Fashion News*," Danielle said through gritted teeth. Without touching her food, she prepared to leave. Scooting back in her chair, she reached for her purse. "I get your point, Xavier. I didn't get the job and you want to rub in all the reasons why I'll probably never get another job. Well, thank you very much for that walk down memory lane, but believe it or not, I have taken that walk all by myself the past two years."

He started to respond, but she cut him off before he could get a word in.

"I screwed up. Are you happy now? I've said it. I screwed up my career." Her voice started to crack and her hands shook, but she fought to keep any other signs of her emotional state at bay.

With a few of the other customers glancing their way, she refused to have a breakdown in front of him. "I've set colleagues against me, and I've estranged everyone who helped me build my career. I even messed up my chance with you. But you know what? I've changed. I'm not that same person who yelled at stylists, had people fired, demanded flowers in my dressing room that had to be flown in from halfway across the world. I'm sorry you can't see that."

Danielle paused to catch her breath and Xavier leisurely raised his hands in front of him and clapped slowly and loudly, his expression indicating that all she said didn't affect him at all. "That was so moving. So emotional. However, according to the people who have already been contracted to work on this show, you *are* the same person. They have nothing that demonstrates to them that you've changed. *I* have nothing to show me that you've changed."

Her shoulders sank and her head dropped. Not in defeat, but in complete exhaustion. What more could she do? What more could she say? The chance she needed to prove herself would never come. The bridges were burned beyond reclamation. With no one to blame but herself, the time had come to face the music. She was over. Done. Finished. Kaput. She'd done too much damage. Hurt too many people. Thrown one too many temper tantrums. The acceptance of this fact emotionally drained and overwhelmed her.

Standing, she put her coat on, feeling tears welling in the corners of her eyes. "Thank you for your time, Mr. Johnston. Obviously there is nothing more to say. I wish you luck with your television show."

This was the moment he'd been waiting for. Counting down the days to. This was the moment he would give Danielle a taste of her own medicine. "We've already made an offer to our host. We expect her to accept today."

The sting of his words pierced her heart. Nodding, she turned to leave. The door was less than thirty feet away. The short walk would be her final bow. No job. No prospects in the industry. No Xavier.

"This show's success hinges on the credibility and the likability of the host," Xavier explained.

Danielle turned to face him and forced a smile, interpreting his statement. "We both know, in the eyes of the fashion world, I have neither of those."

"Every person associated with the show didn't want you—and that includes me. The only reason I allowed you to audition was so that I could be the one to tell you that your career was officially over. You have more people rooting against you than you'll probably ever know. Even the guard at the security gate of the studio didn't look forward to having to check you in every day."

His tone softened slightly and Danielle swore she heard a "but" coming.

"But the screen doesn't lie. The camera loves you."

A small ray of hope rose inside her.

Xavier hesitated. "Unfortunately, the network doesn't know if the fact that you are so controversial will help the show—or seal its fate. They left the final decision up to me."

Any hopes that were raised in her the last few seconds

quickly disappeared. This was the moment he'd been building to. The opportunity to put the final nail in the coffin of Danielle Olivia Kennedy's career. Deciding to take it like the strong woman she was, she squared her shoulders, stuck out her chin in confidence, and straightened her back. "And?"

"We offered the job to Layla Chandler."

# Chapter Three

"It's a little early for that—don't you think?"

Xavier downed the shot and signaled the bartender for another. "I've decided to start happy hour a little early."

Reggie glanced at his watch and raised a brow. "It's three thirty."

Watching the bartender fill the shot glass, Xavier shrugged. "Close enough."

"Vodka?" Reggie said, watching the clear liquid being poured into another shot glass. "Now that's definitely out of the ordinary."

The words went without a response as Xavier threw his head back and swallowed, signaling for another.

Reggie shook his head at the bartender, giving him a silent signal that his younger brother had had enough. "I don't know if that's number three or thirty, but either way, I think it would be a good idea for you to take a break."

Xavier turned to the voice, trying to recall just how many drinks he'd had. Three? Four? "If I needed a father, I'd drive across the bridge to Maryland and visit ours."

Tapping his glass on the bar, Xavier felt his patience for getting his refill wearing thin.

Gripping the Absolut bottle tightly, the bartender stood in front of Xavier. "If your friend is going to drive you home, I'd be glad to serve you. Otherwise, I'll trade you another shot for your keys."

Glancing from the bartender to his brother, Xavier rolled his eyes, mumbling under his breath. All he wanted to do was enjoy his afternoon by having a few drinks, and his brother and the bartender were going to try to mess that up. Taking his keys out of his pocket, he brazenly shook them in front of the bartender's face. Releasing his hold, he dropped them and they landed on the wood bar.

The bartender picked up the keys and handed them to Reggie. "Hold on to these."

Pulling another glass from under the counter, he poured another shot and moved to the other end to help another customer.

Reggie picked up his brother's keys and dropped them in his pocket before taking a good look at Xavier. "It's Thursday afternoon and you're sitting in a darkened bar with what is obviously at least your third drink. What's going on with you? Your message said to meet you here for a celebratory toast."

"That's right," Xavier said, drinking the shot in one fluid motion. "Welcome to my party."

Counting the glasses lined up in front of Xavier, Reggie said, "You usually don't toast good news with hard liquor."

"I can toast with whatever I want," Xavier said, sounding offended by his statement. "Now, are you going to join me or not?"

"This so-called celebration," he said, questioning the true nature of this impromptu get-together, "looks more like you're drowning your sorrows."

"What are you talking about, man?" Xavier said, raising his hands in victory with a silly grin on his face. "Of course I'm celebrating."

The last thing Reggie's baby brother was doing was celebrating, no matter how many times he said it. Whether Xavier wanted to admit it or not, something wasn't right.

Deciding to play along, Reggie ordered a beer. "So what's the occasion?"

Xavier leaned over close to his brother for emphasis. Feeling a little buzzed, he overpronounced his words. "I finally gave that woman exactly what she deserved. Taking from her just like she's taken from others."

Reggie nodded in understanding. Now the picture was becoming increasingly clear. "By 'that woman,' I'm guessing you're referring to Danielle Kennedy."

"Please," Xavier said, raising his hand in annoyance. "Don't even say the name."

The beginning of a smile tipped the corners of Reggie's mouth. So that's what this little celebration was really about. For the past two weeks, the only thing Xavier wanted to talk about was his television show. More specifically, how Danielle wasn't going to be a part of it. Pegging her as the meanest woman in the fashion industry, Xavier had gone on a personal crusade to make her pay for all the wrong he thought she'd done.

The vendetta Xavier had against Danielle sometimes confused Reggie. The business his brother chose to be a part of had its fill of manipulative, egotistical, and dominating people, but none had gotten under his skin like this woman. Reggie couldn't recall a time when Xavier had carried a grudge as deep, or as long, as the one he had for her. Xavier had almost seemed giddy at the prospect of finally putting her in her place. "I guess things went as planned in your meeting?"

"You got that right," Xavier said triumphantly. "She stepped into that restaurant looking fantastic, smelling good, wearing perfect makeup on that perfect face, and flashing a sexy smile." Xavier's voice got a little softer as his words trailed off.

Reggie watched him closely. After several seconds, any hint of softness quickly disappeared.

Xavier, realizing where his thoughts were taking him, shook them off. With an edgier tone, he continued. "I made her sit there and listen as I rolled off a list of all the people she'd ended up on bad terms with over the years. I reminded her of the times she thought only of herself. In plain and simple terms, I let that woman know that she has no idea how to foster relationships."

"Are we talking about in her professional life or in her personal life?" Reggie asked, remembering that they had shared both.

Xavier glared at his brother, appalled at the insinuation. "Why would I care about her personal life?"

Reggie shrugged. "One minute you're talking about how sexy she is. The next minute, you're talking about destroying her. I'm just trying to keep up."

"Then let me make sure you completely understand," Xavier said, signaling the bartender. "That woman built her career on the destruction of others. As a service to all who ever had the displeasure of working with her, I sentenced her to a life of unemployment.

"You should have seen her," he continued proudly. "It was truly a classic moment. She gave some speech about how she'd changed. Learned her lesson. How she was a different person, ready to rebuild her professional career. Her acting was so good at that moment she almost had me believing it. She even managed to look a little distraught when she left the restaurant."

Reggie just listened and noticed the change in his demeanor. What had started out as an attempt to smile victoriously slowly turned somber and the celebration aspect of this gathering seemed to be fading.

"So what's your problem?" Reggie asked lightly, taking a sip of his beer. "To hear you tell it, it couldn't have gone better."

"I don't have a problem," Xavier declared, sounding

as if he might be trying to convince himself more than anyone else. Shaking off the eerie feeling that started to creep up on him, he yelled for the bartender to come take his order. "Like I said, this is the time to celebrate."

To make his point, Xavier stood and raised his empty glass. The quick motion made his head light, and he quickly sat back down. Maybe it was time to switch from vodka shots to something a little less lethal.

Reggie listened to his brother's words and observed his behavior. They didn't match. "Ever since that woman walked out on you, you've been plotting and planning your revenge. Now that you've done it, you just don't appear to be as happy about it as you thought you would be."

"First of all," Xavier started, pointing his finger at his face for emphasis, "let's be clear about that so-called relationship between me and that woman. *She* did not walk out on me. *I* walked out on her—after she embarrassed me on network television. She could have done serious damage to my career. Second of all, I *am* happy. This day couldn't have gone any better."

Reggie slapped Xavier's hand out of his face and stared at his brother for several seconds, wondering if he really didn't see the truth. If what Xavier said was true, and he reveled in his meeting with Danielle, he should have been practically dancing on the tables. Yet, he sat in a bar in the middle of the afternoon, trying to drink his guilt away.

"Just admit it," Reggie said, finally breaking the silence. "You didn't want to do it, and now you feel guilty."

Older than his brother by three years, Reggie felt it was his MO to act as though he had all the answers. As a child, Xavier had looked up to his big brother like a superhero. Excelling in academics, he opted for the entrepreneurial route, starting a computer consulting firm that specialized in helping small businesses stay ahead of the technology curve.

Looking at the two of them, very few people would assume they were brothers. At six feet, Reggie was a couple of inches shorter than Xavier, and with his dark chocolate skin and the short locks in his hair, his football player's body blended with his thick muscles and healthy appetite.

"Guilt?" Xavier exclaimed. "You must have had more to drink than me. You know better than anyone that I've been waiting for years to stick it to that woman. This television show was the perfect opportunity. As the executive producer of the show, I had the final casting decision."

"You may have stuck it to her," Reggie said, "but now you regret it."

Xavier narrowed his eyes and cocked his head to the side. "Have you been smokin' something illegal? The fact that you could even let those words come out of your mouth tells me you've got major comprehension issues. Haven't you been listening to me?"

"I have," Reggie admitted. "I just don't believe you."

"There is no way I regret what I did today," Xavier said. How could he? All the hurt. All the pain. All the suffering he'd experienced because of her had finally been avenged.

Turning the bottle to his lips, Reggie half smiled. "You're lying."

"I am not," Xavier said without hesitation.

"Then why did you ask me to meet you?" he challenged.

"To join in the celebration." That statement reminded him that his latest order from the bartender hadn't been filled, and he yelled again for him.

"Yeah, right," Reggie said, not buying any part of his story. "You wanted me here to tell you that you did the right thing. To ease your guilty conscience."

"There are no guilty feelings to ease," Xavier declared.

His raised voiced told a different story and Reggie chuckled. "Then why are you upset?"

"Because you're ruining my party," Xavier said, finally getting the attention of the bartender.

"You call this a party?" Reggie challenged. "It's more like a guilt-fest."

"Will you stop saying that?" Xavier said, his agitation growing by the second. "And where is the bartender with my drink?"

"Calm down, Xavier."

"I am calm!" he yelled.

Reggie stared at his brother for several seconds, trying to gauge just how out of hand this situation could become. Suddenly, he burst into laughter.

"What the hell are you laughing at?" Xavier asked, completely confused by his behavior.

"You."

"And what makes me so funny?"

"You're either too drunk or too stupid to admit that you regret what you did today."

Xavier rolled his eyes, unable to believe that they were still on this same topic. "For the last time, I do not have a problem with what happened today."

Reggie just chuckled. "If you say so."

"I *know* so."

"Fine."

"Fine."

Xavier started to defend himself again, but thought better of it. If his brother thought he was feeling guilty over how he treated Danielle, the more he denied it, the worse that would make it for him. That's the last image he wanted to portray to his brother. Instead, he decided to change the subject altogether. "How's Melinda?"

The smile on Reggie's face said it all. "She's great. And you're not fooling me by trying to change the topic."

"Can't a brotha ask about his sister-in-law without causing suspicion?" Xavier asked innocently.

"Whatever, man," Reggie said, shaking his head in disbelief.

"What is she now, five months?" Xavier said, hoping to keep the topic of conversation away from what he'd done to Danielle.

"Six," Reggie said proudly. "She thinks she's getting big as a house, but I can honestly say I've never seen her look more beautiful. She's looking forward to dinner tomorrow night. I don't think you two have seen each other in over a month."

Reggie and Melinda had been high school sweethearts and married three years ago. She had been a part of Xavier's life for as long as he could remember. They had become like brother and sister. Melinda and Reggie were expecting their first child at the end of May.

After graduating from college, they carved out a nice life for themselves. With Reggie's computer business and Melinda's career as a corporate trainer, they were living the American dream. It was the type of life that Xavier had avoided at all cost.

The ordinary workdays and the predictable weekends. Who could survive twenty, thirty, forty years of that? Xavier had always had his sights set on something more exhilarating. With his career in entertainment, he got exactly what he wanted.

Attending film school right out of high school, he worked his way up the ladder, taking small jobs and building a reputation for delivering a quality product. Being an African-American in the industry had made his ascent three times as hard and ten times longer, but he fought his way through, proving himself over and over again.

All that work finally paid off. Respected and sought

after, he'd moved from directing to producing, and now he'd gotten the green light on an entertainment show focusing on the fashion industry. To have greater control over what he put on the airwaves, he took a big plunge and built his own studio. Less than a handful of African-Americans owned and operated their own studios.

This show would be the first project to come out of XJ Productions. Choosing Washington, D.C., for the studio location was definitely a risky move, but he believed he could make it work. Growing up in the area, he wanted to give back to his community. His studio would help him do that by employing people and offering training to young people interested in careers in film and television.

Over the years he'd experienced artistic and material success, something people in the field of entertainment didn't always achieve—black or white. Now he wanted to parlay that success into something bigger.

With all the projects that he had in the works, he should have been sitting on top of the world. Instead, he sat on a bar stool, downing shots, trying to convince his brother that he had it all together. "You're going to make a great father, Reggie."

"So will you," he said confidently.

Xavier's mouth curled into a cynical smile. "I don't think so. I'm not cut out for that life."

Not knowing whether to laugh or be offended, Reggie said, "What's that supposed to mean? What's wrong with my life?"

"Some men thrive on building a house in the burbs, having the picket fence and a family dog. I don't," Xavier said. "I'm more of a mover and shaker. Not able to settle down in one spot."

That point of view wasn't alien to Reggie. Xavier had made similar statements on more than one occasion throughout the years. Once he met someone like Melinda, all that would change. Melinda was smart, beautiful, and unwilling to put up with any of Reggie's bad habits. He couldn't imagine living life without her. "Those thoughts will all change soon enough—if they haven't already."

"Don't hold your breath," Xavier mumbled. "I haven't dated anyone for more than a few months in years—and that's for a reason. I don't need a woman getting all needy on me. Expecting me to be home for dinner. Wanting me to cut the grass."

"Doesn't matter," Reggie said. "When she shows up, you'll know it."

"When who shows up?"

Reggie answered without hesitation. "The woman that will make you think about focusing on something other than work. The woman that will make you seriously question signing on for another project that will keep you away from her for long periods of time. The woman that will have you running home for dinner, mowing the lawn, and jumping for joy when she steps out of the bathroom and shows you that the stick turned blue."

"Whatever, man," Xavier said, unable to fathom the thought. "You sound like a Hallmark card—and not a very good one."

"You say that now," Reggie said knowingly. "But you'll see. I'll be proven right."

"And I thought I was the one who had too much to drink," Xavier said. "I don't have time for all the drama that comes along with trying to have a serious, long-term relationship. It's too much of a hassle and I lack the time and patience needed to make it work."

"You had the time and patience to make it work with Danielle," Reggie politely reminded him.

Xavier started to speak, but Reggie continued before he could get a word out.

"If my memory serves me right—and I think it does—

you were crazy about her. You said that you'd never met someone so driven. So committed to her career. You even told me that her reputation, while well earned, wasn't really the true Danielle."

Xavier heard the know-it-all attitude in his voice and had a sudden urge to slap that smug look off his face. "Don't even go there with me. I am not some lovesick guy pining away for someone who epitomizes everything I don't want in a woman."

The lack of conviction in his voice told the real story. "Then explain to me why you are sitting here, feeling bad about what you did today."

"*You* said I was feeling guilty—not me," Xavier pointed out. "I did exactly what I set out to do. The last emotion I'm feeling right now is guilt."

"So what are you going to do now?" Reggie asked.

"I'm going to let you give me a ride home and then—"

Reggie cut him off. "I'm talking about Danielle. What are you going to do about her?"

Xavier wondered why his brother just wouldn't let it go. "Nothing. That part of my life is over."

"Why don't you just call her?" Reggie said.

The words rolled off his lips so casually that Xavier had to take a moment to make sure he heard him correctly. Reggie spoke as if his suggestion were the most natural thing in the world. "We have nothing to talk about. She applied for a job. She didn't get it. End of story."

"I wasn't talking about calling her about a job," Reggie explained. "I was talking about calling her for a date."

Xavier reached in his wallet and threw several bills on the counter. "Pigs would fly over hell just as it froze before I would ever ask that woman for anything— especially a date."

"Umm," Reggie said thoughtfully.

"Don't do that," Xavier moaned.

"Do what?"

Xavier's attention to this conversation was fading fast. "You know what . . . that damn 'umm.' You always say that when you think I'm BS-ing you."

Reggie just stared at him. "You said it, not me."

"Look, man," Xavier said, feeling the need to justify himself, "for the last time, I am not interested in ever dealing with that woman again. Today was about closure. She's probably on a plane heading back to that small town in Georgia to lick her wounds. If everything goes according to my plan, I'll never have to deal with that woman again."

# Chapter Four

Danielle stared out the window of the taxicab as it made its way through the streets of downtown D.C. and into the suburbs of Maryland. The late afternoon traffic already showed signs of a treacherous rush hour. Managing to hold her tears in check when she walked out of the restaurant didn't diminish how stunned she was at the events of the day. Needing some time to gather her thoughts, she spent a couple of hours walking the streets of the nation's capital. Paying no attention to the majestic monuments or memorials, she tried to make sense of all that had transpired today.

When she finally hailed a cab to take her home, she managed a polite smile to the cabdriver as she gave him the address. Once in the backseat, she leaned back against the worn leather seat and closed her eyes. The entire meeting replayed in her mind. From the moment she stood in front of him to the second he delivered the news. And just like that, all her plans for a return to entertainment were squashed. That realization killed any feeling of control she had left, and a few tears escaped her eyes. She quickly wiped them away.

Jobless. Broke. Homeless. Accurate descriptions of what her life had become. All her eggs had been firmly placed in one basket, and it got dumped. *The Fashion Design House* would premiere without her. Layla Chandler would be the one interviewing the newest designers to hit the scene. She would be the one covering the latest shows in New York and Europe. Layla would be the one to show viewers the homes of their favorite celebrity models. Layla's career would go to the next level.

Regardless of the outcome of today's meeting, she had promised to call Michelle with the news. Digging in her purse for her cell phone, she pushed the first three numbers and froze. Not ready to hear the disappointment in her agent's voice when she would have to admit that she didn't get that part, she turned the phone off and tossed it back in her bag.

Michelle had been carrying Danielle for the past couple of years. Keeping her on the roster, helping to get the few auditions she'd managed to scrounge up. But this was her last chance. If this gig didn't come through, there was no one left who would take a chance on her. The next time she talked to Michelle, the only item to discuss would be how to officially dissolve their working relationship. Highly respected in the fashion industry, the Michelle Ford Modeling Agency represented some of the top models in the world. Why would she continue to hold on to Danielle?

Out of the one thousand photos of teenagers that lined the walls of the only mall in the small Georgia town Danielle grew up in, Michelle had found a diamond in the rough in Danielle while conducting a highly publicized talent search for the next new face. Everyone in Danielle's family couldn't believe that she became the chosen one.

Under the watchful and protective eye of Michelle Ford, Danielle, scared and excited, had packed her bags at seventeen and moved to the Big Apple. Together, their success defied all that was expected. Michelle couldn't book her fast enough. The requests were coming in daily and Danielle sometimes did three shoots a day. It was a hectic pace and at the end of some days, she would be physically exhausted, but Danielle loved every minute of it.

Many had tried to warn Danielle that no one stayed on top forever, and that she should be mindful of the people she'd have to deal with on the way down from her self-erected throne. Not heeding the advice, Danielle absorbed everything that fame had to offer. She ate up the hype and publicity surrounding her and reveled in the image of greatness that had been thrust upon her.

The superstar attitude wasn't just reserved for those who worked with Danielle. Her family members had also been subject to her wrath. Constantly throwing her fame and fortune in their face, she never missed an opportunity to let anyone around her know how beautiful, rich, and successful she had become.

Her father told her repeatedly that she was ruining her career by her behavior. She responded by patronizingly telling him that he just didn't understand big business. When her sister stopped talking to her because of her treatment of family and friends, Danielle chalked it up to good old-fashioned jealousy, telling Tanya that she couldn't be held responsible if Tanya lived a boring life as a contract administrator for a construction company.

The friends who had been so dear to her before her fame fell swiftly by the wayside. Danielle just didn't have the time for unsophisticated teenagers from her high school. Traveling the world and attending high-profile celebrity events had became everyday occurrences. What could she possibly have to talk about with high school girls who'd never been out of the state of Georgia?

They say that everything that goes around comes around. That whatever you dish out will come back and smack you in the face. Both of those sayings couldn't have been truer for Danielle. When she needed her family and friends the most—at the lowest point in her life—no one stepped forward to offer support. Her father was too hurt, her friends laughed in her face, and her sister thought she got exactly what she deserved. If it wasn't for her mother, she would have had no one to turn to and no place to live.

Mable Kennedy had been her saving grace. Dankerville, Georgia was far from the glitz and glamour of New York, but that's where Danielle had sought refuge after her professional career and personal life collapsed. Instead of passing judgment on Danielle, or lecturing her on the perils of her ways, her mother just opened her heart, and her home, to give Danielle the time and space she needed to get her life back together.

When she first arrived back in her parents' home, she'd overheard several discussions about her situation. Her father didn't want to see her out on the streets, but he didn't think Danielle should be able to just step back into their lives as if nothing had happened between them. Mable stood up for her youngest child, believing that the sweet, kind, and gentle daughter they had raised was still somewhere in her. With time, love, and support, she would appear again. It took many months, but her mother was right. By the time Danielle got word about this audition, the strained relationship with her parents had been healed.

Which, at this point, was a very good thing, because based on this latest development, Danielle might be headed right back to Georgia. Right back in the nurturing arms of Mother.

All the people she'd ignored over the years, looked down upon, dissed, and treated like dirt had gone on to achieve great things and live wonderful lives. Tanya had reunited with her true love, Brandon Ware, and was busy planning her June wedding. Danielle's high school friends had gone on to become successful lawyers, entrepreneurs, wives, and mothers. Even Xavier had carved out quite a career.

Danielle didn't even have a place to live. With Tanya's wedding just around the corner, staying with her sister wouldn't be an option for too much longer. She'd only asked to come for two weeks while she completed the audition process. Racking her brain, Danielle tried to come up with one person that she could possibly stay with. Amid all the names and numbers that she'd accumulated over the years and that were still listed in her Blackberry, there wasn't one person in it that she could call a friend—except Michelle. But her agent had already done so much for her, she couldn't possible ask her for anything else.

The taxi turned off the main road and started down the quiet residential street. She should have been gathering her belongings, getting the fare out of her purse, and preparing to get out. But she didn't move. Unexpectedly, her throat constricted and she felt short of breath. Panic swelled inside and the reality of her situation hit her like a ton of bricks. The only thing she'd known her entire life—modeling—was over. What was she going to do? How was she going to make a living? How was she going to survive?

Taking deep breaths, Danielle put her hand on her chest, feeling a slight strain. For the first time in her life, fear fully engulfed her. When had she ever not had a plan? A next move? Another direction to go? Even when she lost her fortune, she thought it was only a temporary setback. Even as she struggled through the last couple of years, she'd always held out hope that things would turn around and somehow, some way, someone would give her a second chance.

Her meeting today proved that the industry—and everyone in it—had no intention of giving her anything. They had moved on without her. There were no more options. No more opportunities. No more plans. No more potential jobs. No more what-if scenarios to play out in her mind. She'd reached the end of the line. Michelle had warned her that this audition was her last chance to redeem herself. And she didn't do it—couldn't do it.

One rule in the Kennedy household that everyone had to abide by when she was growing up was church on Sundays. Danielle and Tanya would murmur and whine under their breaths every week as they put on uncomfortable dresses and patent leather shoes, only to spend the morning having to sit still on uncomfortable wooden pews. Danielle didn't remember much from those Sunday school lessons or the sermons, but there was one scripture that her mother always ingrained in both of them: "you reap what you sow."

Danielle had never paid much attention to those words. Instead, she reveled in the mantra "you reap what you take." But the truth has a funny way of prevailing. She'd sown misery, and that's exactly what she got in return.

"Miss? We're here."

Startled out of her thoughts, Danielle glanced out the window and realized they had pulled up in front of her sister's house. The crisp February air, the bare trees, the empty flower beds reminded Danielle of her current state. Dry. Desolate. Without life.

"Are you OK, lady?"

His tone was more agitated than caring, and Danielle snapped out of her daze. "I'm sorry. What do I owe you?"

"It'll be nineteen twenty-five."

Reaching inside her purse, she offered her apologies and handed over her money. She slammed the door shut, and the cab took off before she'd stepped fully onto the sidewalk. For several seconds, Danielle stood frozen in place. Everyone had been waiting to hear the results of her meeting. Her parents. Tanya. And especially Michelle. She'd disappointed them—again.

Making her way up the walk, she tried to concentrate on what she was going to do next. The quietness of the moment reminded her of how different her life was. At the height of her career, she'd had an entourage of at least seven at all times. Now there was no one.

The door opened and Danielle heard someone call her name.

"There you are. I've been waiting for you."

Danielle released a genuine smile for the first time since having lunch with Xavier. Even though it was just after four in the afternoon and Tanya should have been at work, she was here. Waiting for her sister. Emotions swirled in Danielle as she thought it nothing short of a miracle that Tanya now stood to offer her support. Of all the relationships that she'd ruined over the years, this one stung the most.

Growing up, they'd shared everything. Their room, clothes, makeup, and dreams. No one could have been happier for Danielle when she got her modeling contract than Tanya. Over the life of Danielle's career, Tanya bought at least three issues of every magazine featuring Danielle, and five of each one for which she was the cover model. She'd cheered the loudest for every accomplishment and advancement Danielle experienced. Not only had Tanya been there for her in the good times, she'd also been there when she had her moments filled with fears and doubts about her ability to make it in this business. However, their closeness ended when the fame and fortune became more important to Danielle than her friends and family.

Barely on speaking terms with Danielle for the past several years, Tanya wasn't easily convinced that her baby sister had changed her ways. When their mother tried to tell

Tanya that Danielle was no longer the egotistical person they were used to dealing with over the years, Tanya refused to believe her. Luckily, over time, Tanya began to open up her heart to her again. The past few months, the relationship that had appeared to be irreparable just a few short years ago was slowly on the mend.

Nothing made that more apparent than when the opportunity for this job came up; Danielle desperately needed a place to stay during the auditions. She just didn't have enough money to spend on a hotel—no matter how inexpensive it was. Tanya stepped to the plate, offering her a place to stay and encouragement.

Tanya took one look at her sister's face and instantly knew the answer to the question. Still, she'd held out hope. "I didn't hear from you, so I decided to come home. I wanted to be here to celebrate with you if you got it. And, well . . . be here for you if things didn't go your way."

Danielle stared at her sister for several seconds. Her bottom lip quivered and pain moved from her gut, up her chest, and into her head. The emotions of the past two years of her life gushed forward. Her expression faltered and the tears that she fought to hold in check couldn't be contained any longer.

With empathy, Tanya watched the woman who'd always represented strength, power, confidence, and success. Her rise to fame had been swift, and so had her demise. The results of that turbulent life stood before Tanya today. It wasn't a pretty sight. Her baby sister was falling apart. She stretched her arms out, and Danielle walked into them and cried.

Between sobs, Danielle verbalized her fear. "What am I going to do, Tanya? No television show. No job. No money. No place to live."

"It's going to be OK, Danielle," Tanya offered. Somehow she held out hope that her sister would land on her feet.

"No, Tanya, I really don't think it will." Always a positive thinker, Danielle firmly believed that nothing came without first believing that it would. But she was all out of belief. There was nothing left to believe in.

"Let's go inside."

Stepping into the living room, Danielle removed her coat and threw it across the arm of the sofa. Plopping down on the cushioned material, she was emotionally exhausted.

"I'm sorry you didn't get the job."

"Thanks, Tanya. But not getting the job I could have handled," Danielle said, grabbing a Kleenex and wiping her face. "It was that maniac Xavier that's got me falling apart."

"The producer?" Tanya asked. What could he have done that was worse than not giving her the part?

"You should have heard him," Danielle said, getting mad all over again. "It was as if he was taking pleasure in reminding me of my past."

"I don't understand," Tanya said.

Sure that Tanya had heard the rumors about Danielle's demanding ways, and that she had probably read an article or two in the tabloids or entertainment magazines, Danielle still was too ashamed to admit all the horrible things she'd done that Xavier listed for her. "He made me sit through a laundry list of all the enemies I'd made who are now working on this show. One by one he laid out why these people did not want to work with me. Everyone from the director to the writers to the stylists. The whole meeting seemed to give him great delight."

The longer Danielle spoke, the more agitated she became. How dare he sit there like the king of the hill, looking down on her?

"That doesn't sound professional at all," Tanya said. "Why would he do something like that?"

Danielle hesitated before answering. Tanya knew

nothing of her previous personal relationship with Xavier. They were barely on speaking terms when she and Xavier had become a couple. "Xavier and I used to be . . ."

Danielle's words trailed off and that piqued Tanya's curiosity. Sitting forward in her seat, she stared at her sister with expectancy. "Used to be what?"

Standing, Danielle began pacing the floor.

Tanya watched the display and a slow smile curved her lips. She'd never known anyone, man or woman, to get to Danielle. To have her all jumbled up, full of doubt, anger, and possibly attraction at the same time. She had a strong inkling that this was that moment. "You two had a relationship. A very personal relationship."

"What we had was a mistake," Danielle corrected. "I don't know what made me think that man could be someone I could share my life with. I can't believe we lasted as long as we did. Today just proves my point."

Tanya thought Danielle protested a little too much, but decided not to say anything. Instead, she asked, "Why did the two of you break up?"

Danielle stopped pacing and turned to her sister. She opened her mouth to speak, and then quickly shut it. Searching for the right words, she wasn't able to come up with anything that would put her in a positive light.

Noticing her hesitation, Tanya crossed her arms at her chest accusingly. "What did you do?"

Inhaling, Danielle appeared to be offended. "Why do you assume it's something I did? He's the one who obviously can't separate the personal from the business. Because if he did, I would have that part."

Tanya refused to buy into her innocent act. "Spill it, Danielle, because I know it must be a doozy if he's still mad about it and you're getting so worked up about him."

Kicking off her shoes, Danielle sat back down. "Let's be clear about this. He's obviously being the immature one. I have moved on. I am not, as you put it, 'worked up' over him. If I am worked up, it's because he lied to me. He said he would give me a fair shot and he didn't. That's petty, immature, and just plain stupid."

"The question is, does he have justification for his behavior?" Tanya said. "Which leads me back to my original question—what did you do?"

Closing her eyes, Danielle leaned back on the sofa and sighed in frustration. It was apparent that she was not going to get out of this conversation without spilling the details of her failed relationship with Xavier Johnston. "If you really must know."

"Really," Tanya said, trying not to crack a smile. "I must know."

Waiting several seconds, Danielle sat forward, opened her eyes, and nonchalantly shrugged. "I refused to go back onstage during a live show he was directing, causing the designer to threaten a lawsuit, the network to go into a panic, and the sponsors to question whether they'd put the advertising dollars in the right place. Xavier claimed it could have ruined his career."

The room fell silent as Tanya opened her mouth in awe. Shaking her head in disbelief, she searched for the right words. "Damn, Danielle. You were a bi—"

Danielle raised her hand to cut her off. "That was a long time ago. He should have gotten over it by now."

Shaking her head from side to side, Tanya half laughed. "You're kidding, right? Get over it? I don't think so. No wonder he nailed you to the wall today."

"I'd like to nail him to a wall," Danielle mumbled.

"Be nice, Danielle," Tanya said.

"He actually enjoyed watching me squirm," Danielle started thoughtfully. "Sitting across from me like he was the ruler of the world. Just because you look good, have attained some level of success, and have a little power doesn't mean you can treat people any kind of way."

Clearing her throat, Tanya raised her finger to interrupt. "Do I need to remind you of your behavior?"

"My behavior was years ago," Danielle said in her defense. "What's his excuse? It just burns me up that he sat there, with that confident quirky grin and those cute dimples, as if he hadn't a care in the world."

Tanya was surprised to hear the slight wistfulness in her voice. "Do you still have feelings for this guy?"

"What!" Danielle exclaimed. "What I have is a desire to scratch his pretty little hazel eyes out."

"I don't know," Tanya started. "It just seems to me that you're focusing on the personal stuff instead of the professional side."

"So?" Danielle said, trying to follow her sister's line of thinking.

"So maybe it's because the personal stuff is still important to you."

Danielle half laughed. "I don't think so."

"Maybe you should call him."

Gasping at the audacity of the suggestion, Danielle pretended to clean her ears. "Did you say what I think you just said?"

"Yep."

"Why on earth would I do that?" Danielle asked, confused and dumbfounded by the suggestion.

"Because it sounds to me as if the two of you have unfinished business."

The dream from last night flashed in her mind and Danielle cut her eyes downward just as her body temperature rose at least ten degrees. Ignoring the feeling, she waved off her sister's crazy idea. "Believe me when I say that Xavier Johnston and Danielle Kennedy have nothing left to discuss."

The words didn't quite sound as convincing as Danielle had hoped they would.

"Are you sure you still don't have a thing for him?"

"A thing?" Danielle asked, horrified. "Have you gone completely mad? No way would I classify what I feel for that man as 'a thing.'"

"Then how would you classify it?" Tanya asked seriously.

"What?"

"If you don't call it a 'thing,' then what would you call it? Because it's obvious to me that it's something."

"It *is* something—over!"

"Are you sure about that?" Tanya questioned.

"Absolutely."

Tanya tried to approach it from an angle she might be more receptive to. "Maybe he'd be willing to reconsider the part if you contacted him."

Danielle didn't answer right away, wondering if her sister heard her own ridiculous words. "And maybe Layla Chandler will voluntarily step down and hand me her job on a silver platter."

"You should at least call him and—"

"Forget it, Tanya. That man made it quite clear today that there is nothing left for us to discuss."

The room fell silent and the subject appeared to have been dropped. Shifting uncomfortably in her chair, Danielle decided to be proactive on another issue. Taking a moment to gather her courage, she said, "Tanya, I know I asked about staying here for two weeks and that time is up this weekend. But I was wondering . . ."

Tanya didn't have to guess what her next words would be. "It's OK, Danielle. You can stay here as long as you need to."

"It won't be long," Danielle promised eagerly.

"I'm sure you'll come up with something," Tanya said confidently. "Besides, as we get closer to the wedding,

I've been spending more and more time at Brandon's. Most of my clothes are there, and I'm only staying here a few nights a week."

"Thanks, Tanya. I'll find a way to pay you back. I promise."

"Don't worry about it," Tanya said sincerely. "What good is it to have a family if they can't help you out when you need it?"

The words touched Danielle's heart as she remembered all the times that she could have helped and she didn't. She made a silent vow to always be there when her family needed her. "How are things with Brandon? Is he ready to stand at the altar?"

The subject of Brandon Ware and his marriage to Tanya Kennedy always sparked an expression of happiness. "You know, me and Brandon can actually be compared to the situation with you and Xavier."

"How in the world did you come to that conclusion?"

"Think about it," Tanya reasoned. "Brandon and I dated and fell madly in love. He, in a truly selfish moment, lied to me, ultimately causing us to be apart for years. After much groveling and apologizing from him, I decide to give him another chance. And here we are, about to walk down the aisle."

"Nice story, but again, I ask you, what does that have to do with me and Xavier?"

"You two were madly in love. You screwed up and—"

Danielle interrupted. "And this is where the two stories part ways. According to you, the next step would have me groveling and apologizing to Xavier, begging him to take me back. And that, my friend, ain't gonna happen."

"All I'm saying is that if Brandon wouldn't have made the first move, we might not have gotten back together. Don't you want that special person to share your life with? To wake up to every morning? To always have your back, no matter what?"

The dreamy look in Danielle's sister's eyes would probably be mirrored in her own if she had the love of someone like Brandon. He treated her like a queen and always put her first. At twenty-nine, thoughts of marriage often crept into Danielle's mind. However, all those things her sister just described seemed like a distant hope for her.

There weren't any prospects—and with her current professional and financial situation, she didn't have visions of any man beating down her door for the chance to get to know her. "Maybe someday. But right now, I have other priorities to worry about."

The lighthearted conversation they'd had going a few minutes ago had quickly turned back to the matter at hand. Danielle and her future—or lack thereof. Hoping to take her mind off her problems—if just for a little while—Tanya said, "I'm meeting the girls for dinner tomorrow night. Why don't you join us?"

Without thinking about it, Danielle declined. "If I remember correctly, your girlfriends hate me."

"Hate is such a strong word," Tanya said, hoping to change her mind.

"Then how about strongly dislike?"

Tanya heard the sarcasm, but couldn't deny there was some truth to the words. "There have been some issues between you and them, but I've shared with them how much you've changed."

"I'm sure they jumped at the chance to spend an evening with me," Danielle said, rolling her eyes.

"Come on, Danielle," Tanya said, moving to sit beside her. "Don't be so hard on yourself."

Convinced that "the girls" Tanya spoke of included Christine Ware and Natalie Donovan, Danielle had no intention of changing her mind. Her past with these women had been quite checkered and she wasn't sure if she was ready to find out if the three of them could repair their broken fences. "Thanks for the invite, but I really don't think I'd be good company. Besides, they're your friends, not mine."

"And what about you? Where are your friends? You've been here for two weeks going through a very trying time. Who's been there to help you through it? Who's been there to offer you advice, a shoulder to lean on, a chance to vent your frustration?"

Danielle listened and knew that Tanya was right. But she didn't think that Tanya's friends would be the ones to fill that void. The damage had been done.

"You're right, Tanya, but who's to say that Christine and Natalie would want to be that for me?" Standing, Danielle gathered up her shoes and purse and headed for the stairs to go to her room. "I just don't think I'm ready to face them."

"Danielle, you've got to start opening yourself up to friendships. Let people get to know you. To find out what a nice person you've turned out to be."

Danielle started to argue, but then abruptly stopped herself. Why was she putting up such a fight? When was the last time she'd gone out to relax? When she was modeling, all of her nights out revolved around business. Through all of her shows and shoots, she never forged a bond with any of the other models. As a matter of fact, there wasn't one woman she could call a true friend. "You know what? I think I will join you guys."

Tanya smiled. It was nice to see Danielle finally taking a little bit of her armor off. "We're meeting them at Lenny's at seven."

"I'll be ready."

# Chapter Five

The crowd at Lenny's stretched outside the door. The soul food restaurant had become a staple in the community, offering good cuisine with a great social atmosphere. The Friday night crowd filled the waiting area and bar enjoying conversation and networking.

Nervously adjusting the strap on her purse, Danielle was haunted by second thoughts about her decision. The thought of enjoying an evening out with her sister faded as she faced reality. Was she really up to dinner with Christine and Natalie? Last night, all that talk about marriage and friendships had influenced Danielle's decision to come and hang out with the two women. Now that the time had arrived to actually do it, her courage had faded.

No one would argue, including Danielle, that the professional bridges she'd burned were beyond repair. However, those associations paled in comparison to the personal damage she'd done over the years. The two women waiting for Tanya and Danielle were at the top of that list.

Christine Ware and her half sister, Natalie Donovan, had become an integral part of Tanya's life. Close as sisters, the three of them had shared some extraordinary experiences over the years. Sharing in the happiness in the best of times, Tanya had been there for Christine when she met and married Tanya's boss, Damian Ware.

Natalie was there to help Tanya work through her issues with Brandon, Damian's brother, before agreeing to marry him. Both Christine and Natalie had been there to share in helping Tanya with all the wedding plans.

However, in the midst of all the good memories they had had together, the three always had each other's back when the rough times reared their ugly heads. Tanya offered Christine support when she dealt with her abusive past. Natalie had been there for Tanya when Danielle had turned her back on her sister and caused havoc by trying to steal Damian away from Christine.

At the height of her career, Danielle met and got engaged to Damian Ware. But as with all her personal relationships during that time, her selfishness and self-absorption caused her to put her needs before Damian's, ultimately destroying their relationship. Years later, with her modeling gigs drying up and her money not far behind, she tried to rekindle her lost relationship with Damian, hoping he would use his money to bail her out.

It was during this time that Damian had begun dating Christine. Ignoring their blossoming relationship, Danielle unscrupulously threw herself at him, attempting to weasel her way back into his life. When confronted with his courtship with Christine, Danielle tossed her nose in the air, leaving no doubt that she thought Christine was no match for her and that Christine wasn't good enough for him. Afterward, Christine and Damian almost called it quits.

Natalie and Tanya were appalled and angry at how Danielle treated their friend. Christine Ware had every right to hate Danielle—and Danielle believed she did. While Christine and Damian were able to work things out and now had a beautiful daughter, Danielle wasn't quite sure she believed Tanya when she said that Christine had no ill feelings toward her and was open to getting together in a social setting.

Pretending to want Damian back only to use him for his money had been the absolute lowest point in Danielle's life. After that, her career tanked, creditors were hot on her trail, and there wasn't one friendship she'd fostered over the years to help her through this time in her life. Stepping on everyone going up the ladder of success, she was left with no one who had her back when she rapidly descended.

Moving back to Georgia gave Danielle time to examine herself like never before. Clarity came to her and she began to comprehend why other people didn't like her, didn't want to work with her, and actually found joy in her demise. Reliving every misstep, every wrong move, every snub, every moment that she made someone else's life miserable was the hardest thing she'd ever had to do.

Professionally, Michelle tried desperately to ease Danielle back into the fashion world, but couldn't convince others that Danielle had changed. The responses were always the same: It was easy to be nice and appreciative when you were at rock bottom. How would Danielle act if she ever got back on top?

On the personal level, her family had opened their hearts to her, but as she stood outside the restaurant tonight, she wasn't sure if she was ready to find out if some of her friendships could be salvaged.

"Are you OK?"

Tanya's voice pulled Danielle out of her thoughts. "I don't think this was such a good idea. Did you tell them I was coming?"

"I left them messages that you would be joining us," she said, giving her a reassuring smile.

Danielle looked around self-consciously and Tanya didn't need to be told she was second-guessing her decision.

Danielle remembered her business meeting with Xavier.

It had been a complete disaster. Mistakenly assuming that he would focus on the present, she found him using that opportunity to put her in her place. Would Christine and Natalie do the same? Pretending that they were fine with her joining them, only to use this dinner as a chance to let her know that they could never forgive her for what she'd done in the past? "Actually, Tanya, I'm a little tired. I think I'll just go home."

"Don't be ridiculous," Tanya said, gently nudging her toward the entrance. "We're already here."

Danielle didn't respond immediately, wondering how much a cab would cost to take her back home.

Reaching out, Tanya squeezed her hand. "Danielle, I've talked to both of them about you. They know you're not the same person you were a year ago."

The words sounded sincere, but Danielle still wasn't completely convinced. "It took you years to forgive me for all my malicious comments and unscrupulous behavior. How could Christine and Natalie forgive me so quickly?"

The lack of confidence in her voice had become her trademark the past couple of weeks. Where was the go-get-'em woman Tanya had known her sister to be? "I'll admit, it might be a little awkward at first, but once we start talking about my wedding plans, everything will be just fine."

Danielle's expression remained unchanged, but on the inside, her heart sank. Tanya's wedding. Christine, the matron of honor, and Natalie, the maid of honor, probably had a thousand ideas and details to discuss. The location, the food, the dresses—and of course the honeymoon. Once again, Danielle would be the outsider. Tanya hadn't asked Danielle to participate, and with their shaky past, she didn't expect her to.

Raising her hand, she signaled the valet to get a cab. "You go on in. Have a good time. I'll see you when you get home."

"Danielle, don't go. We can—"

Danielle walked toward the curb, her decision final. "I think I'll just go home and get a good night's sleep."

The sadness in her voice tugged at Tanya's heart and she was at a loss as to what would be best for her sister. Sitting in a restaurant or giving her time alone? "If you really don't want to."

"I really don't."

Handing her the valet ticket, Tanya gave her a quick hug. "You don't have to take a cab home. Take my car. I'll have Christine or Natalie drop me off."

"Are you sure?"

"Yeah."

Taking the ticket, Danielle gave her sister a reassuring smile. "I'll be fine. Thanks for the invite. It really meant a lot to me that you would include me."

"I'll see you later."

"Later."


The bottle of wine sat in the center of the table as the foursome prepared for an enjoyable dinner. Their table, situated in the back against the window, gave Xavier the perfect view to watch people come and go. His eyes were fixated on the two women who stood right outside the entrance. With his having to determine the conversation by body language only, it appeared as if Danielle had tried to come inside, but hesitated, looking upset and slightly distraught. He wondered if the news he'd delivered yesterday had anything to do with those expressions.

It had been more than twenty-four hours since he watched her walk out of that restaurant. That meeting represented the moment she would walk out of his life once and for all. But when she disappeared from his sight, she still remained in his mind—and in his dreams.

He was driven from his bed in the early hours of the morning, and neither the five-mile run nor the ice-cold shower could diffuse the overwhelming need to be with her. The decision to go with Layla was the right choice, but he began to wonder if he'd made the right choice in how he delivered the news to Danielle.

As he'd driven to meet her for lunch yesterday, he had a spring in his step and an unshakable smile. The moment he'd been planning for the past two years had finally arrived. But now that he had put Danielle in her place, the satisfaction he'd expected to feel was nowhere to be found. He kept waiting for that feeling of joy to overtake him, but it never came. Seeing her tonight only added to that unsettling emotion. Not able to fully define the feeling, he could only wonder when it would go away.

"Xavier?"

The high-pitched voice caught his attention. How long had she been calling his name? Putting on his best smile, he lightly patted her thigh. "I'm sorry, Tina, did you say something?"

"Yes, I did," she answered, poking her lip out for emphasis. "And you know I hate when you call me Tina. It sounds so . . . so . . . normal."

"I'm sorry, *Catrina*, did you say something?" Xavier asked, trying to keep one eye on the front door.

Rolling her eyes at his sarcastic tone, she picked up her evening bag and stood. "I'm going to the ladies' room. When I get back, I would appreciate it if you would start paying attention to me. Otherwise, I'd feel like I've wasted this Dolce and Gabbana dress."

Xavier watched her make her way down the hallway. The last thing she did to that dress was waste it. At five ten and 115 pounds, she was a designer's dream. The strapless black dress that stopped at least four inches above the knee gave new meaning to the term "the little black dress."

They'd met about three weeks ago at a charity event to raise money for pediatric AIDS research. He'd been a contributor who plopped down $2,500 for a table. She'd been seated at the table beside his. After exchanging pleasantries, they danced and had good conversation. But as he was sitting with her tonight, the only thing he could think about was the woman standing outside.

Not quite sure why his mind had suddenly become occupied with thoughts of Danielle, he'd hoped this night out on the town would extinguish her. But just as he managed to get her out of his head, she showed up in front of his eyes—less than twenty feet away.

"I think I'll join her," Melinda said, giving her husband a quick peck on the lips before following the other woman. "Pregnancy has made trips to the bathroom part of my hourly routine."

Turning her attention completely on Xavier, Melinda continued, "And I suggest you snap out of whatever it is you're in. Catrina seems to be a nice person and you're messing it up with your inattention."

"What are you talking about?" Xavier said.

"Where is your mind tonight?" she said. "You haven't heard one word any of us have said since we sat down."

"Maybe it's because he's still thinking about Danielle," Reggie answered before Xavier could say anything.

At hearing that name, Melinda narrowed her eyes suspiciously. "Danielle? What does she have to do with this?"

Neither man answered and Melinda's curiosity rose. "I hope she's not back in the picture. That woman is bad news. We were all there when she chewed your heart and spit it out. You better think twice if she's somehow weaseled her way back into your life."

"Weren't you on your way to the bathroom?" Reggie gently reminded her.

Glaring at her husband, she turned back to Xavier. "You're lucky I can't hold it much longer, or I wouldn't leave until I got some answers."

Once she was out of earshot, Reggie moved into the seat vacated by Catrina. "I thought going out to dinner would put you in a better mood. So much for that theory. At least you gave up on the vodka shots."

"Give me a break, Reggie," Xavier said, not taking his eyes off the front door, even though the subject of his attention had already left.

Reggie followed his line of vision, but didn't see anything out of the ordinary. "I take it by that annoyed tone, you're still in a funk and feeling guilty about what you did yesterday."

Xavier turned his attention back to his brother. "I am not in a funk."

Reggie raised a questioning brow. The words had come out strong, loud, and harsh.

Lowering his voice, Xavier tried to maintain his coolness. "All I mean is that, contrary to your opinion, I am not feeling guilty, culpable, in the wrong, or at fault. I did exactly what I wanted to do and I have no regrets."

"You also won't have a date if you don't snap out of whatever it is you're in," Reggie said. "Catrina's patience is fading fast."

"The last thing I need from you is advice on women," Xavier said. "Catrina and I are just fine."

"Oh yeah?" Reggie asked, nodding his head to the left.

Xavier followed his gaze, witnessing Catrina standing at the far end of the bar, leaning in close to a brotha with dreadlocks and a designer suit. The sexy smile and the fact that he was buying her a drink told Xavier all he needed to know. He wasn't surprised by her actions or by the fact that he didn't care. The two of them wouldn't have lasted anyway. Catrina still thrived on the nightlife and the parties that were so prevalent in their line of work. At this stage in his life, Xavier found himself wanting to skip more and more of those events. "I think I'll call it a night."

Standing, Xavier reached in his pocket and pulled out his credit card. Before placing it on the table, he paused and put the card back in his wallet. "On second thought, this night is on you."

Reggie's laughter rose above the noise level. "If it's bothering you that much, why don't you just call her?"

"Who?" Xavier said, putting on his overcoat.

"Playing dumb was never your strong suit," Reggie said.

"*Being* dumb was never yours . . . which is exactly how I would classify that idea."

"Just admit that you're still attracted to Danielle and that you hoped by giving her what you thought she deserved, you could cleanse her from your soul."

"Are you ever going to stop talking like a Hallmark?" Xavier said, upset that he could so easily figure out who had been on his mind.

Ignoring the jab, Reggie saw his wife heading back to the table. "All I'm saying is that you have the finest woman in the place on your arm—my wife excluded—and you haven't said more than five words to her the whole night."

"That doesn't mean that I'm pining away for Danielle," Xavier pointed out. "She's everything I would never want in a woman."

"And everything you *do* want."

"How can you say that with such confidence?"

"Because I remember what you were like when you dated her. Love doesn't just disappear because you get hurt."

The words in Xavier's mouth were drowned out by Reggie's next words.

"I'm not saying that the two of you should be together. I'm not saying she wasn't wrong for what she did. All I'm saying is that if you really want to move on with your life, you're going to have to talk to her about what happened."

Xavier stared at his brother, his expression unreadable. "Good night, Reggie."

Reggie decided to let it drop. He'd said his piece. The rest was up to Xavier. "What about your date?"

Xavier watched Catrina giggle and whisper something in the new guy's ear. "I don't think you'll have to worry about her. I'll say good night on my way out."

Reggie watched Xavier say good night to Catrina. She didn't look surprised, nor did she seem bothered or upset by the way her evening had turned out. After several minutes, Xavier waved good night and stepped out into the cool, winter night.

"What is all this talk about Danielle?" Melinda asked when she returned to the table. "And where is Xavier?"

Kissing his wife on the cheek, he picked up his menu. "There's nothing to talk about. Catrina decided to make other plans and Xavier left."

Melinda stared at her husband for several seconds as he read the menu intently. Picking up her own menu, she started to make her selections. But she wasn't fooled. The Johnston men were up to something and she had every intention of finding out what was going on.


Danielle locked the front door and leaned against it. Almost eight thirty. This had been the longest day of her life. Reliving every meeting, every line from her audition, every outfit she'd worn, and the final meeting with Xavier, she wondered if she could have done anything different. Was there any way she should have handled it better that she didn't recognize? She'd asked these questions over and over again the past twenty-four hours, but she kept coming up with the same answer. She would have done everything the exact same way.

Glancing around the entryway, she felt the silence in the house deafening. Hanging her coat in the closet, she went upstairs to change her clothes. Coming back down, she stopped in the kitchen to pick up a bottle of water and the rest of the grapes, before getting settled in her final destination, the living room. Plopping on the couch, she picked up the remote and aimed it at the television. Just before pressing the On button, she put it back on the table. She wasn't in the mood.

Leaning back against the large pillows, she inhaled deeply, studying the room for the first time since coming to stay with her sister. Tanya had bought the house more than five years ago, but Danielle had only visited a few times.

The walls were beige, except the one to the right, facing the entryway. The deep burgundy accent added warmth to the room and framed the fireplace perfectly. Standing, she walked to the mantel and slowly moved her eyes from left to right, staring at the photographs on display. Christine and Damian on their wedding day. Natalie and Tanya at a New Year's Eve party. Brandon and Tanya dressed for an evening out. Christine, Damian, and their two-month-old daughter, Brianna.

Instantly, the outcome of her life choices slapped her in the face. Her sister had built a home, a career, friendships, and love. Tanya had girlfriends she could count on and a fiancé who loved her more than life. Danielle had none of those things.

For all the time she'd been on this earth, she had nothing of value to show for it. No career. No money. No friends. No love. That realization drained the last bit of strength she'd been trying to hold on to. Deciding she'd cried enough the last couple of days, she picked up the remote again and curled up on the couch. Maybe she could find a good comedy to take her mind off her troubles. To make her forget that she was lonely—and alone.

Xavier stood on the porch, hesitating to knock. He wasn't quite sure what he was doing here, but he couldn't stop himself from coming. Watching her walk away from him after lunch yesterday, he had never felt so satisfied—so redeemed. Yet, moments later, the gratification started to melt away, and the smile of victory began to falter. With her head held high and her emotions in check, the outward signs indicated that she was handling the news like a pro. However, when he looked in her eyes, there was no denying it. Disappointment and hurt were reflected in them. She stuck her chin out and swallowed deliberately, but the disappointment couldn't be hidden. He was not sure what he had expected her to do, but it wasn't for her to thank him for his time and walk away looking defeated.

Not ready to admit it to his brother, Xavier was taken aback by the lack of peace from his actions. He wouldn't quite classify it as guilt, but it definitely didn't measure up to the euphoria he'd assumed he'd get after turning Danielle down for the job.

As he had watched her through the restaurant window, there was no sign of the woman he used to know. Walking into a room and claiming it as her own. People standing up and taking notice when she made an entrance—going out of their way to make sure she wanted for nothing. That was the atmosphere that Danielle had thrived in. She not only enjoyed the attention, she reveled in it. But tonight, as he watched her through the window, no signs of that Danielle were present.

Instead of barreling ahead, making a grand entrance fit for a queen, she stood back, hesitating. He couldn't hear the words of the conversation, but her body language said she was having second thoughts about continuing with the evening. That's when he knew something wasn't right. Lenny's was *the* spot to see and be seen in. The Danielle he had known would never pass up an opportunity like that.

If he made sure she was fine, maybe he could put his uneasy feelings at rest. Taking a deep breath, he rang the doorbell. After several seconds, the outdoor light came on.

Danielle peered through the peephole and blinked twice. "What do you want?"

Not quite the reception he'd hoped for, but it was a start. "Open the door, Danielle."

"Why? Did you forget to turn the knife you stuck in my back? Or maybe you have a few more stories about the people I've gotten fired over the years."

Xavier didn't blame her for the comments. He wouldn't deny that he had crossed the professional line yesterday. "I deserved that."

The admission caught Danielle off guard, and she hesitated with a comeback. It almost sounded like he may have regretted his earlier words.

"I just wanted to come by to make sure you were OK," he said, hoping to convince her that his intentions were pure.

Any feelings of forgiveness Danielle had started to feel evaporated with that sentence. "I'm fine," she said through clenched teeth. "It will take more than a few mean words from you to do me in."

Xavier started to answer, but then caught himself. He'd never intended to have this conversation through a door. "Can I come inside?"

"Look, Xavier," Danielle said, ignoring the part of her that wanted to do just that. "I don't know what you're doing here, but if you've come to ease your conscience about what you did to me, forget it."

She tried to sound strong, but he could hear the tone in her voice revealing the emotions that were slipping through her tough exterior.

"You're right, Danielle. I had no right to say those things. To treat you like that. It was immature and vindictive."

Straining her ear against the door, Danielle didn't answer right away. She listened for any hint of sarcasm.

"Please, Danielle," Xavier said, quietly, "I'd like to talk to you."

Several seconds passed and Xavier realized his trip had been in vain. Not sure what he'd wanted to accomplish, he turned to walk away. Just as he stepped off the porch, he heard the click of the lock.

The door opened and Xavier unconsciously sighed in relief. Obviously having changed from her clothes after leaving Lenny's, she appeared on guard in a pair of gray sweatpants and an oversized T-shirt. Her face, already clean from the makeup she'd worn, looked younger than her almost thirty years. The image of a supermodel can be so overshadowing that one can sometimes forget that the person underneath the fancy hair, full makeup, and outrageous designer gowns is a regular person. That's what stood before him.

"You wanted to talk . . . so talk."

Clearing his throat, he said, "Can I come in?"

Trying to gauge his intentions, she waited. After several seconds, she stepped aside and motioned with her arms.

She headed to the living room, him following close behind.

She sat on the sofa as he took a seat on the chair across from her, and silence ensued.

Danielle waited for him to speak, mainly because she fought an internal battle that prevented her from saying anything. When she'd looked through the peephole and seen him standing on the other side, a part of her wanted to tell him to go away, while the other part had a flashback to her dream from last night. Her anger battled with her attraction, and at this precise moment, she had no idea which side was winning. But then she thought of their lunch earlier in the day, and the angry side began to take the lead. "Unless you're here to offer me a job, I don't think we have anything to discuss."

The cold tone of her voice indicated that her feelings about him were anything but friendly. "The job still belongs to Layla."

"Then what are you doing here?"

"I saw you at Lenny's."

Surprise registered on her face. "So?"

"You appeared not to be doing so well."

Offended, Danielle stood. "You have some nerve. First, you tear me down. Then, you give away a job you know I deserved, and now you have the audacity to look me in my eyes and tell me you're concerned about how I'm doing?"

Hearing it put that way, Xavier didn't blame her for the reaction. "I just thought—"

"No, you didn't, Xavier. You didn't think." Her voice started rising, but she didn't care. She'd spent the last couple of years trying to make up for all the wrong she'd done, and at every corner she was met with someone unwilling to give her a chance, unwilling to believe that she'd become a different person. At this moment, all the anger and frustration she'd experienced at trying to get her life back together were firmly being spewed at the man sitting in front of her.

"You think that I can't handle myself? You think your

rejection is going to affect me so much that I won't be able to go on? Well, I've got a news flash for you. I'm going to be just fine. I don't need you and I don't need your stupid job."

Storming past him, she opened the front door. "Good night."

Xavier was close on her heels. Watching the exaggerated rise and fall of her chest, he could just feel the adrenaline pumping through her veins. "Danielle, I . . . we . . . could—"

"Could what, Xavier?" Danielle yelled. "Be friends? Hang out? Shoot the breeze? Let me tell you what you thought. You thought you could come here to ease your conscience. Make yourself feel better about what you did to me . . . how you treated me. Well, guess what? I'm not going to let you off the hook that easy."

Xavier couldn't argue with her point. He'd come here to somehow absolve his guilt, and he'd failed. Resigned to the fact that this was how it was going to end—not just this conversation, but their relationship—he nodded in understanding. "Good luck, Danielle."

"I don't need luck, Xavier," she said, with renewed confidence. "I fought my way to success before, and I can do it again."

Opening his mouth to respond, Xavier realized there was nothing else to say. He'd intended to ruin her career. To put her in her place. To punish her for what she'd done to him. But now he understood his plan had backfired. He didn't destroy her—he made her stronger. With her fiery eyes daring him to say something, the realization that she didn't need him sank in. With or without him, she was going to be just fine. The fact that she would probably do it without him disturbed him the most.

Danielle slammed the door with brute force and refused to watch him get in his car and drive away. Pacing the hall, she hadn't been this worked up in a long time. Determination coursed through her veins like never before. An hour ago, her pity party had reached an all-time high. Singing the woes of her life to anyone who would listen, she'd had one depressing conversation after another. But five minutes with that man had changed everything. Now, more than ever, she was determined to do something productive with her life. And when she did— she would parade her success in his face.

Returning to the living room, Danielle was too wired to watch television. Grabbing a pen and paper, she decided to plan out the rest of her life. Not quite sure what she was going to do, she opted to write down her assets and skills.

The exercise didn't take long. Once she listed modeling, fashion, and a sense of style, she was at a loss. *Is this really all I have to offer?* Tossing the pad of paper on the coffee table, she sat back, crossing her arms across her chest. How was she going to ram her success down his throat if there was nothing she could do outside of modeling?

Stretching out against the oversized pillows, she exhaled loudly in defeat. *Lord, what am I going to do?*

# Chapter Six

The rays of sun cascaded into the room, warming the side of her face. Slowly opening her eyes, Danielle started to sit up when she noticed the blanket that had been laid on her. Tanya must have covered her up sometime during the night.

Yawning, she glanced at her watch. Just after nine A.M. She figured Tanya had already left for her wedding gown fitting scheduled for ten o'clock. Stretching, she squinted trying to block out the bright sunlight. She'd only awakened once during the night because of him. The dream had been like all the others. Passionate. After their heated discussion last night, how could he still take over her dreams?

Throwing the cover off her body, she sat up cautiously, dreading the stiffness in her body from sleeping on the couch. Standing up, she turned her neck from side to side, pleasantly surprised that nothing seemed rigid. Out the window, the golden sky seemed filled with hope and unexpected pleasures. Spring was just around the corner.

Glancing at the coffee table, she saw the words on the paper that she'd written last night, which instantly reminded her of her current situation. This time, however, she didn't have the panic, fear, and shame that normally accompanied her thoughts about her situation. In a roundabout way, she had Xavier to thank for that. Last night, he'd gotten her so riled up that she found herself completely changing her perspective. Who did he think he was? Coming to her to ease his guilty conscience. Insinuating that his one television show would completely break her—ruin her. Did he really think his one little show had the power to completely put her out of the game? Destroy all hope of having a satisfying career?

Picking up the paper, she reread her three skills. Was this all she really had to offer? Dropping the paper back on the table, she leaned her head back against the cushioned back of the sofa and closed her eyes.

*Modeling. Fashion. Sense of style.* Those three things kept swirling around in her head. No college degree. No formal training. Just *modeling, fashion, sense of style.*

There had to be something there. There had to be an opportunity somewhere in those words. They might not seem like much to others, but they were her gifts and there had to be purpose for her in them. A way to use them in a productive manner.

Suddenly, she felt her spirits lift. So busy wallowing in her situation, she had narrowly based her future on what she had done in the past. But what if there were other possibilities for her to explore? What if she could find success by taking a completely different path? What if she had been limiting herself?

Opening her eyes, she sat forward and picked up the paper again. Each word became ingrained on her brain and a picture quickly flashed in her mind.

"Oh my God," she screamed to the empty room. "That's it!"

Jumping up, she began pacing the floor as the idea began to take shape. The more she thought about it, the clearer the fuzzy picture became. Calming herself enough to sit down, she picked up the paper and pen again.

For the next hour, Danielle jotted down notes and

ideas until her fingers started to ache. Not caring what others would think, or whether she had the ability and resources to make it happen, she let the ideas flow page after page.

Dropping her pen, she leaned back and reread her notes. Even though some of her writing was barely legible, and some ideas could already be thrown out, it didn't matter. A slow grin creased her lips, as she had the beginnings of an amazing plan.

Grabbing the phone, she dialed. Keyed up, she misdialed twice before getting all the numbers right. It was Saturday morning, but there was usually a skeletal staff there. Michelle claimed it was the one time she could get work done without trying to put out fires.

"Michelle Ford's office."

The perky voice on the other end had been the same one that had answered this phone for the past ten years. "Hi, Stacy. It's Danielle. Is your boss available?"

"One moment, Ms. Kennedy," she replied dryly.

The old Danielle would have told her she needed to adjust her attitude, but the new Danielle understood why Stacy didn't roll out the welcome mat for her. In line with all her other professional relationships, she'd been impolite and difficult on many occasions with Stacy. She would often come to the office and completely ignore her, or if she did take the time to acknowledge her, it only resulted in treating her like a second-class citizen. "Stacy?"

"Yes?"

"I don't think I've ever said thank you."

"Umm . . . excuse me?" There was no hiding the confusion in her voice.

"For the past ten years, you've helped Michelle keep my appointments straight, some of my paperwork in order, and I know you had to rave about how wonderful

I was to clients, even though you and I know that was a big lie."

The silence on the other end of the phone didn't come as a surprise to Danielle. Stacy probably wondered if Danielle was delirious.

"In any case," Danielle continued, "I just wanted to say thank you. My career would not have been as successful, and as organized, without you."

"You're welcome."

Danielle couldn't tell whether Stacy actually believed her, but at least she'd had the chance to apologize.

"Where have you been? I've been calling you on your cell phone since yesterday."

Danielle could hear the mix of worry and relief in Michelle's voice. "I wasn't in the mood to talk yesterday. I was a little down in the dumps, but . . ."

"I'm sorry about the audition, honey." She'd heard through the grapevine that Layla got the part. "Are you OK?"

"If you had asked me that question twenty-four hours ago, I would have answered with a definite no, but . . ."

"I can't believe they chose that girl. She's as stiff as a board," Michelle said.

Danielle's shoulders relaxed and she easily laughed right along with Michelle. Her agent was absolutely right. Layla would need a lot of coaching to make her a natural in front of the camera.

There was a long pause as Michelle tried to get her next words together. "Danielle, we've been together for a long time."

Closing her eyes in anticipation of what was coming next, Danielle felt flutters in the pit of her stomach. Ready to move on to a new phase in her life didn't exempt her from feeling nostalgic at the conversation that was about to take place. "I know, Michelle. There's no need to say it."

"I love you as if you were my own daughter. But the work—"

"Is just not there for me anymore," Danielle said, finishing her sentence.

"I'm really sorry, Danielle," Michelle said. Over the twenty-five years that she'd been in the business, clients had come and gone. She'd forged strong professional relationships, and even some wonderful friendships, along the way. But nothing touched the professional accomplishments and personal relationship she and Danielle had developed.

"So I guess this is it," Danielle said, resigned to accept the situation. "You're dropping me as a client."

Michelle never could have predicted this day would come. She had expected Danielle to beat the odds, remaining in the entertainment industry long after her runway days had ended.

"I can remember you telling me that nothing lasts forever. I didn't want to believe you," Danielle continued. Her faraway tone said she vividly remembered those conversations. "When I was working the catwalk and shooting commercials, I couldn't see my career ever ending." Danielle paused. "I finally get the picture." And she did. Over the past few months, she had dreaded the idea of being without an agent. That would represent her final disconnect with the world she'd been so entrenched in just a few short years ago. Now that the words were spoken, they didn't have the sting she thought they would. "It's OK, Michelle."

Michelle had been so successful in this business because she didn't pull punches. She'd promised herself early on that she'd always be honest with her clients. "I'd always hoped you'd continue to work in other areas of the industry."

"Me too," Danielle admitted. "But I have no one to blame but myself."

"If there's anything I can do . . ." Michelle offered.

"You've done so much for me. It's time I started doing for myself."

Her prophetic words hung in the air.

"I have a few papers for you to sign. They'll go out FedEx to you."

Danielle thought of all they'd been through over the years. It just didn't seem right to end it by signing some forms through the mail.

"Why don't I come to New York? We can have a drink, dinner, and finalize everything at that time." Even though her funds were limited, the train ticket would be well worth it to say good-bye to something, and someone, who had been a part of her life for so many years.

"I think that's a fabulous idea." After a short pause, Michelle said, "What are your plans?"

Eyeing the notes in front of her, Danielle wasn't quite ready to share them with anyone—including someone as close to her as Michelle. "I'm working on something."

"Really?" Michelle said, surprised, pleased, and curious. She didn't think there was one project out there that would be interested in having her, but if she found something on her own, nothing would make Michelle happier. "Is it anything I can help you with?"

"No," Danielle said, not forthcoming with any additional information. "This is something I have to do on my own."

Pushing aside some papers on her desk, Michelle leaned forward. "You've got my interest. Tell me about it."

Like a baby in its infancy, Danielle felt a little protective of her ideas. She wasn't ready to share them with the world yet. Not until she got comfortable with them herself. "I'm still trying to figure everything out."

"An independent film? Overseas work?" Michelle inquired.

"Actually, it has nothing to do with the business," Danielle said, hedging.

That statement blew Michelle away and she didn't know what to say.

"Once I get it sorted out, I'll tell you all about it."

"That's a deal," Michelle said, reluctantly respecting her wishes. "Let me know when you're coming to the city."


The following Friday, Xavier sat in his office staring at the contract in front of him. What should have taken him an hour to get through was quickly approaching the three-hour mark. With a production meeting scheduled for noon and a train to catch at two, his day was quickly slipping away from him. Rubbing the bridge of his nose, he berated himself for wasting time. With so much on his plate, he could ill afford to lose hours out of his day for any reason—and he especially shouldn't be wasting time because of one particular reason. Not only did she continue to invade his nights, she'd now preoccupied his mind during the day.

His ringing cell phone became a welcome distraction, until he saw the number on the caller ID. He'd already ignored two calls. Pushing the green button, he exhaled loudly. "What?"

"Is that any way to greet family? It makes me think that you don't want to talk to me."

"If the next words out of your mouth include Danielle, your feelings aren't too far off," Xavier warned.

"It's been a week, and you haven't made any attempts

to contact her," Reggie said. "Unless you talked to her and didn't tell me."

The frustration in his brother's tone didn't faze Xavier one bit. "Look, Reggie. She's moved on. I've moved on. Here's a piece of advice—you should move on, too."

The conversations with his brother hadn't changed much since the night they had dinner at Lenny's. Xavier told him about visiting Danielle that night with the goal of finally getting closure. But Reggie didn't believe him. "You still have some unfinished business with her."

"Finished or unfinished, she's not interested in talking to me."

Not sure if Xavier heard his own words, Reggie smiled. "But you're interested in talking to her?"

"Give it a rest, man, or you're in real danger of losing a brother."

"It's just that I've never known you to give up on something that you wanted."

When would his brother get the message? "Who says Danielle Kennedy is something that I want?"

Reggie's laughter boomed through the line. It was obvious to him that his brother had a severe case of denial. "I saw the way you looked at her at Lenny's a week ago. That's right—I saw who you saw. I didn't say anything then because I figured you'd come to your senses. Anyone could see it—including my wife."

Xavier hated when his brother spoke in riddles. "See what?"

"That you still care. That you still have feelings for her."

Xavier didn't disagree right away. After leaving Danielle that night, he'd been more confused than ever. For so long, he'd wanted her to suffer. But now? He wasn't so sure what he wanted.

When the auditions had started a month ago, she

walked into that studio dressed to a tee in a magenta pantsuit that accentuated every great feature of her body. Long legs. Small waist. Beautiful smile. The entire room went silent when she stepped on the soundstage and began her taping. Confident, dazzling, and articulate. If she had been any other person, she would have had the job locked. But she wasn't just anyone else.

The focus groups and the research showed that the public still had a negative response to Danielle. When shown the different tapes from the top three people in the running for the job, the audience tuned Danielle out—which meant they would turn the show off. The television shows that highlighted her most infamous diva moments obviously still lingered in people's minds.

He also made a few calls to industry insiders, preparing to set up segments in which they would be the featured guests. Not surprisingly, the people he spoke with weren't that excited about having Danielle do those segments.

Unfortunately, keeping Danielle out of his show didn't keep her from showing up in his dreams. In the past week, she'd made quite a few appearances. Last night, he'd awoken in a sweat after visualizing them making love on a deserted beach. The sound of the waves crashing on the shore was their serenade and the moon was their candlelight. Thank God he never told his brother about the dreams. That bit of information would never get Reggie off his back.

Reggie waited for his brother's response. When he was met with silence, he decided to try another approach. "The least you could do is see if there's something you can do to help her career. After all, you did have a hand in destroying it."

Those words bought Xavier out of his thoughts. Help Danielle? She'd made it quite clear that she didn't want to see him again. "Are you serious? The last thing she would want from me is my help."

"Then maybe you shouldn't talk with her. Doesn't she have an agent?"

Making her way up the stairs of Penn Station, Danielle stepped onto the busy New York street. Staring at Madison Square Garden, she heard the sound of car horns and watched the hustle and bustle of the sea of people on the streets. The mix of tourists, with their slow pace and ever-ready cameras, contrasted with native New Yorkers, moving at breakneck speed to their destination.

Pulling the collar on her jacket closer, she decided to walk the six blocks to Michelle's office building. As she passed a couple of magazine stands, several subway stops, and a hot dog vendor, the energy around her made Danielle realize how much she missed the fast pace of city life.

Entering the building, she removed her jacket and tossed it across her arm. Opting for comfort, she'd settled on a pair of blue jeans and a sweater. Even with the ordinary look, the black boots, light powder, and neutral lip gloss couldn't hide the characteristics that made her a highly sought-after model.

Making her way to the security area, she smiled and waved to the uniformed guard. "Hi, Jason."

Jason had been working that security desk for the past six years. Always polite and offering a smile, he reached for his clipboard and turned it out toward her. "Good afternoon, Ms. Kennedy. I haven't seen you in a while."

"I haven't been to the office in about a year. I've been spending time with my family."

If Jason knew the true story behind her absence, he didn't let on. Responding with a nod, he pushed a few buttons on his laptop and a visitor's pass printed out. Sliding it into a plastic protector, he handed it to her across the counter. "You have to have this visible at all times."

Hooking the badge on her sweater, Danielle waved and headed for the elevators. Pushing the Up button, she thought about the thirty-five-page document in her bag. The butterflies in her stomach and her loss of appetite were only a few signs of the eager nervousness she felt.

On the one hand, she was coming to officially end her professional relationship with her mentor and agent, but she was also about to embark on another part of her life. Ready to share her idea for a new adventure, Danielle had prepared to lay out the blueprint for her future plan.

For the past week, she'd spent every waking hour putting the project together. Tanya offered her support, as well as volunteered Christine and Natalie's. With the three of them, they had enough experience and information to make Danielle's job much easier. After thinking it over, Danielle decided to pass. Not only because she wasn't ready to face the other women, but because she wanted to see how much she could do on her own.

The hard work and sleepless nights had been worth it. Her t's were crossed and her i's were dotted. Focusing on this project also served as a great distraction from Xavier. Thinking more and more about his visit of last week, she wondered what could have been if she'd decided to hear him out. But that part of her life was over. Her future rested in the plans she'd been putting together.

The Michelle Ford Modeling Agency took up more than half of the twenty-first floor. In business for almost twenty-five years, the agency and its owner had a reputation for developing some of the best talent in the modeling business. Michelle had started out just trying to help a friend who needed moral support for a modeling audition.

At twenty-two, Michelle had an English degree and no job. Moving to New York from Chicago, she planned to make her mark in the literary world. After seven job interviews at various publications and no offers, she started tagging along with her eighteen-year-old roommate, Angela, as she tried to break into the fashion industry.

Hanging out in waiting rooms and backstage at photo shoots and fashion shows, Michelle observed everything that went on during each phase of the process. As Angela got work and got turned down for some gigs, Michelle deciphered what made a model employable. By helping to keep her friend's business and appointments organized, she began acting as a combination personal assistant, business manager, and agent. As she got to know the other models, they soon began asking for her help in keeping their schedules structured and in booking jobs. Today, Michelle's business savvy and reputation established her as one of the best in the business.

Stepping off the elevator, Danielle made her way down the hall she'd traveled so many times during her twelve-year career. At seventeen, fear and excitement had ruled her emotions. Never having been out of Georgia, she'd found New York City quite overwhelming. Living in an apartment with three other models, and a very watchful guardian, Danielle didn't think she fit in. The other models, though her same age, seemed to have it all together.

Confidence, a strong fashion sense, and professional savvy were attributes that Danielle greatly admired. After the first few months of watching and learning, she developed some of those same characteristics and her career took off.

By the time she turned twenty-four, she had become the admired one, moving through the modeling business with confidence, style, grace, and attitude. At the top of her game, she had more people working to keep her happy than she could count. Designers begged for her, cosmetic companies vied for her endorsement, and younger women coming into modeling begged for her time, a little advice, and words of encouragement.

When she turned twenty-seven, the tides began to change. With her no longer working the runways, the time had come to parlay all that hard work into television and movies. But that plan was not to be. She'd never forget the day she walked this same hall after being summoned by Michelle. The tone in her agent's voice told Danielle it wouldn't be good news.

Having created some bad blood over the years with other models and industry insiders, Danielle had started to hear rumors that some of the auditions she'd been going on were a moot point because people weren't interested in working with her.

But lack of work wasn't the only thing on her agent's mind that day. The news Michelle delivered was the most unforeseen news Danielle ever expected to get. To this day, it remained the most shocking moment of her life—and she remembered it as if it were yesterday.

Late summer, she hadn't worked in about three months and was starting to get a little antsy about the status of her career. She'd hoped that the meeting Michelle called was to share good news concerning her endorsement contract. Wearing a comp dress from Prada, she breezed past Stacy without so much as a hello and walked into Michelle's office without knocking. Impatiently waiting for Michelle to finish a phone call, Danielle took a seat. As soon as Michelle hung up the phone, Danielle jumped right in.

"I hope this meeting is about L'Oreal. I can't believe the renewal contracts haven't been finalized and sent over. Probably the legal department holding it up. Getting them to get something out the door on time is next to impossible."

Michelle stared at Danielle and took a deep breath. An agent had the great job of telling their clients they'd just booked them on a great assignment, secured a national commercial, or closed the deal on a major endorsement. But they also had the daunting task of being the messenger when things weren't so good.

Deciding it best not to beat around the bush, Michelle opened some files and leaned forward, not a trace of joking in her expression. "Danielle, you're just about broke."

For several seconds, Danielle said nothing. She had come to talk about signing a multimillion-dollar endorsement contract and her agent had just said the words that strangely sounded like she had no money. "What?"

Michelle's phone buzzed and Stacy announced a call. "Take a message, Stacy, and hold all my calls."

Turning her attention back to Danielle, Michelle saw by the blank look on her client's face that her words had come as a complete shock. "Danielle, I'm really sorry, but things don't look good for you right now. Careerwise or financially."

"What do you mean?" Danielle said, panic starting to make its way through her body. Standing, she walked over to the window, trying to make sense of the words that were coming out of her agent's mouth. "That's impossible. I've made millions of dollars over the past ten years. Hell, I made three million last year alone. There's no way I can be broke."

"You grossed about three," Michelle explained. "That part is true. However, you netted about four hundred thousand."

Rubbing her temples to counter the onset of a major headache, Danielle frantically tried to think back to her last meeting with her business manager—almost seven months ago. "How is that possible? Marty said—"

Softly, Michelle spoke. "I got a call from the authorities

yesterday. They've had several complaints against Marty and were calling to see if I've heard from him. They've been looking for him for almost a month."

Danielle turned and stared at Michelle in confusion. "Looking for him? What is that supposed to mean?"

Michelle's stomach churned. If she could end this discussion right now, she would. But she had to let her know everything. "Marty has disappeared."

"Disappeared?" Danielle repeated the word so softly Michelle could barely hear her. "That's impossible," she said, trying to invoke a little more confidence in her voice. "He left me a message about two weeks ago, saying that he wanted to arrange a time to get together to go over my latest financial statements."

Michelle sympathized with her client. There were going to be no more calls and no more meetings. At this point, she could guarantee that she would never hear from her business manager again. According to the authorities, he'd gotten away with about twenty million dollars. That was enough money to disappear for quite a while. "Have you tried to call him? When was the last time you spoke to him? When was the last time you actually saw him?"

Danielle shut her mouth and stopped arguing. Frantically searching her memory for a date or time when she could place herself and Marty face-to-face, she drew a blank. The last words anyone wanted to hear was that their business manager had "disappeared."

"How could this happen?"

Michelle knew her client was hurting, but she also needed to hear the truth. "I tried to warn you, sweetie. You were spending too fast. Not paying attention. You let that man basically run your entire financial life."

Danielle had heard the underlying message in her statement . . . "I told you so."

\*\*\*

The hairs still stood up on her neck each time she thought about that fateful day. From the moment the ink had dried on her first contract, people tried to offer her advice about her money. When she first came into the business, Michelle had handled all of her finances, but Danielle found her too conservative, doling out cash to Danielle like allowance.

Explaining to Danielle that the million-dollar endorsements and the runway shows paying five figures would dry up—probably before she was thirty—proved futile. Warning her to set aside a nest egg to secure a financial future was met with resistance.

Danielle was having too much fun living the high life to listen to her. Keeping Michelle as her agent, she turned over her finances to Marty Stimper, a well-known manager handling several other models. Danielle loved Marty's philosophy immediately. Claiming his investments of her money would keep her well into her old age, he allowed Danielle to spend at will.

Her friends, family, Michelle, and even Damian Ware tried to deter her overindulgences, but she ignored all of their advice. Instead, she traveled the world, hosted expensive parties, drove exotic cars, and indulged in every luxury available, including four-hundred-dollar facials and twenty-thousand-dollar vacations. Her friends and family were right. Her money was gone, her career had stalled, and she'd alienated everyone she ever cared about. But all of that was about to change. Danielle Olivia Kennedy was on the comeback.

# Chapter Seven

Opening the glass doors that led to the reception area, Danielle flashed a smile and waved at Stacy, who was busy talking on the phone and so was unable to stop Danielle from heading down the hall, where she made a beeline for the last office on the left. Passing several cubes and offices, she nodded and acknowledged a few people she recognized, being sure to ask how they were and how things were going. Shocked by her sudden kindness, most responded with a hesitant nod, trying to figure out why she was being so friendly. In the past, she'd barely had two words for the staff when she came to the office. If she did speak to them, it usually involved asking them to do something or get something for her.

Passing a conference room with a glass door, she slowed her walk just a little. A tall, lanky girl not more than fifteen years old, with blond, shoulder-length hair, walked back and forth as a couple of people watched. Danielle recognized the look on her youthful face, a mix of excitement, fear, and anxiety. The young woman probably believed her entire future depended on this one moment. An older lady stood in the far corner, no doubt the mother, hoping and praying that her daughter would have the "thing," the one trait, characteristic, look that the agency was searching for.

As the girl struck a pose, one of the men took a Polaroid.

Her casual ensemble of cargo pants and a tank top showed off her good bone structure and excellent posture. The pouty lips indicated she had the right attitude. With the connections and power that the agency had, Danielle might have just gotten a peek at the next supermodel.

Pausing at the last door, Danielle took a deep breath. She patted her bag one last time to confirm that her document was still there. She'd never wanted something so much in her life, and she hoped Michelle would see her vision and believe in it. With a quick knock, she didn't wait for an answer before opening the door. "I hope you're decent, because . . ."

She took two steps inside before her words trailed off and she froze in place.

"Danielle, you're early," Michelle said, quickly realizing that this was going to be an awkward moment.

Danielle opened her mouth to speak, but nothing came out. Clearing her throat twice, she finally found her voice. Her words were directed at Michelle, but her eyes were focused on him. "I, um, I got in early and thought I'd surprise you. I guess that was a bad idea."

Xavier stood and picked up his coat. "We were just finishing up."

Michelle stood as well, reaching out to shake Xavier's hand. "Thanks for coming by. I'll definitely consider your idea and try to get back to you by the end of next week."

Watching the two shake hands agitated Danielle. What was he doing here? This was her territory, not his. What idea did Michelle need to consider? It was bad enough that Danielle couldn't get him out of her dreams, but now he was turning up during her waking hours?

Casually dressed as he was in brown slacks and a crew-neck sweater, there couldn't be any denying the understated attraction that seemed to follow him wherever he went.

"I look forward to hearing from you." Xavier turned his attention from Michelle and focused on Danielle. Dressed down in a pair of jeans and an off-the-shoulder cashmere sweater, she looked relaxed—and beautiful.

"Are you here to ruin someone else's career?" Danielle said, unable to carry over her newfound attitude of niceness with him.

Any amount of sympathy he might have started to feel for this woman evaporated with that sarcastic comment. "It's that snooty attitude that has kept you out of work the past couple of years."

Danielle placed her hands on her hips, refusing to let him get away with those words. "Maybe it was your blackballing me that kept me out of work."

"Yeah, right," Xavier said with a short laugh. "I'm sure it was my fault that people got tired of your crazy demands and childish behavior."

His obvious refusal to admit to having anything to do with her challenges in finding work only incensed Danielle more. "For your information, my attitude with everyone else in this world is just fine. It's just you that brings out the worst in me."

"Lucky me," he mumbled under his breath.

"Children, do you mind?" Michelle said, acting as referee.

Both turned their attention to Michelle, and Danielle spoke first. "He started it."

"Oh, please, Danielle," Xavier said. "You started it two years ago when you put my television show on the line because of your spoiled attitude."

"Give me a break, Xavier," Danielle said, feeling her last bit of patience break. How long were people going to hold her past against her? "My career is in the toilet and I'm broke. Shouldn't that make you happy enough that you could let that one incident go?"

Her words struck a chord with everyone in the room, and there was complete silence.

That soft spot she'd first touched at lunch, and then that night at Lenny's, had just been struck again. He'd been ready to combat whatever snide remark she was going to dish out, but he couldn't. When he'd gone to see her last week, he got a glimpse of the pain she was in, but today, he got to see all of it.

"What's the matter, Xavier? Cat got your tongue? Trying to come up with more insults?" Danielle was proud that her voice didn't crack, even though emotions swelled to an all-time high inside her. That fact gave her an unexpected boost of confidence.

Xavier started to respond.

"Save it, Xavier, for someone who cares," she said, raising her hand to stop him from speaking. "I may be down, but I ain't out."

"What is that supposed to mean?" Xavier asked, hearing a hint of a challenge in her words.

"It means I've got a plan," she said proudly. "Did you really think that your job would be the only work I could possibly do for the rest of my life? I have moved on, and believe me, it's going to be a success."

Hearing her speak the words with such conviction, Xavier believed her. With all her faults, the one thing Danielle had down pat was how to fight. If she wanted any semblance of her previous life back, she'd have to battle like hell to make something happen.

It was at this moment that Xavier finally admitted to himself how much he admired her—cared about her. It mattered to him what was going on her life. It mattered to him whether she succeeded or failed. It mattered to him whether she would be able to rebuild her professional career.

That revelation took his breath away and he needed

a few moments to get himself back together. His brother was right. He still had deep feelings for her.

Hurt by her betrayal years ago, he'd let the sting of that moment dictate his behavior toward her for years. But now he found himself in a different position with her. He was rooting for her. Not sure what to do with this new-found revelation, he gathered up his coat andpapers. "Then I wish you luck."

The tone in his words caused Danielle to narrow her eyes in suspicion. If her ears were working correctly, she would have sworn she'd heard a hint of sincerity in his voice. Where was his comeback? The insult? The angry response?

Not wanting to appear to be the petty and immature one, Danielle simply said, "Thank you."

Xavier stared at Danielle a few more seconds before turning his attention back to Michelle. "Well, I'll let you two get on with your meeting."

Walking toward the door, he stopped in front of Danielle. Leaning in close to her ear, he whispered, "I really do wish you the best."

The deep, breathy voice caused a sense of comfort to pass through her. Swallowing deliberately, she gave a quick nod in acknowledgment of his words. A few seconds later, he was gone.

Danielle stared at the closed door for several seconds. He still had the most amazing eyes she'd ever seen in a man. The dark brown center was slightly hidden by his lids, outlined in long, naturally curled lashes. When they had been a couple, she would wake up to find him staring at her, all of his emotions evident in them. It only took a quick glance in his eyes to see what he was feeling—devotion, love, anger, annoyance. But today, they were unreadable. She had no idea whether his good wishes were sincere or not.

"If I'd known you were coming to the office, I would have met with him earlier," Michelle said, taking blame for the scene that had just played out. "I thought we were meeting at the restaurant."

Turning her attention back to Michelle, Danielle tried to appear nonchalant. "No problem. Xavier Johnston doesn't bother me in the least."

"Umm," Michelle said. Having seen Danielle with many men, she thought Xavier was the only one who could handle her. With Xavier, Danielle had been able to let her guard down fully. In the public eye so much, Danielle constantly felt like she had to prove herself over and over again. Xavier gave her a refuge from that life, and she seemed to thrive in it.

Even after their breakup, Michelle held out hope that the two of them would find their ways back to each other. As she watched them today, it became clear to Michelle that maybe too many things had been said and done that could never be taken back.

"What did he want?" Danielle asked casually.

"I thought you didn't care."

"I don't," she said, a little too quickly. "I'm just wondering what he could have to talk to you about."

"He was here to find out about you," Michelle said, watching her reaction.

"Yeah, right," Danielle said. "The last thing on that man's mind is me. He made that quite clear when he ever so politely turned me down for *The Fashion Design House.*"

"I don't think so," Michelle said, taking a seat.

"Did he tell you something different?"

Michelle raised a brow at her question. Danielle may have tried to keep her tone level, but the interest couldn't be disguised.

"He came here under the pretense of talking to me about scheduling an upcoming segment on his show, but we'd only been in my office a few minutes before your name came up."

Danielle took a seat in the chair that Xavier had just vacated and she immediately regretted it. The scent of his cologne still lingered and she couldn't help but close her eyes and inhale deeply. A creature of habit, he rarely wore any other fragrance.

"It does sort of linger, doesn't it?"

Danielle opened her eyes and shifted uncomfortably in the chair as Michelle stared at her with a knowing grin on her face. "I don't care about his cologne or him."

"It wouldn't be the worst thing if you two started seeing each other again," Michelle said, trying to get the idea out in the open for discussion.

"Ugh," Danielle said, opening her bag and pulling out her document. "I can't believe you let those words come out of your mouth. I have a better chance of being the *Sports Illustrated* swimsuit issue cover model at thirty than me and that man ever having another personal relationship. And I don't have to remind you how bad my last shoot with *SI* went."

Michelle moved some files around to make some room. At forty-nine, she'd given up on trying to keep a clean desk. There were too many things going on in her life to worry about things like that. She made a habit of keeping things simple. That's why she kept her strawberry-blond hair cut short, her glasses on a chain around her neck, and her clothes usually consisting of two pieces. Trying to accessorize and coordinate bags and shoes took up too much time. Michelle could always be found with the same diamond stud earrings and black, low-heeled shoes. "You guys had a rough breakup, but you were so good for each other when you were together. He seemed to help you loosen up. Get rid of part of that chip that had lodged itself on your shoulder."

Danielle had to admit that she had a point. He was good for her.

Michelle watched her face soften. "He's staying the night in the city. I know where he's staying."

"Michelle," Danielle warned, "no matter what our relationship was, it's over. He can't forgive me and I can't forgive him."

"Are you telling me there's no chance? That you're completely over him?"

Danielle didn't answer, hoping that if she ignored the question, Michelle would get the hint that this was one conversation she wasn't interested in having.

"If there's any chance that the two of you could work things out, don't you want to at least try?"

When Danielle still remained silent, Michelle reluctantly agreed to drop the subject. "So what's this bright idea you have for a job?"

Danielle exhaled and set a copy of her business plan on the desk.

Michelle, not having expected anything written, opened up the binder and started reading.

Danielle stood, unable to contain her excitement.

After reading a couple of pages, Michelle raised her eyes filled with questions.

Before she could say anything, Danielle exclaimed, "I'm going to open a boutique."

"I see that from this business plan you set in front of me." Michelle didn't mean to sound so surprised. She wasn't quite sure what she'd expected Danielle to say, but this definitely wasn't it. What did she know about running a business?

"Just think about it a minute," Danielle said, hearing the shock, and doubt, in her voice. "Over the years, I've had the privilege of working with some of the greatest designers—Halston, Sean Jean, Phat Farm, Chanel, Chloe, Gucci. But

I've also been privy to some of the lesser-known designers looking for their big break. They have fantastic designs, but no showcase. They don't have enough money for fashion week, and haven't been able to work for other designers. I want my store to sell their designs."

"That sounds like a good idea, Danielle, but New York is filled with boutiques, most of them not quite successful. Not to mention that you don't have a business background." Michelle watched her expression change, losing some of its excitement. "I'm not saying it can't be done, I just don't think it will be as easy as you think."

"First of all, I'm not opening in New York. I'm going to open it in D.C.," Danielle said. Having realized the fierce competition and expense involved in opening a store in Manhattan, she'd already ruled it out. "I've been checking out the fashion scene the last week or so, and I think there's a market for upscale business attire that's fashionable, yet not too outrageous."

"I'm with you, Danielle, but it can be tough to get a business off the ground. Most new businesses don't make it five years." Michelle thought back to her early days as an agent and wondered how she made it through. There were more tough times than she could ever recall.

"I'm not saying I won't have to work hard, or that I don't need some business advice," Danielle admitted. Her research had pointed out all the core statistics about the chances of her store succeeding, but it also provided all the information she needed to make sure her business was a success. "I love fashion and helping people look and feel good about themselves. This is one way I know to combine all those things."

Flipping through her copy of her business plan, she directed Michelle to several sections, including marketing, analyzing the competition, finding suppliers, expenses, and projected income.

"You've done your homework," Michelle said, unable to hide her surprise at how well thought out the plan was.

Danielle could tell that Michelle was impressed. "I've been busting my butt the last week, putting this together. I learned a lot as I developed it. I know I can do this."

Setting the plan to the side, Michelle clasped her hands together. "Are you sure you want to commit your time to this? How will you fit in time to audition, make casting calls, or take advantage of media opportunities if you take on this project? I know the outlook on your career is bleak right now, but if Paula Abdul's career can be resurrected, anything is possible."

Danielle smiled at her attempt at humor. "I totally understand the commitment this boutique will take—in time, energy, and money. And I'm ready to make it. My modeling career? I'm just not interested in that life anymore. My time has come and gone. It was a wonderful journey and I appreciate all the opportunities it afforded me. But you and I both have to face reality. It's over—and I'm OK with that. I accept it. I'm ready to let that part of my life go."

"So you're telling me that if I got a call today for a commercial, a shoot, anything—you wouldn't be interested?"

Danielle sat back in her chair. If that question was posed to her a couple of weeks ago, the answer would have easily rolled off her lips. She would be ready to take on any project that would put her name back in lights. But that was then. "Honestly, I would say no."

Michelle studied her for a moment, trying to gauge whether she was being honest with herself. "OK, for the sake of argument, let's say you have what it takes to run this business. Where are you going to get the money from? You need to secure a location, build it out, purchase store fixtures, have advertising money. Need I go on?"

Danielle sat quiet, digesting everything her mentor

said. The up-front capital she needed far exceeded the money she had. "I plan to go to banks and the Small Business Administration for loans. They have programs for minorities and women specifically for situations like this."

At times, Michelle felt more like a mother to Danielle than her agent, and this was one of those moments that called for tough love. "You had to file bankruptcy when your finances fell apart. The discharge was not even two years ago. I don't think you'll be able to get financing from those sources."

Danielle thought she'd prepared herself for the hard road ahead of her in opening up her business. The task would probably be more daunting than she'd imagined, but that wouldn't deter her. "I'm going to at least try. My business plan may help convince the powers that be that this is worth the investment."

Michelle admired the determination in her voice. "I could help you look into some nontraditional financing options, such as private investors." Michelle rose from her chair and walked around her desk. "In the meantime, you know you're welcome to stay with me."

Financing such a venture would be tough in the ideal situation, and Danielle's was far from that. In light of that, the offer from Michelle should have been great. But Danielle couldn't accept. "Thanks, Michelle, I really appreciate it, but if I'm going to open up a shop in D.C., I really need to be there."

Michelle agreed that was probably the best solution. A bittersweet moment for Michelle, she thought back over the past twelve years they'd spent together. Danielle had been a big part of her life. Even some of her other clients were jealous of the friendship the two of them shared. Never having much luck in the love department, Danielle had become the child Michelle never had. Now it was time for her to move on.

In Michelle's mind, it all made sense, but her heart was having a hard time digesting the information. "Are you going to stay with Tanya?"

Nodding yes, Danielle sat back down. "She told me there was no rush to leave, but it feels weird staying there."

"I thought things were going well for you two."

"They are," Danielle said. "It's just that I've already imposed on her. With her upcoming wedding, I just don't want to get in the way."

Michelle could see the frustration mounting in her protégée. "Are you completely out of money?"

The bankruptcy had offered her some protection, but the funds were dwindling fast. "I'm down to about five thousand and I'm holding on to it for dear life."

Michelle gave her a hug. "I'm really sorry about how things have turned out for you."

A year ago, Danielle would have responded by telling Michelle how her situation was not her fault. How the industry had done this to her. Now Danielle knew that that was not the case. She was where she was in life because of the choices she'd made, and if she wanted to get her life back on track, she'd have to make different choices.

For the next few minutes, Danielle signed a variety of papers that officially dissolved their working relationship.

"I won't be done here for another hour or so," Michelle said. "Do you want to wait here?"

Gathering her belongings, Danielle headed for the door. "I'm going to take a walk. We can meet at the café you like so much for dinner."

"I'll be there."

Danielle walked across the lobby, dropping off her badge with Jason. It would probably be a long while before she walked back into this building again. As she stepped onto the concrete, the late afternoon sun was hidden behind the tall buildings. As it was now cooler than when she'd arrived, she buttoned up her jacket. Taking two steps, she heard a voice from behind.

"Want some company?"

# Chapter Eight

There was no need to turn around. She recognized the voice immediately. "What are you still doing here?"

"Waiting for you."

The answer sounded simple, but the meaning behind it could lead to nothing but complications. "Why?"

"Because you seem a little upset with me and I wanted to know why."

Danielle finally turned around and placed the palm of her hand on his forehead. "You don't have a fever, so you can't be delirious."

Xavier laughed and reached for her hand. Bringing it to his lips, he gently kissed her fingers. The gesture surprised both of them. "All I'm asking for is a cup of coffee."

She snatched her hand away, and the shivers from the cold that she'd felt a few moments ago dissipated from the warmth of his lips. Her decision to accept or decline had nothing to do with her personal wants, but more with whether the two of them could be around each other for more than five minutes without causing a scene that would end up being embarrassing to both of them.

"There's a Starbucks on the next corner," he offered, hoping to make the decision easier.

Crossing her arms at her chest, Danielle still wasn't convinced. "What could we possibly have to talk about?"

Nonchalantly, he answered truthfully, "The attraction we still have for each other."

Danielle didn't know whether to laugh at the absurdity of his statement or admit that he had spoken the truth.

"If you say no," he said, "I'll have to keep showing up at the most unexpected moments asking you for a few moments of your time."

"And if I say yes, will you disappear from my life afterward?"

"Only if you want me to."

The five-minute walk was made in an uncomfortable quietness. The only words either of them spoke involved telling the cashier how they liked their lattes. Stepping in front of him at the register, Danielle paid for her own coffee before he had the chance. She wasn't a charity case.

Once they were seated, she didn't wait to take a sip of her coffee before saying, "We're here. So talk."

Xavier leaned back in his chair and released a slow grin. "My brother says that real attraction between a man and a woman is usually masked in the snide comments they make to one another."

"Is that so?" Danielle asked sarcastically. "Maybe snide remarks can be a reflection of how one truly feels."

Slowly nodding his head in agreement, Xavier said, "So which is it for us?"

For the past week, Danielle had dedicated her days to putting together her business plan, but when the lights went out and she lay in her bed, he always crept into her dreams. When the dreams started around the time she began auditioning, they were always making love. But lately, those dreams had them taking walks on the beach, enjoying a ride at an amusement park, and sharing intimate dinners.

A psychologist would say that she was harboring feelings for him, but the reality was she was lonely and hadn't been in a relationship since they broke up. What she needed was to meet someone new. "It's neither. We were thrown together because of work, and now that we won't be working together, we can each go back to our separate lives."

Xavier took a sip of his coffee as he thought about her statements. It sounded as if it was the best decision they could make. They'd tried to be a couple and it didn't work. Being back in her life these past few weeks probably just stirred up some of those old feelings. They could leave this coffee shop and, theoretically, never have to see or deal with each other again. "Is that what you want? Because I'm not sure if that's what I want."

She couldn't believe what she was hearing. Did he actually want her to give them another chance? After all that they'd been through? All the things they'd said to each other?

Reaching across the table, he grabbed her hands. "Don't you think if we decided to give us a try, it might be worth it?"

The request caught her completely off guard and she had no idea how she wanted to respond.

"For the record, it was the focus groups that determined your fate in relation to *The Fashion Design House.*"

That admission only helped ease her anger at him slightly, but he wasn't out of the doghouse yet. "It wasn't the focus groups that took me to lunch and took pleasure in delivering the news."

Xavier dropped his head in shame. After several seconds, he looked her in the eye. "I'm sorry, Danielle. I was still so angry with you for what you did to me. I couldn't get past it. But watching you these last few weeks made me realize how wrong I was for treating you that way."

She removed her hands out of his touch. "So this conversation is not about us getting back together, it's about me accepting your apology to ease your guilt."

"Danielle, that's not what I meant. . . ."

Gathering her belongings, she couldn't believe she almost fell for it. "Have a nice life, Xavier."

Balling up his napkin in frustration, he watched her disappear down the street. She read his intentions all wrong. He had finally admitted that he still had feelings for her, and she wasn't interested in hearing anything he had to say. Was she right? Should they just move on with their lives? If it wasn't for the audition, would he even be thinking about her?

But then again, maybe the audition was the means to getting them to give each other another chance. If that was the case, how was he going to convince her?

Monday morning, Tanya walked into the kitchen dressed for work in a dark green skirt and matching blazer, her hair pulled back in a neat ponytail. Working as a contract administrator for Ware Construction four days a week, she also helped out Natalie one day a week at her nonprofit association that helped people plan how to start businesses. Danielle had shared her idea for opening a boutique, but hadn't asked for any advice.

For the past week, she'd been working day and night on her business plan, researching late into the evening. Tanya made an offer to take a look at it, but wasn't offended when Danielle declined. She had an inkling Danielle was trying to accomplish something on her own. "Any good news in there?"

Without looking up from her newspaper, Danielle marked a spot on the page. "I'm reading the employment section."

Tanya's hand froze in midair as she reached for the coffeepot.

Glancing up, Danielle caught her stunned expression.

"That's right. I'm looking for a job—preferably at a boutique or small clothing store. That way, while I'm working on looking for financing, I can be gaining some real experience."

Tanya tried to cover up her surprise. This was a scene she'd never thought would be played out. "Do you see anything?"

"Quite a few ads for department stores, but just one or two for smaller boutique-type stores. I'm going to visit them today."

Tanya filled her cup and sat across from her sister. "Danielle, I'm really proud of what you're trying to accomplish."

If those words had come from anyone else, Danielle might have seen it as condescending, but Tanya was rooting for her to succeed. "Thanks."

"Things have been hectic with work and planning a wedding, but if you need my help with anything, just let me know."

Getting up to refill her coffee, Danielle said, "That means a lot to me, Tanya."

Returning to the table, Danielle continued her job search.

Tanya was starting to leave when she stopped and turned back to her sister. "I'm going to be getting back together with Christine and Natalie for dinner soon. I wanted you to join us. We're going to be making final decisions about the wedding—the dresses and the flowers."

Danielle understood that Tanya was trying to include her to help her continue to build their relationship, but she just wasn't ready to deal with Christine, Natalie, or a wedding she wouldn't be participating in.

Folding the paper and setting it to the side, Danielle tried to think of a nice way to decline the offer. "I'm so busy with looking for a job and getting my business off the ground that I have no idea what my schedule will be. So go ahead and make your plans. If I can make it, fine. If not, don't let me hold you up."

Tanya's forehead wrinkled as she appeared to be in deep thought. "That's really putting me between a rock and a hard place."

"How?" Danielle said, wondering what difference it made if she joined them or not.

Exhaling loudly, Tanya pretended to pout. "I need to make sure that all my bridesmaids agree on the choices."

It took a few moments for her words to sink in. The corners of Danielle's lips moved upward and the sparkle in her eyes grew brighter.

"I didn't ask you sooner because I didn't know how you felt about participating," Tanya admitted. "But I'd really like you to be a part of this."

Growing up, Tanya never would have imagined walking down the aisle without her sister by her side. Since their relationship had been so strained over the past couple of years, she originally had no intention of even inviting Danielle. However, over the past few weeks, Tanya has gotten a glimpse of their old relationship and it was growing stronger every day. With the big day just a few short months away, she wanted her sister to be there.

Danielle wrapped her arms around Tanya and the connection that had been so severely severed over the past few years was repaired. Things in Danielle's life were finally on the upswing. "I would love to participate. Maybe Brandon has a good-looking groomsman to be my escort."

Tanya half smiled and asked, "Have you talked to Xavier?"

Thinking of their time in the coffeehouse on Friday, she said, "Why do you ask?"

"We talked about you contacting him, so I was just wondering if you did."

"*We* didn't talk about calling him, *you* talked about it," Danielle reminded her. "I saw him Friday."

"In New York?"

"He was there on business."

"And?"

Danielle relayed the details of her time with him, including his apology.

"Are you going to see him again?"

"No," Danielle said without hesitation. "That ship has sailed."

Opening up her newspaper, Danielle indicated that this conversation was over.

Tanya didn't want to push it, so she let the topic drop.

Two hours later, Danielle walked into Sara's Closet, an upscale women's clothing shop nestled in the heart of Washington, D.C. The eclectic neighborhood streets were filled with homes, shops, and restaurants. The ad said they needed a full-time sales associate. When she called, the assistant manager told her to come in at eleven for an interview.

The bells above the door chimed and a middle-aged woman with brunet hair in a short layered cut appeared from the back of the store. She was wearing black pleated pants with an aquamarine silk button-down blouse, and the color complemented her complexion. The look was stylish and sophisticated, confirming Danielle's selection of a straight skirt and button-down blouse as a good choice.

"May I help you?"

Taking a quick short breath, Danielle mustered all the confidence her nervousness would allow. She hadn't been this tense since getting ready for her first cover photo shoot. "Yes. I'm responding to your ad for a sales associate."

The women extended her hand. "Patricia LaRue."

"Danielle Kennedy."

"Nice to meet you. The manager just stepped out for a moment," she said, walking toward the back of the store. "Why don't you take a few minutes and fill out the application? She should be back by the time you're done."

The request caught Danielle off guard. She'd never had to fill out a job application. "Uh, sure."

Taking the clipboard from the woman, Danielle sat on the dark mahogany cushioned bench by the dressing room while Patricia greeted a customer that just walked in.

Glancing around the store, Danielle made a mental note of the inventory. With summer just a few months away, the front of the store showcased the latest in warm-weather wear. The center of the store seemed dedicated to the professional women. Designer skirts, pants, and blazers would be a perfect fit for any boardroom meeting. To the right, several racks of evening clothes lined the wall. The styles ranged from the simple black cocktail dress to sequined ball gowns appropriate for most formal affairs. The area directly in front of her housed the items that must have been left over from the previous season. Still great clothes, just greatly reduced in price. Although about half the clothes in the store were too conservative for Danielle's taste, the other half she could work with.

Flipping through the pages of the form, Danielle couldn't believe how much information they were requesting. Completing the section asking for her name and address was a breeze. It was the experience section that threw her for a loop. Last job? Annual salary? Duties and responsibilities? After thinking for several seconds, she started writing. If she was going to make a fresh start, she needed to be completely honest. She finished up just as the manager came in and stood in front of her.

"I understand you're here about the sales associate position."

Danielle stood and came face-to-face with a woman who looked to be in her fifties, if not her sixties, with her graying hair pulled into a tight bun and reading glasses hanging from a chain around her neck. The black skirt and jacket stylishly covered most of her body, her slim lips had bright red lipstick, and her light green eye shadow matched her eyes. "Yes. I saw the ad in the paper."

"I see," she said with a polite smile. "I'm Elaine Bartlett, the manager and owner."

Her straight back, serious tone, and small smile did nothing to help Danielle to relax. They shook hands and sat.

As the woman reviewed her application in silence, Danielle watched her flip pages back and forth several times. Periodically glancing at the woman's face, Danielle nervously bit her bottom lip.

Finally, Elaine turned the pages of the application over as if she was looking for more info. "Is this some kind of joke?"

"Excuse me?" Danielle said.

"Besides your name, address, and phone number, there's nothing else written on here that could possibly be true." She placed the paper in front of Danielle, who waited for her to elaborate on her concerns.

Danielle leaned forward, looking at the words she'd written. "I signed the last page that affirms that what I wrote is true and correct."

Elaine flipped to the last page and the signature. "Yes, I can see that," she said, sounding as if she still had doubt.

"What specifically do you have questions about?" Danielle said.

Turning to page two, she pointed to the middle section

labeled "previous employment." "Under experience, you have 'supermodel' as your last position."

Danielle nodded. "That's true."

Staring for a moment at Danielle, Elaine slowly moved her eyes back to the paper. "Modeled high-end designer clothes in Milan, Paris, and New York?"

"Correct."

She didn't speak immediately, but once again tried to figure out if the woman sitting in front of her had a few screws loose. "Annual salary from last position—three million dollars?"

"That was gross," Danielle said, realizing just how crazy this must all sound to the woman.

Elaine put the paperwork to the side and folded her hands in front of her. "If you were, as you've put it, a supermodel, what are you doing in D.C. applying for a job that pays ten seventy-five an hour?"

Elaine had no idea how many times Danielle had asked herself that same question today. But the facts were the facts. Without anyone willing to give her a chance in the industry, she understood she'd have to rebuild herself. She'd beaten the odds before by becoming one of the most sought-after African-American models ever, and she could beat the odds again, by learning the boutique business and opening up her own shop. "I'm aware of the pay for this position. I also understand that you pay by commission, which could greatly increase my salary."

Elaine stood. If what Danielle told her was true, she probably wouldn't last a month—too privileged. If what she listed on her application was a lie, she definitely wouldn't be getting any job offers from her. "Thanks for coming in, but we're looking for someone with sales experience."

Believing her opportunity was slipping away, Danielle refused to stand. "I may not have direct sales experience, but I can bring so much more to this job. I know fashion, I understand trends, I—"

Elaine interrupted. "Yes, well, could you please explain to me again why you're here? I'm sure some of your 'supermodel' friends would have better job opportunities than this."

Danielle didn't miss the sarcasm in her voice and it began to grate on her nerves. Taking a deep breath, she remained calm. "I'm here because I need a job."

Raising a brow at not only the comment, but the tone of voice, Elaine didn't respond. Was that desperation or sincerity?

Realizing it wouldn't do her any good to lose her patience, Danielle regrouped and gave a relaxed smile. "What I meant to say, Ms. Bartlett, was that I'm no longer working in the fashion industry in the capacity I was in the past. I am now seeking other opportunities. Working in this boutique will help me gain the experience and skills I need to move to the next phase of my career."

Elaine wondered if she understood the tasks of working retail. "This job is not just helping customers on the floor. It includes unpacking shipments, dusting displays, vacuuming floors before opening—"

The condescension in her voice made Danielle more determined than ever. "I'm prepared to do all the duties associated with this job."

"Excuse me, Elaine."

Both women stopped talking and turned their attention to the woman standing in front of them.

"Mrs. Lucas," Elaine said with a genuine smile. Gone was the accusatory and condescending tone in her voice. It was replaced with pleasantries. "How nice to see you. Are you here to pick up your dress for your husband's award dinner this evening?"

"Yes," Mrs. Lucas said. "I didn't mean to interrupt, but I wanted to try it on one more time since it's been altered."

"Of course," Elaine said, taking the gown out of the customer's hand. Removing the plastic, Elaine used a key hooked on her waist to open one of the dressing room doors. "Why don't you go ahead into the dressing room? I'm sure you'll be pleased with the length of the hem and the trim we added around the collar and sleeves. It will be perfect with the evening bag and shoes you said you have at home."

Danielle watched Mrs. Lucas shut the wooden door behind her. Not wanting the interview to end this way, she said, "I can wait while you assist Mrs. Lucas."

Giving Danielle a polite smile, Elaine picked up her application. "Actually, this may take a while. But thank you for coming in, Ms. Kennedy. I'll review your application and I'll be sure to give you a call if we're interested."

Danielle stood to leave, fuming on the inside. She'd given enough of her own kiss-offs to know one when she heard it. The tight expression on Ms. Bartlett's face sent a clear message that Danielle would never hear from her again. "I know it seems like this job would not be a good fit for me, but I'm telling you, I would make a great sales associate."

"I'm sure you would, Ms. Kennedy," she said, already turning her attention away from here. "Like I said, I'll be in touch."

Danielle decided it was time to go. This interview had gone like the rest of her life the past couple of years. She just couldn't catch a break. With no modeling jobs, heracting career in the tank, and no money to start her boutique, what was she going to do now?

While Danielle was gathering up her coat and purse, Mrs. Lucas came out of the dressing room.

Stepping onto the raised dais, she turned from side to side, getting a look from all angles.

"You look great, Mrs. Lucas," Elaine said, fussing with the hem of the gown.

"Thank you, Elaine. As usual, your recommendation is a winner." Turning to Danielle, Mrs. Lucas asked, "What do you think?"

Danielle glanced at Elaine, who watched her with careful eyes. Taking this opportunity to prove that she should be the one to get the job, Danielle dropped her items back in the chair and walked around Mrs. Lucas, examining her from head to toe.

"I'm sure she would agree that you look absolutely perfect," Elaine said, wondering what Danielle was up to.

"Actually," Danielle started, "black can be a little over-done, especially with a sequin top. With your husband receiving such a prestigious honor tonight, you don't just want to look great, you want to look spectacular."

"What I think Ms. Kennedy is trying to say—" Elaine started, fearing she was about to lose a sale.

Flashing her million-dollar smile, Danielle stepped up on the dais with Mrs. Lucas. "You have such beautiful green eyes and lovely legs. We should build on that."

A little hesitant, Mrs. Lucas tried to visualize what she was being told. "I don't know. I'm almost fifty. Showing off my legs is not my style."

"Oh, not showing off, but accentuating." Jumping down, Danielle headed for the front of the store. "Give me five minutes. If you don't like it, you can go with the black dress. After all, you do look great in it."

"I don't think . . ." Elaine said, trying to control her rising temper. This unemployed supermodel was going to cost her a good customer.

"It's OK," Mrs. Lucas said, waving off the concerns of Elaine. "I have five minutes."

Danielle moved between two racks before she came to what she was looking for. She'd noticed the top when she first entered the boutique and thought it would be perfect for Mrs. Lucas. Quickly heading to the front counter, she shifted through the accessories and pulled out a pair of chandelier earrings and a matching necklace. Topping it off with an evening bag, she headed toward the dressing room, swooping up a pair of dressy pants in the process.

Mrs. Lucas took one look at the colorful top with the long black flared pants accented with a fake split up each side and couldn't hide her skepticism.

"Trust me," Danielle said confidently, hanging the items in her dressing room. "Just step out when you're done and we'll see what you think."

Elaine stood next to Danielle as they waited for Mrs. Lucas to reappear. Leaning over, she whispered in her ear, "I hope you know what you're doing. Mrs. Lucas is not only one of our best customers, she often refers her friends and associates to us."

For a split second, Danielle doubted herself. Things had been going so wrong for her lately, would this be one more embarrassment she'd have to deal with? But just as quickly as those thoughts entered her mind, they disappeared. Raising her head and squaring her shoulders, she gave Elaine a look that said "I got this." If it was one thing Danielle knew . . . it was how to put a look together.

After a few minutes, which seemed more like an hour, Mrs. Lucas emerged from the dressing room. Elaine gasped and Mrs. Lucas's look of reservation increased. Stepping onto the dais, she turned into the mirror. Slowing, she turned from side to side. The corners of her mouth tilted up and creased her face. "I love it!"

Danielle released a breath she didn't realize she had been holding.

"I never would have chosen such a colorful top, but it's very balanced with the solid black pants. The fake splits on the side make me look taller . . . and slimmer."

Stepping onto the dais with her, Danielle began to fuss with the top. "I've selected an evening bag that will be perfect, along with earrings and a necklace. The clothing is just the canvas. The accessories are what bring the outfit to life."

Twenty minutes later, Danielle stood to the side as Mrs. Lucas completed her sale. Wrapping her jewelry in tissue paper and covering the clothes in plastic with the Sara's Closet emblem on it, Elaine wished her and her husband a great evening.

Before leaving the store, Mrs. Lucas turned to Danielle. "Thanks again for your help, Ms. Kennedy."

"Oh, please, call me Danielle."

After a thoughtful few seconds, Mrs. Lucas said, "My husband and I are attending a fund-raiser for his hospital's children's ward. It's an afternoon luncheon and art auction. If you see anything you think would be appropriate, please let me know."

"I'll be sure to do that," Danielle said, refusing to look at Elaine. "Enjoy your evening."

As the satisfied customer exited, Danielle turned to Elaine, not giving her a chance to speak. "I believe the black dress she originally was going to buy was four hundred ninety-five dollars. She not only left with a top and pants that cost six hundred and seventy-two dollars, she also took home the earrings, necklace, and evening bag, which totaled just under three hundred dollars. Do you still need time to consider my application?"

Elaine hated to admit that Danielle had a definite eye for fashion and a certain boldness about her. She had wanted to recommend something more daring for Mrs. Lucas when she came in last week, but had backed down at the last minute, afraid of losing a customer if she didn't like the recommendation. Danielle had sweetened up Mrs. Lucas just enough to make her feel comfortable in trying something new, while letting her know that the worst-case scenario would put her in the dress she originally came in for—being sure to let her know that she would look great either way. "When can you start?"

Danielle wanted to scream with excitement, but worked to maintain her cool. "I'm available immediately."

"Why don't you come in tomorrow morning at ten? We'll discuss your schedule at that time."

Shaking hands, Danielle couldn't hide her enthusiasm. "I'll be here. Thank you, Ms. Bartlett. You won't regret it."

"Please, call me Elaine."

Danielle could have sworn the smile she gave her this time was real.

Elaine watched Danielle walk through the door and down the street. She'd never made such a spur-of-the-moment decision. She only hoped Danielle was right—she wouldn't regret it.

"Why did you give her such a hard time?" Patricia asked, who'd witnessed the entire scene from the front of the store.

"A supermodel?" Elaine said, still unable to believe what had just transpired.

Patricia laughed. "You used to be a corporate lawyer before taking over this store. So this isn't so strange."

"I guess not," Elaine said thoughtfully. "I just hope this works out."

"Don't worry, it will."

"I hope you're right, Patricia," Elaine said thoughtfully, staring out the door, no longer able to see Danielle. "I hope you're right."

# *Chapter Nine*

Xavier sat in the waiting room flipping through the latest issue of *Image* magazine. In New York on business, he'd decided to stop by Michelle's office to discuss the segment they would be shooting for the third episode of *The Fashion Design House*. He could easily have done this by phone, e-mail, or fax, but took a chance that she would be able to fit him into her schedule.

"Michelle is ready for you now. You can go on in."

"Thanks, Stacy."

Michelle's office, an organized mess, had papers and pictures everywhere. Xavier took a seat after handing her the info.

"I didn't expect to see you," Michelle said. "We could have talked about this by phone."

"I know, but as they say, I was in the neighborhod. It was just as easy to bring it by."

"Umm," Michelle said.

"Once you have a chance to review the information, you can call me and we—"

"She's decided not to go back to Georgia, but instead is staying with her sister."

Her interruption caught him off guard. It wasn't hard to figure out whom she was talking about, but he decided to play dumb. "What are you talking about?"

"Oh, please, Xavier," Michelle said, leaning back in

her chair. "You only came by here to get the latest scoop on Danielle."

"That's not true," he said. "I couldn't care less what she's up to."

Michelle didn't believe him. "I remember when you two were a couple. I thought you guys would really make it."

"Yeah, well," he said, thinking of their last conversation at the coffeehouse last week, "I also thought Vanilla Ice would make a comeback."

Michelle had watched Xavier's career develop over the years. Initially directing commercials, he'd carved a niche for himself in directing television shows, several movies for cable networks, and a couple of documentaries. He broke into the big screen by directing three commercially successful movies, and now he was trying his hand at producing. Opening his own production studio was a risky move. To make it, he couldn't just depend on his own production; he needed others to buy into his vision as well. He was taking one step at a time, and *The Fashion Design House* was the perfect opportunity for him.

"Let me ask you something," she said.

Xavier sat back in his chair. "Shoot."

"What's the real reason you didn't choose Danielle to host your show?"

Xavier didn't answer right away. No matter what he said, he would come out looking like the bad guy . . . which wouldn't be too far from the truth.

"You want to know what I think?" Michelle asked, seeing the thoughtful look in his eyes.

"No," he said.

"I think you wanted to pay Danielle back for the way she treated you, and now that you have, it doesn't feel as good as you thought it would. That's why I can't get rid of you. You're trying to find a way to make things right."

Xavier decided not to deny the truth. "You're half

right. I do feel bad about what I did. But I've already tried to make it up to her. She made it very clear that she's not interested in hearing anything I have to say."

"Michelle, Pierre Serlion is on line three." Stacy's voice boomed over the intercom. "He says they've been set up for the shoot for almost an hour, but there's no sign of Gabrielle."

Michelle let out a few expletives before reaching for the phone. "Another MIA model. Excuse me, I have to take this."

Michelle put her headset on and hit the line on her phone. Prepping herself for a fuming-mad photographer, she could only imagine how much this delay was costing. Standing, she put a smile on her face, hoping it would come through on the phone and help calm him down. "Pierre, sweetheart. What seems to be the problem?"

Xavier watched Michelle turn to face the window. While she tried to appease the photographer, there was no doubt that Stacy was launching a full-fledged hunt for Gabrielle. Thinking her call could take a while, he reached across her desk to review the taping schedule one more time. That's when another document caught his attention. The title on the cover read "Danielle's." Glancing at Michelle, he saw that she paid him no attention. He grabbed the binder and began reading.

"Do you make it a habit of snooping on other people's desks?"

So engrossed in the document, Xavier didn't realize Michelle had ended her call and was now staring at him, irritated.

"Is she serious about this?" he asked, pointing to the pages in front of him.

Not wanting to betray Danielle's trust, Michelle wasn't sure how much info she should reveal to Xavier. "More serious than I've ever seen her."

"This is a great plan," he noted. "I skimmed most of the sections. She really has a good handle on this."

"She worked hard on putting it together," Michelle said, remembering the number of hours Danielle said she put into it.

"Wait a minute," Xavier said, surprised at that bit of information. "Are you telling me Danielle wrote this?"

"Every word."

He turned a couple of pages and read a few more lines. "The marketing plan. The sales projections. The staffing needs."

Michelle didn't take offense at his disbelief. She'd had those same thoughts after she read through it. "I've never seen her so focused on anything—and I've known her a long time. Hopefully, she'll be able to overcome her challenges."

Closing the business plan, he placed it back on the desk. "What do you mean?"

"I don't think she'd appreciate me sharing her personal business with you. Unless," Michelle said, leaning forward and narrowing her eyes, "you're sincerely interested in helping her—especially after how you treated her when you didn't select her for the show."

"Like I said, I've tried talking to her—even suggested we take some time to talk things out. She turned me down flat. So believe me, if there was any way I could help, I would."

Michelle relaxed at his admission. "She's having problems getting the money together."

"Are you serious?" Xavier said, not hiding his surprise. "From what I've read, she's put together an excellent business plan. Who wouldn't jump on this opportunity?"

That's what Michelle thought, too. "No one in the industry is interested in helping her out and the banks won't give her a second look. Without her having a business background, some private investors are a little skeptical."

Xavier's heart sank. He hadn't realized how much he wanted Danielle's happiness. "How's she been taking it?"

"She's a trooper," Michelle said. "It's been hard for her to accept just how many enemies she's made over the years. Fortunately, she's working hard not to dwell on the negative."

"How?"

"The old-fashioned way," Michelle announced proudly. "She got a job."

Xavier cracked a smile at the comment. "As in a nine-to-five?"

"That's not very nice," Michelle said.

"I'm sorry," Xavier said, unable to hide his amusement. "I just can't imagine what kind of job Danielle would get."

"Modeling is a job," Michelle not so politely reminded him. "And if my memory serves me correct, she was pretty damn good at it."

"You're right, Michelle," he said sincerely. "I'm sorry. What is she doing now?"

"She thought investors would feel more comfortable if she got a job in the retail industry."

Xavier nodded in agreement. Experience was the best approach when looking to start a business venture. "Did she get on as a buyer with a store?"

"Not exactly," Michelle said, hedging.

"A district manager with an upscale store?" Xavier said, thinking of the number of department stores located in the Washington, D.C., area.

"Not quite."

"Something along the lines of a store manager?"

Michelle hesitated before answering, "More along the lines of sales clerk."

This time, Xavier couldn't contain his laugh. "Did you say clerk, as in cashier, as in floor salesperson?"

"You sound surprised, " Michelle said, scolding him with her eyes. "All of those positions are respectable jobs."

"I don't deny that. I just can't imagine Danielle working the bottom rung of retail."

"In all honesty, Xavier, neither could I. But she's been there more than a week and she couldn't be more excited."

"What's the name of the store?"

Michelle hesitated and raised a suspicious brow. "Why?"

"Just curious," Xavier said, even though she probably knew his intentions.

"I'm not sure if Danielle would want me to give out personal information."

"Come on, Michelle," Xavier said, leaning forward. "Give me something. I won't do anything stupid."

"Sara's Closet."

Thoughtfully, Xavier stood. "Thanks. I've taken up enough of your time." Waving the business plan in the air, he headed for the door. "Do you mind if I hold on to this for a while?"

"I don't know. If Danielle found out . . ."

"I may be able to help."

Michelle stared at Xavier. She decided he might be able to reach people who could help Danielle that she couldn't, so she nodded her approval.


Danielle glanced at the clock when her stomach growled. Almost two o'clock. She had yet to take a lunch break. On the job for almost two weeks, she loved every part of it. From helping customers pick out the perfect outfits, to restocking inventory, to closing out the register at the end of the day. Fascinated by every aspect of running a business, she'd worked just about every day since she'd been hired.

This afternoon, she unpacked several cardboard boxes containing sweaters from a designer in Italy in the stockroom. Throwing the tissue paper to the side as she removed each sweater, she hung them on a hanger and set them on the rolling rack.

"I'm headed out to grab a sandwich. Do you want anything?" Patricia yelled from the dressing room area.

"Turkey on wheat, no mayo, would be great," Danielle yelled back.

The two of them worked together most days. With two grown daughters who were married and raising their own children, Patricia enjoyed working with the customers at the store. A widow of three years, she'd found her work a godsend as she dealt with living alone.

Patricia stood in the doorway and watched Danielle work with a vengeance. She was pleasantly surprised by Danielle's commitment to her job; she had proven to be a hard worker showing great customer service. Even Elaine had to reluctantly admit that she had no complaints about her new employee. "Elaine won't be in for another hour, so be on the lookout for any customers."

"Sure," Danielle said, not stopping her work. A few seconds later she heard the bell over the door signaling Patricia's departure.

Finished with the box, she quickly broke it down with a small knife and moved on to the next one. The silk tops were perfect for the spring and she hung them up and plugged in the steamer. There was no way she would put them on the selling floor with that many wrinkles. Just as she started to steam, she heard the doorbell. Setting the steamer on the table, she patted her hair and reached for her suit jacket. "I'll be with you in just a minute." She slipped her left foot back in her pump.

"Take your time."

Danielle lost her balance as she tried to put on her other shoe. It was the voice. She'd heard it before—many times before. It couldn't be. What would he be doing here? Quickly slipping on the other shoe, she checked herself in the mirror outside the dressing room before berating herself for doing so. Making her way to the front of the store, she found her worst fear confirmed.

"What are you doing here?" she hissed. She was glad he was the only customer in the store. That meant she could be as rude as she wanted.

"Is that any way to greet a customer?" he asked, studying the front rack of casual tops. "As a sales associate, I thought you would know better than to be obnoxious with a customer."

"I do know how to treat my *customers*, but you don't qualify."

"Of course I do," he said, making his way farther into the store.

She watched him pick up a pair of pants and put them back down, only to move to the next rack where he held up a dress to examine it. Snatching the item out of his hand, she returned it to its proper place. "This is a *women's* clothing shop."

Taking a step closer to her, he leaned in. "I need to buy a birthday present for my mother," he said lightly. "I think she would classify as a woman."

His nearness set her off balance and she inhaled the scent that sent her body scrambling. When she had walked out of that coffee shop, she intended never to see him again. But he kept showing up in her dreams, and now he stood in front of her. Upset that she let him affect her this way, she took a step back. "This is April."

"And your point?" he asked.

"Your mother's birthday is in June," she said pointedly.

Pleased that she remembered details about his family that they'd shared when they were a couple, he took one more step closer. "I shop early."

"Fine," she said, stepping around him. The closer he stood, the more her senses went on high alert. He was wearing that cologne that turned her on. She had to put some distance between them. Ignoring it, she said, "What can I show you today?"

Shrugging, he glanced around the rest of the store. "Something dressy, but casual."

Danielle spent the next fifteen minutes pulling together various looks that would suit his mother's style and taste. Having met her during their courtship, she remembered her to be about five feet six, a size twelve, and very active. Her hair, having gone gray years before, had not been dyed, giving her a distinctive look. Since Xavier had insisted on invading Danielle's space, she made sure he was going to pay for it.

When she laid it all out, Xavier had to admit that he liked her choices. The skirt, blouse, and casual jacket fit his mother's style to a tee. "You're not too bad at this."

"What did you expect?" she said, secretly pleased that she impressed him.

"I'm not sure," he said thoughtfully as he watched her ring up his purchase. With her having talked him into two scarves to go along with what he'd already selected, he handed over his credit card, silently complimenting her on her up-selling skills. His original purchase, just over four hundred, had somehow inched up to five hundred and sixty-two dollars.

"We have some wonderful scarf clips that many of our customers use to change their look from day to cocktail. I think—"

"I think you've sold me enough," Xavier warned. "My mother will be quite happy with what I've gotten."

"If you say so," Danielle said, placing the clips beside the scarves to show how well they blended together. "It's just that the scarf clip is the piece that completes the look."

Xavier caved. "Fine, I'll take two clips—whichever two you recommend."

The smile on Danielle's face increased, as did his total. Six hundred twenty-two dollars and sixty-three cents.

Once the items were carefully wrapped and placed in a gift box, Danielle moved from around the counter and crossed her arms at her chest. "Now, why don't you tell me the real reason you're here?"

Xavier hid his surprise that she could see right through his act. "I came to ask you to dinner."

Dropping her hands to her side, she walked around him and began straightening the table that held several handbags. "No, thank you."

"Aren't you going to take a minute to think about it?"

"Don't need it."

"I detect a slight hint of agitation in your voice."

Stopping her task, she turned to him and took a step toward him. "Then you have obviously misread me. What you should have detected is downright anger."

"Why would you be angry with me?" Xavier asked, casually leaning back against the counter.

"You know what?" Danielle said, throwing her hands up in defeat. "On second thought, you're right. Why should I be angry at the fact that I was the best person for that host job and you cut me out?"

"You were good, Danielle, just not the right person for this project," Xavier said honestly.

The words only incensed Danielle more, but before she could respond, the bell over the door rang, indicating another customer. "I believe you've gotten all you're going to get today. You can show yourself out."

Xavier watched Danielle's entire demeanor change as she helped a woman pick out the perfect ensemble for a dinner party. Charming and attentive, she joked and laughed with her customer, all the while adding more and more to the purchase. She was none of those things with him. Standing against the wall, he took note of her ability to make the customer feel like a friend, while also making the sale.

Danielle tried to ignore his presence as she continued her work. Feeling as if her every move was being watched, she hoped her discomfort didn't show to her client. Why didn't he just leave?

"Thank you for coming, Shannon. Let me know how the dinner party turns out."

Xavier had seen enough of Danielle in a variety of moods to know that her enjoyment of working with that customer was genuine. Owning a boutique just might be the perfect job for her.

"Are you still here?" The sarcasm magically reappeared in her voice as soon as the customer was out the door.

"I didn't get a chance to tell you what time I'd pick you up for dinner," he said, confident that she would agree.

Placing her hands on her hips, she couldn't believe his audacity. "That would be unnecessary information, since I'm not going to dinner with you."

Just then, the bell sounded again and Elaine entered the store.

"Please, Xavier. Leave," she whispered, nervously glancing at her boss. "I'm not interested in seeing you tonight or any other night."

Elaine tipped her head in a silent greeting and stepped behind the counter and began checking invoices for the day.

Noticing her reaction, Xavier whispered, "Is that your boss?"

Grabbing his arm, Danielle pleaded with her eyes. "Just go, OK?"

"I will if you have dinner with me," he countered.

"No."

"Not even if I have information about someone interested in investing in Danielle's?"

The words caught her completely off guard and she narrowed her eyes in suspicion. "What do you know about Danielle's?"

"I know that you put together a great business plan, but you have no money and no one interested in giving you money."

The bell over the door rang and another customer entered.

Danielle greeted the customer, letting her know that she would be right with her. "Did Michelle say something to you?"

"You have a customer waiting. But I promise you, I'll tell you everything . . . over dinner."

"Fine," she relented. "I get off at seven."

"I'll be here."

"I'd prefer to meet you."

"That's not my style. I'll be here at seven."

Danielle watched him leave with that confident swagger that she used to find endearing. Now it just irritated her. But still, she couldn't contain that sliver of excitement at seeing him again.

# Chapter Ten

Danielle checked her watch for the third time in only a few minutes.

"Are you OK, Danielle? You seem a little nervous."

Silently berating herself for being so anxious, Danielle turned her attention back to adding up her personal sales receipts for the day. "I'm fine, Elaine."

Elaine didn't believe her for one minute. She'd been at the front counter for almost an entire fifteen minutes and Danielle had added that same stack of receipts at least five times. She didn't even think Danielle realized what she was doing. "It's just that ever since that customer left this afternoon, you've walked around on edge."

Danielle heard the curiosity in her voice and chose to ignore it. Even though Elaine spoke the truth, Danielle would never admit it.

Now that some time had passed, her anger at Xavier was subsiding. In its place, feelings of attraction had started to develop. It was bad enough that he'd become a permanent fixture in her dreams, but spending an evening with him might prove to be more than she could handle.

They broke up because she'd been blinded by success. Now that she'd matured, it didn't take much for her to clearly see what a good man she had let go. But if she was going to make a new life for herself, she had to leave her past behind—once and for all. Xavier Johnston was a part of that past. "What customer?"

The fact that Danielle didn't look up when she spoke told Elaine that she was pretending to be in the dark about what she was asking. "The gentleman who was here when I arrived."

"Oh, him?" Danielle said coolly. "That was just a customer."

Danielle didn't say anything further and Elaine decided to push it. "Do you know him?"

Shrugging nonchalantly, Danielle stacked her receipts and stapled them. "He used to be somebody I worked with."

Elaine raised a brow at that statement. "Since the last job you had was as a supermodel making three million a year, I guess it's safe to say that he's from the world of the rich and famous."

"Very funny," Danielle said, beginning to gather up her belongings. "I'm not scheduled to come in tomorrow, but Mrs. Norton is coming in to pick up two suits I set aside for her. Can you give her the thank-you card I put under the register?"

"No problem," Elaine said, moving in front of Danielle, blocking her from stepping out from behind the counter. Reaching out for her, she held her hand much the way a mother would. "I haven't asked a lot of questions, because I figured if you wanted to share your past with me, you would."

The concern in her voice caused Danielle to feel a little guilty about her short answers. "I'm just not ready to—"

Elaine cut her off before she could finish. "I can see that, but you have to admit that if the roles were reversed, wouldn't you be a little curious?"

Aside from what Danielle had put on her application, she had been less than forthcoming with details about her previous life. Most of her conversations with Patricia and Elaine revolved around work. Danielle admitted silently that Elaine was right. If the roles were reversed, she'd be dying to know what the deal was.

"I have a confession to make," Elaine said.

Those words caught Danielle's attention and her eyes narrowed in curiosity.

"I almost Googled you, but I stopped myself because whatever your experiences have been, they are just that . . . yours."

"Thanks, Elaine," Danielle said, squeezing her hand. "I appreciate you respecting my privacy."

"Well . . ." Elaine said, wanting to lighten the mood. "I'll respect your privacy in your past professional life. But in this store, personal lives are fair game. So tell me, who was that fine-looking man that was in here earlier? I'd bet money that there's something personal between you two."

"And why would you want to lose your hard-earned money?" Danielle asked, picking up her purse and keys.

"Oh, I wouldn't lose," Elaine said with a knowing look in her eyes. "I could see it by the way he was looking at you."

Two customers walked in and Elaine greeted them, letting them know she'd be right with them. Focusing back on Danielle, she said, "I may be from another generation, but I know attraction when I see it. That man, as you young people like to say, has the hots for you."

Danielle stepped around the counter and headed for the door. "You're mistaken. He just wanted to get a birthday gift for his mother."

Elaine hesitated before speaking. "You've only been here a few weeks, but you have yet to take a day off—even when you have one scheduled. You volunteer to open when one of us has an appointment, and you've stayed late to help customers."

Glad for the sudden change in the topic of conversation, Danielle said, "I thought that was the kind of commitment bosses looked for in their employees."

"Commitment, yes. But just don't let that turn into hiding out."

Danielle paused at the strange terminology. "Hiding out? From what?"

"Life."

Just then, the doorbell rang again and Elaine headed to the sales floor to assist the customers, leaving Danielle to ponder the meaning behind her words.

It was a clear, cool night. She waited a few feet from the entrance of the store, the bumper-to-bumper traffic inching its way out of the city and into the suburbs. The foot traffic was heavy, tourists and residents blending as they moved up and down the streets. The variety of shops and restaurants offered something for everyone.

Couples held hands, laughed, and joked with each other, and Danielle thought about the last time she'd been in a relationship that had her feeling that secure and carefree. It didn't take long for her to pinpoint it. Xavier.

He was different from any other guy she'd ever known. In a business that rewarded those who were tough and cut-throat, Xavier had managed to craft a career by not back-stabbing too many people along the way. Always saying that he didn't want his day job constantly spilling over into his nightlife, he'd often convinced Danielle to skip industry events and opt for more normal dates. They enjoyed simple dinners in great restaurants and silly movies weeks after they'd had their star-studded premieres, and he even took her bargain shopping at secondhand shops for items he used to decorate his apartment. But above all else, he made her laugh—not take herself so seriously.

Thinking of the good times they'd had together, she wondered what her life would have been like if they'd stayed together. Marriage? Children? Danielle snapped out of her daze and glanced around as if others could read her thoughts. What was she thinking? This man gave new meaning to the word *lowlife.* Elaine was wrong. She couldn't have seen attraction in his eyes, because if he still had feelings for her, how could he treat her like he did at lunch?

Glancing down the street, she wasn't sure if he planned to park and have them eat at one of the restaurants nearby, or scoop by and pick her up. Either way, she would make this meeting short and sweet. If it wasn't for Xavier mentioning possible investors for her business, she wouldn't be here to begin with.

The black Mercedes pulled up, and Danielle's memory automatically took her back. He'd been eyeing the S class for almost a year, debating whether to buy it or not. When one of his movies premiered number one at the box office, ultimately surpassing the one-hundred-million-dollar mark, he decided to treat himself. Danielle stood by him when he signed the papers at the dealership. They broke it in by driving to a secluded bed-and-breakfast, spending the weekend using more of the bed than the breakfast.

Just thinking back caused a slight intake of her breath. The nights they shared were filled with passion. On many occasions, they lay in bed planning their future. At the time, it was hard to imagine that future without both of them in it.

Opening the driver-side door, Xavier jumped out and trotted around to the other side. "Don't let it be said that I lack chivalry."

He opened her door and waited for her to reach for her seat belt before he closed it.

Once he got back in the car, Danielle thought it best

to remind him of her intentions up front. "I want you to know that this is a business meeting."

Xavier put the car in drive, but didn't pull off. "Business meeting? I thought this was a date," he said, giving her a wink and a wide smile.

She could find no humor in this situation. "Why would I go on a date with you?"

Merging into the traffic, Xavier didn't look at her. "Because that's what people who like each other do."

Danielle refused to acknowledge that statement with a response.

After driving for several minutes, they headed out of the District and into Virginia.

Xavier pushed the Play button on his CD changer. The smooth sounds of Luther Vandross filled the air.

Danielle eyed Xavier out of the corner of her eye, but he continued to stare ahead at the road. Luther was her all-time favorite artist; his voice had been their constant companion when they were a couple—especially at night.

"The Power of Love" came on and Luther's voice boomed through the system.

> *When I say good-bye it is never for long*
> *'Cause I know our love still lives on.*
> *It will be again exactly like it was*
> *'Cause I believe in the power of love.*
> *When you're close I can feel the power.*
> *When it's love I can always tell.*
> *Love for me is the best thing now.*
> *It's something that I know so well.*

Danielle pounded the Stop button and the car became eerily silent. The words of the song touched too close to home.

"Problem with my musical selection?"

His innocent tone didn't fool Danielle. As a matter of fact, it only irritated her more. There was no question he played that song on purpose. "Don't forget—this is a business meeting."

"How can I?" Xavier said, turning the radio on to a local hip-hop station. "You won't let me."

Quiet the remainder of the ride, they passed the Pentagon, heading into the city of Arlington. "Where are we going?"

"I chose some place quiet, out of the way." He glanced at her; it was obvious she didn't like the sound of his description. Too romantic. "So we could discuss our business without interruption."

Turning off the main road, he pushed the button on his sun visor and the gated multilevel parking garage opened. Pulling into a space, he cut the engine and opened his door.

"This is a residential building?" Danielle said, taking note of the numbered parking spaces.

"My condo," he said, as if he was surprised she asked. "I moved in about a year ago. Great location. Close to the airport, shops, restaurants."

"Are you out of your mind!" Danielle screamed. He had been rambling on like a real estate agent looking to make a sale. "Why on earth would I want to spend an evening with you in your condo?"

"For the same reason you wanted to spend the evening with me two minutes ago," he reminded her before getting out. "To talk about your business plan."

Cursing under her breath, she unhooked her belt and stepped out of the car. Following him to the elevator, she wanted to smack that smug grin off his face.

The ride to the seventeenth floor was made in complete silence, but Danielle was the only one uncomfortable. It wasn't that she didn't trust him—she didn't trust herself. No way would she admit this to anyone, but the moment she'd spotted him in the studio at their first meeting about *The Fashion Design House,* she constantly thought about what could have been.

Even when she'd stormed out of the restaurant, blazing with anger at his decision to go with Layla, she still found him amazingly attractive. When she'd stepped into Michelle's office and he turned to face her, he took her breath away. She remembered every whispered word of love they shared, every intimate dinner, every breakfast in bed, and every declaration of love.

When he'd hopped out of the car tonight to pick her up, he appeared to have stepped out of the pages of *GQ.* The stone-washed black jeans hugged his thighs just right. The crisp button-down shirt hung loosely, covered by a three-quarter-length leather jacket. If she didn't still hold a grudge against him, she might find herself giving in to his desire to give their relationship another chance.

The elevator doors opened and he motioned for her to exit first. "Try to keep your hands to yourself tonight. After all, this is a business meeting."

She heard the teasing in his words and as she walked past him she patted his cheek like a child. "Don't worry. It won't be that hard."

His laughter filled the hall and Xavier watched the slight sway of her hips as she made her way to his door. Not telling her where they were eating was his way of keeping her from saying no. Choosing his condo, he'd hoped it would give them an opportunity to talk about their relationship without interruption, but watching her from behind, coming to his condo might not have been such a good idea.

The slacks and suit jacket she wore to work today couldn't hide the sexiness that oozed from her. It didn't matter if she had on a potato sack or a twenty-thousand-dollar designer gown, she would always be gorgeous. Whatever skin care and exercise regimen she used, it was, without a doubt, working. She'd gained a little weight since her modeling days, though the extra pounds filled her out in all the right places. She was more beautiful today than when she strutted for the cameras.

After he opened the door, she stepped into the foyer, and the aroma wafted to her nose.

Taking her jacket, he opened the closet. "Why don't you have a seat in the living room? I'll check on dinner and get us a glass of wine."

"I don't think wine will go with the 'business only' theme we've already established. I'll have water."

Xavier reached for her hands and was surprised when she didn't pull away. "Things have been rough for you lately. Why don't you just take one evening and relax?"

Danielle didn't look convinced.

"If what I saw at the store today is any indication of how hard you've been working these past couple of weeks, then I know you can use a nice, relaxing evening."

Nudging her toward a positive answer, Xavier added, "It will still be a business meeting."

The compliment didn't slip past Danielle, and the corners of her mouth curved into a small grin. Elaine and Patricia had praised her over the past few weeks. Sales were up and she'd developed a rapport with several of the customers. But the compliment from Xavier meant just as much to her.

With the emotional roller-coaster ride she'd been on the last couple of months, maybe he was right. A relaxing evening just might be what she needed. Thoughts of her finances, her living situation, getting a job, and opening a boutique had started to take their toll. "OK, just one glass."

Xavier hesitated before going to the kitchen. For some

reason, he'd expected a smart remark, or an outright demand that they get down to business. Pleasantly surprised, he showed her to the living room and then disappeared to the other room.

Returning, he handed her a glass of Chardonnay and placed the bottle on the coffee table.

Picking the bottle up, she glanced at the label. Her favorite.

"I hope you're hungry," he said, raising his glass for a toast. "I have lasagna, Caesar salad, and French bread—oozing with butter."

She waited a few seconds before finally clinking his glass. "What exactly are you trying to do tonight?"

"What do you mean?"

His questioning gaze would lead an outsider to believe that he truly had no idea what she was talking about. Danielle wasn't an outsider. "Interesting choice of foods."

"I took a chance that it would appeal to you."

The low, sexy timbre of his voice caused her to smile slightly. "You knew it would."

When they'd dated, Danielle had strict dietary instructions that she had to adhere to. Maintaining her weight was a number-one priority. Makeup could cover up skin flaws, tracts of hair and wigs took care of bad-hair days, and a bevy of tricks was available to handle other imperfections. But there was nothing that could slide a body into a sample-size dress if the body was too big. An extra five pounds was the difference in getting a show or not.

Living off vegetables, chicken, brown rice, and fish, Danielle rarely had trouble maintaining the desired weight. But every now and then, she just had to satisfy her cravings for all things bad. Every couple of months, Xavier would make his homemade lasagna and French bread. He'd toss a Caesar salad with as much cheese as he could fit in the bowl, and they would pig out—not worrying about the calories or the fat. The next day, they would faithfully hit the gym and Danielle would work out twice as hard and three times as long. But she didn't care. It was all worth it.

Taking a seat on the sofa, he pulled her with him, sitting thigh to thigh. "That's not the only thing I remembered you liked."

He cut his eyes down to her lips and seductively smiled. "Guess what I've got for dessert?"

Danielle watched as he trailed his hand up her thigh, moving into dangerous territory. Her mind told her to get up, but her body wouldn't obey. "What?" she said breathlessly.

"Betty Crocker devil's food cake with double chocolate icing. And of course you can't have that without Breyer's vanilla ice cream."

"Ohh," Danielle moaned. She had a penchant for all things chocolate. "I haven't had that in years . . . not since . . ."

Her words trailed off and they just stared at each other, the electricity almost crackling in the air. The last time she had that dessert was with him. One week before they broke up.

Xavier licked his lips and lowered his head.

"Shouldn't you check on the food?" she said, standing and walking across the room to the fireplace.

Xavier exhaled deeply at what could have been. Never had he been so desperate for a kiss. He'd dated several women since Danielle, trying to recapture the magic that he'd shared with Danielle. But no one measured up.

When he heard through the grapevine that she was going through a rough time financially, he couldn't count the number of times he picked up the phone, wanting to offer help. But anger had a funny way of being all-consuming. It blinded him from seeing clearly enough to do what was right.

They'd both made mistakes in the past, but now that they had another chance, he wanted to take full advantage of it. Tonight was the first step in that direction. He only hoped Danielle wanted the same thing. "I'll be right back."

Danielle watched him go and took another much-needed sip of her wine. Releasing a slow breath, she rested her head on the mantel. *This is business, Danielle. You've got too much going on in your life right now to get involved in a relationship—no matter how fine the man.*

Feeling as if she'd regained some sense of control, she picked up a few of the pictures on the mantel. The older couple she recognized immediately. The first time she'd met Xavier's parents, they were celebrating thirty-five years of marriage. Relatives from all across the country had come to join in the festivities.

From the moment the introductions were made, his mother was cool and aloof. It wasn't until a few hours later when they were alone in the kitchen that Catherine Johnston made her position crystal clear.

Preparing coffee to go with the cheesecake she was serving for dessert, Catherine politely told Danielle that she wasn't impressed by her pretty face, fancy clothes, or celebrity lifestyle. The tabloids and entertainment news had told her more about Danielle than she cared to know—and it was all negative. Catherine promised to maintain an appropriate demeanor with her because it was obvious to her how much her son cared about her. Before heading out to join the others, she said her final words.

"The good news is, I don't think this relationship will last. The bad news is, it'll tear my son apart when it ends."

How right his mother had been. Placing the picture back in its place, Danielle surveyed the rest of the room. The layout had sophisticated bachelor written all over it.

The oversized sofa and matching love seat were dark blue, accented by multicolored throw pillows. On the opposite wall, a high-tech entertainment system took stage, built into the wall and anchored by a flat-screen television. Soft music played through speakers she couldn't even see.

When they'd dated, he had homes in Los Angeles and New York, similarly decorated. Danielle always felt comfortable when she stayed with him. It had been a safe haven from the crazy world she lived in. Looking around the room today, she had that same feeling.

"We should be eating in the next few minutes."

His return startled her and she pushed down the sentimental thoughts about him. "Great, I'm starving."

Noticing both their glasses were running low, he refilled.

She started to object, but decided against it. When was the last time somebody cooked for her? Served her? Not somebody she was paying to do it, but someone who was doing it because they wanted to? Searching her mind, she couldn't come up with anyone recently. The last person to take the time to make her feel special was standing in front of her.

Xavier thought back to the first time he met her. Was it just three years ago? On the last day of fashion week in New York, he had just wrapped on a documentary that was scheduled to air on HBO. Getting the green light earlier that day that gave him his first feature film to direct, he, and everyone else in the city, was in the mood to party. With champagne flowing and the music blasting, models, designers, movie stars, pop singers, photographers, and the media mingled well into the night at the hottest club in Manhattan.

Working hard at his craft, he'd been linked to several actresses and singers, but none of his relationships had lasted more than a few months. Not because they weren't nice and interesting, but because he feared them getting too needy. There wasn't time in his life to coddle a relationship, to take it from the budding stage to the blossoming stage. Most women said they understood when he explained his position up front. He found out the hard way that that was not true.

Just having called it quits with someone a week before, he swore the last thing he had on his mind was meeting someone new. The entire exercise of breaking up could be exhausting and he didn't think he was up for another woman telling him she could handle the parameters for what he could give to her, and then becoming frustrated when she couldn't change him.

Needing a break from the music and the people, he headed out onto the balcony. Though he'd given up smoking a year ago, this was one of the few times that a craving hit him. Fighting the urge to bum one from someone, he stepped to the rail to look out over the skyline.

She stood off to the side. Her jade silk slip dress dipped low in the back and had to be the shortest dress he'd ever seen on anyone. Her tall, slim figure gave her profession away and it only took a second to admit that she was the most stunning woman he'd ever laid eyes on.

Forgetting the deal he'd made with himself about getting involved with another woman, he couldn't resist at least finding out her name.

In his line of work, attractive women were a dime a dozen. It was what was on the inside that separated the pretty face from the truly beautiful person. Having been in this business for a long time, he'd been fooled several times by the pretty face. The moment he saw her, he prayed that this wouldn't be the case with her.

When he walked up to stand behind her, she didn't turn around, even though he was sure she could feel his presence. "I should be intimidated talking to someone as beautiful as you, but I figure, since I'm so handsome, we'd make a fabulous couple."

Danielle initially ignored anyone who was obviously arrogant. She'd modeled in nine shows in the last three days and her exhaustion level reached an all-time high. The only reason she'd agreed to make an appearance at this party was that she'd had a little incident with the designer of the last show, and one of the major sponsors of tonight's activities.

Michelle had warned her that she needed to "make nice" with him if he was going to use her again. That translated into apologizing for her behavior, attending his party, and raving to everyone who could hear about what a wonderful line of clothes he was putting out this season. She even agreed to wear two of his designs to the next couple of events she would attend where the chances of her being photographed were high.

After smiling all night with strangers and listening to Michelle give her yet another speech on her behavior, the last thing Danielle wanted to deal with was some guy trying to pick her up. Deciding that she'd been nice enough for one night, she turned to face him, letting him know, in a not so polite manner, where he and his pickup line could go.

When her eyes focused on him, her response quickly changed. A few inches taller than her, he casually leaned against the railing as if he didn't have a care in the world. Normally, the men who approached her, no matter how successful they were in their professional lives, somehow seemed intimidated. That was the last impression she got from the man standing in front of her tonight. And that, added to his fantastic looks, made him interesting. "Lucky for you, you're right."

They both burst into laughter and a great relationship was born.

Too bad his mother was right. It was doomed to fail.

# *Chapter Eleven*

Xavier began to pick up the magazines. "I'll move some of this stuff off the coffee table and we can eat Japanese style. It won't take but a few minutes to bring the food out.'"

Danielle glanced around the room and took note of the cozy fire burning in the fireplace, the soft jazz playing in the background, the oversized sofa with its comfortable large cushions, and the bottle of wine that was almost empty. It was a scene set for seduction, not a business meeting. She started to suggest they eat in the dining room, but he'd already disappeared back to the kitchen.

Almost an hour and another bottle of wine later, Danielle put down her fork and patted her stomach. "I haven't eaten this much food in my life. I can't believe I had two big servings of that lasagna. My time at the gym tomorrow will definitely be doubled, if not tripled."

Xavier stacked their plates up and started to stand. "Thank you."

"Let me help you." Danielle grabbed her plate and jumped to her feet. Moving too fast, she felt the rush of the wine and lost her balance.

Seeing her about to fall, Xavier reached out for her, just before she would have hit the floor. Both fell back on the couch, her plate falling to the floor.

Trying to stop her dirty dishes from hitting his light-colored carpet was useless, as they got more entangled with each other. The dishes landed facedown, the remnants of cheese, tomatoes, and salad dressing no doubt starting to penetrate the rug.

Shocked registered on her face and for a split second, she felt bad about it. Then, she burst into laughter. "I'm sorry, Xavier. I think I've stained your carpet."

With his arms wrapped around her waist and her leg on top of his, their compromising position caused them both to take pause. For a moment, neither moved. Removing her leg, Danielle scooted away from him.

Picking up the dishes and putting them back on the table, he surveyed the damage. Just a few small spots here and there.

"Don't worry about it," he said. Judging from her reaction, he doubted that she did. "You practically licked your plate. There wasn't much left on it, anyway."

Danielle heard the teasing in his tone and waved her finger at him, attempting to scold him. "Serves you right for bringing me to your house, fixing my favorite foods, and trying to get me drunk."

Xavier chuckled at the slight slurring of her words. "First of all, eating here provided us the privacy to discuss business. Second of all, the food was just my way of making sure I cooked something I knew you would like. Finally, I didn't try to do anything. You willingly indulged. But having said all of that, there's no doubt about it. You are well on your way to being drunk."

Looking at the two empty bottles still sitting on the table, Danielle tried to remember just how many glasses she'd drunk. "What about you? You had just as much wine as I did."

That part was true. It just didn't yield the same results. "You know as well as I do that I can drink three times as much as you and barely feel the effects."

"Whatever," Danielle said, wondering why he didn't seem the least bit off balance.

"Remember that night in Miami?" he said. "You'd just completed a shoot for the Gucci layout for *Vogue*. We danced the night away at The Cantina."

How could Danielle forget? They had been dating for almost six months and he agreed to join her in Miami for a long weekend. She'd had a rough shoot and wanted to hang out and relax. Hitting the club a little after midnight, they prepared to party well into the morning.

"I think you had a couple of Long Island iced teas," Xavier continued. "I had to keep you from dancing on the tables."

"Yeah, but I had to keep you from knocking out that guy that kept flirting with me," Danielle reminded him. As she'd made her way back from the ladies' room, an older man, looking like a linebacker for the Dallas Cowboys, tried to stop Danielle for a little conversation. Telling him she wasn't available only seemed to encourage him more. When she realized that a polite "not interested" wasn't going to work for him, she just turned and walked away. He reached out for her arm and that's when Xavier appeared, telling him to get his paws off of her.

The shouting match that ensued quickly escalated when the fists were raised. If security hadn't separated the two, there would have been bloodshed. Danielle only hoped it wouldn't have been Xavier's.

"He deserved to be knocked out," Xavier said, remembering the jealousy that raced through him at the thought of her with another man.

"Between my attempts at climbing on the table and your pension for fighting, we were asked to leave well before the party ended," Danielle said, thinking of how much fun they'd had in the midst of all the drama.

"Asked to leave?" Xavier said, remembering that wild night. "Don't you mean kicked out?"

They both broke into laughter as they remembered Big Earl, the bouncer, escorting them out to the limo.

"He was kind enough to let us know that he would be working the door the rest of the night, just in case we decided to come back," Danielle said.

Xavier leaned back and stared at Danielle.

Danielle watched him watch her and her laughter died down as her face grew serious.

"What happened to us, Dee-Dee?" Xavier asked. "Why didn't we make it?"

Danielle kicked off her shoes and pulled her feet underneath her. Xavier was the only person she allowed to call her by that nickname. He gave it to her the night they met. It was his way of reminding her that regardless of what the media told her about herself, no matter how many people catered to her every need, she was just plain old Dee-Dee. It was his attempt to keep her grounded.

That questioned had swirled around in her more times than she cared to admit. Too ashamed at how she treated him, she never would have posed the question out loud. "Too much ambition. Too many dreams to chase."

Reaching out, he stroked the ends of her hair with his fingers. "Was it worth it?"

"What?" she said, trying to concentrate on the conversation as his hands moved from her hair to massage her neck.

"Our careers," he said quietly. "Were they worth destroying what we had? Our friendship? Our support? Our closeness? Our love?"

She scooted to the other end of the couch, out of his touch. Her body was crying out for him and she didn't think she had the power to resist. "That's such an unfair question."

Xavier moved closer to her, prodding her to let him cradle her in his arms. She gave in and rested her head against his chest. "Allow me to answer first. It wasn't worth it for me to hold on to the anger I felt toward you. It wasn't worth it to see how I hurt you last month. It wasn't worth the time we've wasted being apart. It's not worth it to continue to be apart."

Before Danielle could figure out what was happening, he leaned forward and placed a soft kiss on her lips.

His touch, so delicate and sweet, barely lasted a second. Leaning back, he tried to gauge her reaction. She didn't scratch his eyes out, so he took that as a good sign.

"What are you doing?" she whispered, the quandary of emotions swirling in her head and her heart.

Stroking her cheek, he kissed her neck. "What I should have done the moment you walked back into my life."

"Xavier, I don't think this is such a good idea," she said, even though she enjoyed it.

Pulling back slightly, he looked surprised. "Really? Because I think it's the best idea I've had in a long time."

One of her dreams flashed in her mind and her body reacted to the power of the attraction. Snapping out of the spell he was casting, she clumsily stood. "I . . . I . . . I have to go."

Reaching out for her, he held her hand in his. He stood and pulled her body close to his. They stood that way for several minutes, neither one saying a word or making an effort to move.

Xavier peered into her eyes. "Don't you ever wonder? Don't you ever question whether we should give us another chance?"

His breath caressed her ears and tingles coursed through her body. Even though the wine had taken effect, she understood exactly what was happening—exactly what she was doing. "Xavier, we had our chance. I blew it."

It was said so softly he barely heard the words. The resignation in them indicated that she had given up hope on them. "*We* blew it."

Stepping back, she looked around for her shoes. "It's too late for us."

Shaking his head from side to side, he refused to accept her answer. "There's no limit on how many chances we can give each other."

"I think I should go."

Xavier released his hold and sat down, resting his head in his hands. He'd gotten the message loud and clear. A relationship between them was not to be. Without looking up, he said, "Danielle, I was so hurt years ago when we broke up, but the moment you walked in for that audition, I thought the best way to rid you out of my system once and for all was through revenge."

Raising his head, he continued, "After I delivered the news that I thought would put me at peace when it came to you, the reality was that it only made things worse."

Reaching up for her, he traced his fingers up and down the side of her arms. He pulled her in between his legs and hugged her, resting his head on her stomach. "If you tell me you feel nothing for me, I'll accept it. But if you think there's any chance for us, you owe it to us to try."

Hearing his confessions made her heart flutter. All the dreams, all the sleepless nights, all the times she'd awoken in a cold sweat, yearning for his touch—could be satisfied tonight. Maybe this was what *she* needed to get him out of her system once and for all. One night.

"Xavier, maybe we could—"

Before she could continue, he stood and hungrily captured her lips and swallowed whatever words she was going to say. Holding her as if his life depended on it, he molded his body against hers. Every part of him reacted to the power of the magnetism. Slipping his tongue inside her mouth, he moaned at the complete gratification.

Having her back in his arms provided a level of peace and contentment that had been absent during their time apart. His dreams didn't come close to reality. All the restless nights, the cold showers, and the fantasies couldn't compare to what he was feeling at this moment. With her in his arms, everything was right. This was where she belonged, right here with him.

Guiding her back, he eased her down on the couch, lying on top of her. Moving her hair out of her face, he smiled down at her. "This is quite a compromising position."

With the bulge in his pants pressing against her, there was no doubt of his attraction for her. So long since she'd been in his arms, tasted his kisses, and savored his touch; she decided to take her night. Tomorrow she would deal with the consequences, but for right now, she gave in to the raw, animal attraction that she felt for him. "All the more reason to take advantage of it," she said, reaching up and putting her arms around his neck.

The statement left no room for misinterpretation, but Xavier wanted to be sure. "Danielle, you've had quite a bit of wine tonight."

"I'm not that drunk, Xavier," she said, stroking the nape of his neck. "I know exactly what I'm doing . . . exactly what I want."

"And what's that?" he asked.

"You."

Her sultry voice almost whispered the word and her gaze, filled with wanting, sent Xavier over the edge. As he captured her lips, all of the passion that had been held inside for the past two years came pouring out.

Reaching under her top, he slid his hand up her waist, until he cupped her breast. As he massaged gently, her back arched and her nipple hardened. Not in a rush, he wanted to reacquaint himself with every part of her. Starting at the top of her head, he nuzzled in her hair, inhaling the fresh scent. Slowly moving down, he kissed her ear before letting his tongue lick and nibble on it.

"You are so beautiful," he whispered, before going lower to her neck. His hand, not to be left out of the reacquainting process, released her breast and moved down until it touched the top of her pants. Unhooking the belt and unzipping them, he slid inside her underwear. When his fingers caressed that special spot, she groaned out his name in delight.

"Do you want to take this to the bedroom?" he asked, in between kisses.

Unbuttoning his shirt, Danielle seductively smiled. "Uh-uh, we're fine right here."

Removing his shirt, she ran her hands across his chest. "Oh yes, baby."

Going lower, she unhooked his pants.

He pulled her top over her head and flipped the clasp on her bra, tossing it across the room.

They both wiggled out of the rest of their clothes and Xavier reached in his wallet for the small foil packet before tossing the wallet to the side with the rest of the clothes. Sitting up, he quickly protected them.

Danielle, overwhelmed by the power of the moment, became the aggressor. Placing a bronze leg on each side of him, she pushed him back against the sofa.

The moment he entered her, the dreams Xavier had experienced became an instant reality. The dreams had pushed him out of his bed to seek the relief of a cold shower. But tonight, he needed nothing but her. Sinking into a rhythm they never seemed to have lost, neither could contain the moans of satisfaction.

"I've dreamed about this moment," Xavier admitted, reaching up to run his fingers through her hair.

Danielle couldn't believe his confession, and decided to make one of her own. "I haven't had a good night's sleep in a month either."

Realizing how much they both desired each other sent them over the edge. Danielle's body convulsed and the most satisfying feeling overtook her body. Just a few seconds later, he followed with his own release.

After several minutes of both of them trying to get their breathing under control, Danielle was the first to speak. "I can't believe we just did that."

Xavier listened for a hint of regret and said a silent prayer of thanks when he didn't hear it. Kissing her on the lips, he said, "Neither can I, but I'm not complaining."

Danielle attempted to move when he pulled her closer. "No, not yet. Having you in my arms again is like a dream come true."

As she rested her head against his chest, the protection and refuge that had been so prevalent in their relationship returned. Danielle had no idea how long they stayed that way—just holding each other. When he suggested they head to the bedroom, she didn't object.

The moonlight beamed in through the window, casting a soft glow. Leading her to the bed, Xavier gently guided her down. The uncontrollable, raw power that they'd shared in the living room was now replaced by the sensuous touch of a man in no hurry. Kneading, massaging, and giving special attention to each part of her body, his lovemaking was unhurried, allowing their connection to take place at every level—body, spirit, and soul. By the time they drifted off to sleep, they had both entered a state of euphoria.

\*\*\*

Danielle awoke to a darkened room and the feel of a strong arm around her waist. As she remembered the passion they'd shared through the night, her lips curved into an easy smile. Marvelous was too mild a word to describe the last few hours of her life. It almost seemed surreal. After a year of loving each other, then despising and hurting each other, they finally found their way back to each other.

Slightly sitting up, she glanced at the clock on the nightstand. Her body ached, but it was the best kind of pain. The pain that said someone cared, wanted, and needed you.

Almost six A.M. Her eyes focused on the paper beside the clock. Carefully extracting herself from his touch, she picked up the business plan for Danielle's. The feeling of euphoria she'd felt a few short moments ago slightly diminished.

Putting the document back, she slipped out of bed and went to the bathroom. Closing the door, she turned on the shower. The multiple shower heads sprayed her body from six different angles, giving her a much-needed minimassage.

A million thoughts ran through her mind. The boutique was at the top of that list. Finally finding something that gave her purpose again had been the motivating factor in taking positive steps to get her life back on track. Opening and running a business would require so much of her time. There was already the daunting task of raising the capital. Did she really want to have the added pressure of a relationship?

Elaine had been so pleased with her work and talked of letting Danielle handle more and more of the business side of things. Elaine's offer was exactly what she needed to get a full understanding of the entire business.

The magnetism that drew her to Xavier could not be ignored. Her intentions had been for them to share one night together. If she let it become any more than that—could she still focus on her business? With no answers to her silent questions, she lathered up.

The steamy glass door opened and Xavier stepped in. His body, rock solid with a broad chest, flat stomach, and runner's legs, took her breath away. Locking his gaze with hers, he took the soap and washcloth out of her hand and began to wash her body one part at a time. Moving in a circular motion, he started with her shoulders. Continuing down her arms, he paid special attention to them before moving on to her stomach. Reaching behind her, he washed her back, adding just the right amount of pressure that caused her to close her eyes in enjoyment.

Tossing the soap and washcloth to the side, he pushed her completely under the shower heads to rinse her body. Cupping her breasts, he leaned down, taking one in his mouth. His skilled tongue sent a wave of desire through her as the water continued to work the soreness out of her muscles. His head lowered, kissing her belly button. Reaching behind her, he squeezed her butt, inching her closer to him.

As his head continued its descent, all thoughts of businesses and boutiques left her mind. When he reached her core, he caressed her with his tongue and her attempt at holding in a scream failed. As he stroked and licked, every part of Danielle succumbed to the pure bliss he was giving. Just when she thought she couldn't take it another minute, her body trembled and sexual gratification consumed her from top to bottom. Calling out his name, she let the power of the moment take over.

A half hour later, Danielle joined Xavier in the kitchen. With no curling irons, blow-dryer, or a decent supply of makeup, she had to make do. Putting on a pair of his sweatpants and one of his old sweatshirts, she looked more like a ragamuffin than a former model.

"I made us breakfast. I know you don't eat a lot of meat, so I have veggie omelets and waffles." Before he finished setting the food on the table, he went to her, giving her a kiss on the lips. "You look gorgeous."

"Yeah, right." She didn't buy into that compliment. She'd taken a look at herself in the mirror.

Xavier waited for her to sit before he addressed her sarcastic response. "I meant on the inside. You have a certain glow about you. I hope I have something to do with that."

Taking a seat, Danielle noticed her business plan on the table. All the doubts about getting involved with him came rushing back. Now that she'd finally found something to give her purpose again in her professional career, could she afford to get sidetracked with starting another relationship with Xavier? The time needed to start and run a business could be all-consuming.

Xavier watched Danielle's somber expression and wondered if she regretted last night. There was no way either could deny the connection they had with each other. But that was last night. Did she still feel the same this morning?

He caught her eyeing the business plan. "I really did have some news about your business plan."

Danielle took a bite of her omelet. "That's good to know, because my store is very important to me."

Something in her tone sent warning bells to Xavier. Was there a hidden meaning in her words? "I understand you've been having some trouble with financing."

Whenever she had to discuss her money situation with people, she couldn't help but feel embarrassed. It was impossible to count the number of times people had asked the same question over and over again. How could someone who'd made over twenty million dollars be broke? She usually responded by telling them to talk to MC Hammer.

Hearing the question from Xavier, however, didn't

invoke those same feelings. She didn't think she was being judged. "I had to file bankruptcy, and with no business experience, it's been difficult, to say the least."

Xavier acknowledged her response and kept eating. He had no idea how badly out of sync her finances had gotten. Taking a bite of his food, he said, "Tell me about the boutique."

Danielle opened the document and turned to the first section. "I start with—"

Taking the document out of her hand, he closed it and put it to the side. "I read the plan, but I want to hear you tell me about your vision for your store."

Forgetting about the food in front of her, Danielle launched into a monologue about her plans for the up-scale clothing store catering to professional women who also had family lives and hobbies. Everything from the décor, to the layout, to the grand opening had been meticulously thought out in her mind. There wasn't one detail she hadn't planned out.

"What would make your store different from any other women's clothing store?" Xavier asked, getting caught up in her enthusiasm.

"I'd market it as having the inside track to what's going to be the next hot fashion wave."

"How?" Xavier asked, having read what she just said in the plan.

"I'm going to target up-and-coming designers who are close to hitting it big. Having mini fashion shows, allowing designers to showcase their new lines, and giving them an opportunity to deal directly with customers will entice them. Giving my customers the chance to meet designers and buy great clothing at a fraction of the well-known designer's price will lure them into the store."

Her animated expression lit up her eyes. Still, there were quite a few things that hinged on the success of her plan that he wasn't quite sure she'd thought out. "How are you going to get designers to agree to this? You're not exactly someone listed as one of their all-time favorites."

At least this time, Danielle didn't hear any malice in his question. Besides, it was a valid point. Anyone interested in helping her would want to know the same thing. "Fortunately, there are some really great new designers that haven't been touched by my misguided attitude. I've already started contacting a few and they seem interested in hearing more. And, if by chance, they do get word of what an ogre I used to be, I'm hoping the prospect of sales and exposure will overshadow whatever they might have heard."

Reaching across the table, he stroked her hand, smiling proudly. "It sounds like you've got a winner on your hands."

Danielle eyed their entwined hands before extracting hers completely from his touch.

He noticed the gesture and that sinking feeling returned.

They'd both stopped eating as she tried to get her words together. "It's going to take a lot of work to get this off the ground, and even more work to make it a successful venture."

That tone was back in her voice and Xavier braced himself for whatever would be coming out of her mouth next.

"The most important thing to me right now is doing what it takes to make this dream a reality."

He had an inkling where this conversation was going, but wanted to hear it from her lips.

"Anything that takes away from this project is not an option for me right now," she said, casting her look downward.

"Including me." It was a statement, not a question.

Raising her head, she stared into his beautiful eyes. "Xavier, last night was wonderful. You were right. There is something special between us."

"I hear a 'but' coming," he said.

"I just don't see how I can work on a relationship at this time in my life."

Standing, he started to clear away the dishes. It was a safe bet that neither was going to eat the food that had already grown cold. "Couples do it all the time. You don't have to choose between your business and me. You can have both."

Danielle hesitated. The last thing she wanted to do was appear as if she was putting her professional life before him again. "This isn't about the boutique and it isn't about you. It's about me. For the first time in my life, I believe I've found the right path. I'm on track to accomplish something I can be proud of, something that makes me feel good about myself. I hope you can understand that."

As much as he wanted to scream that he didn't understand, that they could make it work if she wanted to, he couldn't. "I do understand, Danielle. When I decided to build my own studio and production company, everyone in Hollywood told me I was a fool. And in D.C.? I could kiss my career good-bye. But I wanted to do it—had to do it. For myself."

Walking to her, he kneeled and squeezed her knees. "I'll give you space to accomplish your goal. Just don't automatically write off a personal relationship between us."

Danielle didn't know whether she was thankful or disappointed. He'd given her exactly what she'd asked for, but somehow that didn't make it any easier.

Standing, he put the business plan in front of her and

sat across from her. "But a professional relationship, on the other hand, is an entirely different situation."

"What do you mean?"

Turning to the financial section, Xavier pointed out several figures. "I reviewed the numbers for your start-up costs and first two years of operations, before you expect to turn a profit. I had it reviewed by my accountant and my attorney."

Danielle's heart started to beat faster. "Do you know someone interested in investing?"

"As a matter of fact, I do."

Jumping out of her chair, she ran to him, almost knocking him over with a hug. Kissing him all over his face, she screamed in joy. "Oh, Xavier, thank you, thank you. I know this doesn't necessarily mean they'll say yes, but it's the best lead I've had. When can I meet with them? Do they need additional information? Should I contact them today?"

"Whoa," Xavier said, trying to calm her down. "One question at a time. They don't need additional information. They already have a copy of your plan, and with their own knowledge of business and some knowledge of the retail business, they think this is a great opportunity."

Clasping her hands together, Danielle did a complete turn, unable to contain her burst of energy. "That's fantastic. When can I meet them?"

" 'Them' is a 'he' and you can meet him right now." Stepping back, he held out his hand for her to shake. "Xavier Johnston. Investor."

Danielle stared at the outstretched hand, trying to comprehend what had just taken place. Was he serious? "No . . . uh-uh . . . no way."

Dropping one hand to his side, he scratched his head in confusion. "What do you mean no?"

"I just told you that it would be too complicated to get involved with you right now," she reminded him.

"Yes, you did," he agreed. "But that was getting involved with me on a personal level. What I'm offering is a professional relationship."

Could they really separate the two? "Are you saying you're willing to give me the money I need to start my business?"

"No."

Confusion caused Danielle to take a seat.

"I'm not *giving* you anything," he said. "I'm investing. And to that extent, I want a piece of the profit pie."

"Why are you doing this?"

"You've not only put together a great business plan. I watched you at the store. You have a knack for customer service and a definite eye for fashion. It's a solid investment."

Danielle still looked skeptical.

Xavier relaxed his stance and smiled at her. "I care about you, Danielle, but not enough to give you this much money for something I didn't think would work."

For a moment, Danielle was thrown off balance by his choice of words. Care. Not love. After telling him that she didn't want to pursue a relationship with him, it shouldn't have bothered her, but for some reason it did. "I appreciate the offer, Xavier. But I can't."

"Why?"

"I want to do this on my own."

"That's the point of this conversation, Danielle. You can't do it on your own. You need money from somewhere."

Danielle couldn't argue. But take his money? "I'll have to think about it."

"Will you also think about us?"

"Xavier—"

"Just think about it, OK?"

Danielle sat back in her chair. She didn't believe anything would change it, but she agreed anyway. "Yes, Xavier. I'll think about it."

# Chapter Twelve

Danielle turned the key to the front door. Before she walked fully through the entrance, the door swung open and she was pulled inside.

"Where have you been?"

The slight grin on her sister's face told Danielle that she was more joking than anything else. "I left you a message."

"At eleven o'clock. The only thing you said was that you were OK and wouldn't be home until today."

"What more did I need to say?" Danielle played the innocent role. She hadn't done much in the way of social activities since she'd arrived back in D.C. Staying out would definitely have been out of the ordinary for her. She didn't want her sister to worry, but she wasn't sure how much of her evening she was ready to share.

Playfully pushing her into the living room, Tanya figured there was more to this story than she was telling. "You can start with that man in the black Benz."

Danielle stopped and turned to her sister. "What do you know about a black Benz?"

"I called the store yesterday and Elaine told me about the customer that came in earlier in the day and that you had a date."

"Can I at least take off my jacket and relax a minute?"

"Sure you can," Tanya said, pretending to be sorry for

the way she'd attacked Danielle as soon as she walked in. "Sixty, fifty-nine, fifty-eight, fifty-seven . . ."

Tanya laughed at her countdown and took a seat on the sofa. "To set the record straight, it was not a date. It was a business meeting."

"A business meeting that lasted all night?"

When the trust and friendship they'd shared was destroyed years ago by her behavior, Danielle longed for the times they'd sat in each other's rooms as teenagers, gabbing and sharing what was going on in their lives. This provided the perfect opportunity for them to start creating those moments again.

"I spent the night with Xavier."

Tanya didn't respond, but stared as if she'd heard incorrectly. Pretending to clean her ear, she paused and waited for more. When nothing else came, she sat beside her sister. "Are you talking about the Xavier Johnston that you can't stand the sight of? The Xavier Johnston that you planned never to see again? The Xavier Johnston who you claimed had nothing in this entire world to offer you?"

Danielle twisted her fingers in her lap. "That's the one."

Tanya leaned in, eyes widened in expectancy. "How? When? What?"

"Wait a minute. One question at a time," Danielle declared. "He found out about Danielle's and said he could help."

"And you ended up spending the night with him?" Tanya asked, still trying to put two and two together.

"Something like that," Danielle said, still trying to make sense of it herself. Her intentions had been crystal clear. Find out what he knew about Danielle's and how he could help her get if off the ground. But those plans got sidetracked when she finally admitted that she was still attracted to him. Still cared for him. Still loved him.

The night was everything she had imagined it to be. There was no denying the fact that they shared a very special connection. The question was whether this was the time to pursue that connection.

"I'm not sure what to say except that I hope you're happy and that I'm glad you two were able to work out your differences."

"Umm," Danielle said thoughtfully.

"What's that mean?"

Explaining that her number-one priority was the store, she told Tanya that pursuing a personal relationship with Xavier wasn't in the cards for her.

"How can you say that? You said you just spent a wonderful night with him. Can you just turn off your emotions like that?" Tanya thought it impossible to understand where her sister was coming from.

"I don't have a choice," Danielle said, wanting more than anything to prove that she had what it took to make her boutique a success.

"Of course you have a choice," Tanya said. "How could you come to the conclusion that this was all or nothing, that you could only have one at the expense of the other? It's not that hard to pursue a professional life and a personal relationship at the same time. You can choose the boutique and love."

Thinking of Xavier's use of the word "care" instead of "love," Danielle pushed down the feelings of disappointment. "I don't have that luxury right now. If I'm going to make my plan come to fruition, I need to dedicate all my efforts toward it."

"And how does Xavier feel about this?"

"He said he would honor my wishes," Danielle answered, remembering her discontent when he didn't put up much of a fight.

"Which means he doesn't agree," Tanya stated.

"There's something else," Danielle said, deciding to put it all out there.

Exhaling deeply, Danielle stood and moved about the living room, both excited and fearful at the same time. "I have an investor interested in Danielle's."

The words were said so calmly that it took a moment for them to register with Tanya. As soon as they did, Tanya jumped up, almost tripping over the coffee table. Hugging her sister tightly, she yelled and screamed for joy. "Did I hear you correctly?"

"That's right, sis. The offer came in today."

After several minutes, Tanya finally calmed down and took a seat in a chair opposite Danielle. "When did this happen? How did this happen? Who invested?"

When Danielle finished telling her sister what Xavier offered to do for her, Tanya was confused. "Let me get this straight. You sleep with a man and he offers to finance your business venture?"

The accusation in her voice wasn't lost on Danielle and she couldn't hide the fact that she was offended. "What are you insinuating?"

Tanya realized what she'd just accused her sister of and quickly backtracked. "I'm not implying anything. It's just that you spend the night with someone you apparently can't stand and now he's giving you money."

The progress Danielle thought she'd made with her sister had just been eliminated with that one statement. How could she even suggest that Danielle would exchange sex for money? "I think this conversation is over." Danielle headed upstairs to her room, fuming on the inside with anger.

"Danielle, wait . . ." but it was too late. The damage had been done. Tanya jumped when she heard the door slam.

\*\*\*

Xavier impatiently rang the doorbell several times before knocking. Peering into the side window, he looked for movement to show that someone was home. Normally, he didn't make a habit of just dropping by unannounced, but he needed to talk to someone.

Last night went far beyond anything he planned. The goal of the night was to get Danielle talking about the possibility of giving their relationship another try and for him to offer help with the boutique.

The first night they'd met, there was a sexual pull so strong it took all of his strength not to act on it. Surprisingly, for all the sexy clothes that Danielle wore and the constant partying and the need to be in the limelight, she was unexpectedly old-fashioned. He found it refreshing that when he suggested a picnic in the park, a movie marathon, or a night at the bowling alley, she readily agreed.

When they broke up it took him months to get over what Danielle had done to him. The mood swings must have agitated everyone around him. One day, his anger would be so strong that he would take it out on the people he was working with, causing delays in production. The next day, he would be somber, barely speaking to anyone.

There were a lot of "I told you so's" from his so-called friends. Most of his associates and acquaintances wouldn't let him forget how they had tried to warn him. There were some who believed he got exactly what he deserved. It was a painful way to learn a lesson.

With all the evidence stacked against her, Xavier had to finally admit to himself that she was just as devious, evil, and selfish as everyone had pegged her to be. Those feelings were what kept him going the past couple of years.

"The way you're bangin' on my door, there better be a fire."

The door swung open and Xavier walked in without as much as a hello, ignoring Melinda, who said hello as she sat in the living room with a book.

Reggie held the door open, dumbfounded by his brother's behavior. "Come in," he said, waving his arm to the empty hallway.

He watched Xavier go down the flight of stairs to the basement, open the refrigerator and grab a beer, and then take a seat at the bar.

"Please, help yourself," Reggie said after the fact.

Xavier, about to take a sip, put it down before getting one drop. "Do I look stupid?"

"Is this a trick question?" Reggie said, taking a seat beside him.

"I told myself that I just wanted to see if there was a chance for us to start again . . . to see if what I was beginning to feel was based on true feelings or guilt."

Reggie knew his brother well enough to know that this was not the time to interrupt. He had no clue what he was talking about, but if he let him keep talking, the situation would be clear.

"Once we started talking, it was just like old times."

At least Reggie could figure out that this was about a woman. Was he talking about Danielle?

"When we woke up this morning, there were still issues to be worked out, but I didn't think there would be a problem we couldn't solve—regardless of what it was."

Putting the pieces together, Reggie decided he had obviously slept with a woman who didn't share his expectations for what their relationship should be.

"Even when I offered her the money—"

Reggie's ears perked up and he couldn't remain silent any longer. Maybe Xavier wasn't talking about Danielle after all. "You spent the night with a hooker?"

"What!" Xavier said, focusing on his brother for the

first time since he'd started his tirade. "Haven't you been listening to me?"

"Yes," Reggie said. "And what I heard was sex and money."

"Are you crazy?" Xavier said, appalled that the thought would cross his brother's mind. "I'm talking about Danielle."

"Danielle Kennedy?"

Both men turned to the voice and Reggie groaned.

"Are you saying that you spent the night with the woman who dumped you like a hot potato?"

"Melinda," Reggie said, hoping to cut off what was potentially a volatile situation. "I don't think this is the time."

Stepping fully into the room, Melinda couldn't believe what she was hearing. "What is going on with him, Reggie? Doesn't he remember what she did to him?"

Reggie went to his wife and gave her a hug. "We all know how you feel about Danielle."

"We should all feel that way about Danielle," Melinda said, losing her patience with the conversation. "She's selfish, vain, egotistical—"

"I think his feelings for her might have changed, and we should be supportive of whatever decision he makes."

"You've got to be kidding me," Melinda said. "How could they? What is he thinking?"

"Um, excuse me," Xavier said, "I'm sitting right here. You don't have to talk about me like I'm not."

Both of them turned to face him and Melinda opened her mouth to speak.

Reggie jumped in. "Melinda, why don't you give us a minute?"

Reluctantly, she agreed and headed back upstairs.

Reggie turned to his brother and apologized with his eyes. "Tell me what happened."

"We met for dinner at my place," Xavier started.

"Your place?" Reggie said, unable to let that detail slip

through. "Why would you do that? As delicate as your relationship was with her, why would you do that?"

"Do you want to hear this or not?" Xavier said.

"Fine," Reggie said. "Continue."

"Anyway, after dinner, one thing led to another, and—"

Reggie interrupted, not interested in the intimate details. "I got that part. What about the money?"

"I got my hands on a copy of a business plan she put together for a boutique."

Not wanting to cut off his story again, Reggie couldn't stop himself this time. "Boutique?"

Explaining how he came across her business plan and why he thought it was a good investment, Xavier told him about his offer to invest. "She put together a fantastic proposal and I've seen her work in a store. She's great with customers."

"How much?"

Xavier finally took a sip of his beer. Hearing him tell the story out loud made him realize how crazy the entire situation sounded. He hoped Danielle didn't view this offer as payment for services rendered or as a bribe to continue seeing him.

Watching his brother's expression, Reggie could easily tell he was stalling, which made Reggie wonder exactly what type of situation his brother had gotten into.

"Five hundred thousand dollars."

Reggie's mouth dropped. "That must have been some good—"

Xavier interrupted. "Reggie! It wasn't like that. I would have made the decision to invest regardless of what happened between us."

"I would hope so."

"If you have something to say, just spit it out." Xavier found it hard to sit still. Standing, he walked to the leather couch and took a seat.

The two of them had shared plenty of laughs in this room. Designed to be a man's room, this area was typically off-limits to Melinda, with its pool table, leather furniture, fully stocked bar, and a big-screen television. They'd watched more ball games and told more exaggerated stories about their lives than could ever be true. But the relaxed feeling he always had when he came here eluded him today. This day, his stomach was in knots and he had no idea what his next move would be.

"With XJ Productions just getting off the ground, do you really want to do that to your cash flow?"

"I have it all worked out."

Reggie hoped he did. "If you guys had such a fabulous night and have decided to go into business together, why did you show up at my door in a panic?"

Taking objection to his choice of words, Xavier defended his actions. "I am not in a panic. I'm just frustrated."

"Because?"

"Because she's not interested in a relationship with me—personal or business," Xavier said, the reality of it causing him more pain.

"I thought you said you were back together?" Reggie asked, more confused than ever.

"What I said was that we slept together," Xavier corrected.

Reggie cracked a smile. "Are you saying that . . ."

Hearing the humor in his voice, Xavier decided it was time to leave. "I should have known better than to come over here for advice and support."

"I'm sorry," Reggie said, unable to control his laughter. "I just don't think there's ever been a time when a woman had you so messed up. You're the one who wants something more, and she's blowing you off."

"Thanks for that recap," Xavier said, tossing his empty beer bottle in the trash. "I'm outta here."

"Whoa, wait a minute, bro." Reggie waited a few minutes for him to calm down before continuing. "I'm trying to help."

Xavier couldn't believe his current dilemma. All the hate and anger he'd carried around with him over the years had been a cover. The women he'd dated, the plans he'd set to get back at Danielle—all in vain. Xavier could no longer ignore the truth. He hadn't fallen in love with Danielle—he'd never fallen out of love.

But Danielle was a different person, with different priorities. The modeling career had gotten her life out of balance and out of perspective. Now she wanted to gain some of that back with her boutique. This was her opportunity to shine. Not only to show the world, but to prove to herself that she had what it took to run a business on her own.

"You know what? I'm just going to abide by her wishes."

Reggie didn't think he sounded too convincing. "If you have feelings for her, you have to let her know."

"For what? What good would it do? She would only think I was trying to distract her from her business goals."

Reggie sympathized with his predicament. "But what if she does feel the same way? What if she loves you, too?"

"I don't want to have to make her choose."

"Between you and the boutique?" Reggie said. "I don't think it would be that cut-and-dry. She can easily have both."

Xavier shook his head. "Danielle doesn't think so— and right now, her perception is her reality. She made it abundantly clear what the number-one priority in her life was. It wouldn't be fair of me to expect anything more from her right now."

"I disagree."

Xavier smiled. "Won't be the first time."

Resigned to the fact that Xavier had made up his

mind, Reggie only hoped that he didn't lose out on the only woman he'd ever loved. "So what's next?"

"I just have to let her know that I'm there for her. That whatever she needs—personal or professional—I'm more than willing to give it."

"And what if she doesn't need anything?"

Xavier didn't even want to entertain the thought.

The soft knock on the door went unanswered. "Danielle, open the door."

Not getting a response, Tanya knocked again. "I want to apologize, but I won't do it through a closed door."

Still nothing.

"Fine. I'll be downstairs when you're ready to talk."

Before she made it to the end of the hall, she heard the door open.

The two sisters stared at each other for several seconds before Danielle motioned for her to come in. Danielle sat on the bed, and Tanya took a seat on the bench that accompanied the vanity table on the opposite wall.

"I can't believe you would think that I would sleep with someone for money."

The crack in her voice told Tanya how deeply she'd hurt her.

"I know I've done some horrible things in my life," Danielle continued. "I've connived, schemed, and plotted to get what I wanted out of my career. I thought the way to the top was to make sure I was the only one up there."

Danielle remembered how she couldn't have cared less what people thought of her. But that was before things started getting out of hand. "The reporters started mixing truth with a little bit of made-up drama, and suddenly my antics became ten times bigger than they actually were."

"Why didn't you fight back?" Tanya asked. She didn't think her sister would stand for it. "Challenge the tabloids, the magazines, and the television shows?"

Danielle gave a cynical laugh, remembering that people outside the industry had no idea what it was like on the inside. "That wouldn't have made one bit of difference. I was no angel, so it probably would have done more harm than good."

A stack of magazines and papers in the corner of Tanya's basement gave a blow-by-blow account of all of Danielle's activities—the good, the bad, and the very ugly. "I remember reading and hearing all about you. It was hard not to believe it all."

There had been a time when Danielle would pick up any paper or magazine that featured her. Loving seeing her name in print, she'd been a firm believer that any publicity was better than no publicity. But the media had its own way. The love-hate mantra. They could turn on anyone in an instant. One day you're the toast of the town. The next, you're wondering how they could print such lies. Lies that included that she used sex to get as far as she'd gotten.

The first time Danielle heard the rumor that she had been sleeping her way to the top, she was so outraged and appalled that she did contact the piece of trash they called a news magazine, letting them know that they had their facts all wrong. But her words just got twisted and the situation grew worse. From that moment on, Danielle just let them be. It was rarely worth the fight. "Just remember, sis, I was bad . . . but never as bad as they portrayed me."

"I'm sorry, Danielle. I didn't mean to insinuate that you slept with Xavier for the money. The words just came out without me thinking," Tanya said. "I didn't mean to offend you."

If the shoe had been on the other foot, Danielle

probably would have wondered the same thing. With all that her sister probably read about her, it wasn't a stretch that she would jump to that conclusion. "It's okay."

"So what is the relationship between you and Xavier?"

As teenagers, the sisters had shared with each other their first crushes. Mark Bills had been Danielle's. Two years older than Danielle, Mark played on the football team and the day he said hello to her, she thought her life was complete. She'd missed that kind of closeness with her sister. Tanya was the one she could always talk to. There had never been another girlfriend to replace that.

Danielle spent the next half hour relaying to her sister everything that had transpired the last twenty-four hours, leaving out some of the most intimate details of her evening with Xavier. "But it was one night. That's it."

"Nothing is usually that black and white," Tanya said. "No matter how much you may want it to be."

"That's my point. If I continue to stay involved with Xavier, it will only get more complicated."

"How so? It's obvious that both of you care about each other."

"For someone who accomplished so much at one point, I'm here today feeling like I haven't done much of anything with my life. Opening up this store would prove that I have what it takes. Anything that takes my attention away from that wouldn't be good right now."

Tanya thought about her upcoming wedding to Brandon Ware. After their initial attempt at a relationship failed, he came back into her life determined to prove that they belonged together. They had gone through several challenges as he tried to convince her that the love they shared was true. In the end, he was 100 percent right. They loved each other completely, and she couldn't wait to make it official in a few short months.

Tanya tried to understand what her baby sister was going through now. Obviously, there was a man who adored her and wanted to see if they had what it took to make a lifetime commitment to one another. But Danielle could be as stubborn as Tanya, and if she fought him on the issue as hard as Tanya had fought Brandon, they might never know if they truly belonged together. "Don't you think you can open your business and explore a relationship with Xavier at the same time?"

"I'm too scared to try," Danielle admitted. "If things didn't work out, I'm not sure I could handle it."

"What about the boutique?" Tanya asked. "Why didn't you take the money?"

"I don't know," Danielle said honestly. "It felt like I was taking a handout. I want to see if I can do this on my own."

"That doesn't make sense, Danielle," Tanya said, trying to comprehend her logic. "You're letting your feelings get in the way. He's not giving you a handout. He's giving you an investment—because he believes in you."

"I have a couple of appointments with banks and a meeting with the Small Business Administration," Danielle said, recalling all the forms she'd completed over the past few weeks.

"What if those don't pan out?" Tanya asked cautiously.

After talking to Michelle, she'd realized that her chances of any of these options panning out were slim. But she owed it to herself to try. "I'll cross that bridge when I get to it."

# *Chapter Thirteen*

The following Wednesday, Danielle sat in the customer service area of the bank waiting for her appointment with the branch manager. The paperwork had been completed a week ago and she was going to get a decision today. This was her fourth bank in the last three days. Glad that she wasn't turned down based on her paperwork alone, she took it as a good sign that they wanted to talk to her. If they were on the fence about whether she deserved their money, an in-person interview could be the thing that made their decision positive. If this loan fell through, she was down to her last hope—the SBA.

The forms and information had been downloaded and sent in to the Small Business Administration. Since the SBA took longer for a decision than commercial banks, her appointment was scheduled for Friday. Having made some minor changes to her business plan, including her recent experience, she hoped that would be enough to sway the SBA to give her the money she needed.

Working at the store was supposed to keep her busy and help take her mind off the night she'd spent with Xavier last week. She counted on long days at the store to tire her out enough so that she would sleep through the night without him invading her dreams. But that plan was hard to carry out when Xavier showed up at the most unexpected times.

The first time was two days after their date. He came into the store under the pretense of buying a gift for his sister-in-law. She reminded him that a woman eight months pregnant had no use for any of the items in Sara's Closet. Xavier simply shrugged, reminding her that Melinda would return to her normal size at some point.

After making him spend another three hundred dollars, he complimented her on her selling skills, and then proceeded to let her know that he was ready to pick up where they left off as soon as she was.

The next day, a dozen roses arrived at the store for her. The card read, "The perfect flower to remind you of our perfect night."

Patricia and Elaine seemed quite interested in why she was receiving gifts, but didn't say anything. Hoping Danielle would share what was going on in her life, they didn't push her.

Yesterday, his black Benz was illegally parked across the street when she got off work.

"If I show up one more time, I think that technically classifies me as a stalker."

Danielle accepted the single rose and agreed. "That's true."

"I don't want to be where I'm not wanted, so this is my last attempt. After today, if there's going to be a chance for us—whether it involves the personal or the professional— it will have to come from you."

Danielle heard the finality of his words. He was leaving the ball in her court. The next move was hers.

Patiently standing in front of her, Xavier had hoped that she would say something to indicate she was ready to give them a chance.

Danielle's hand wanted to reach out to him, stroke his cheek, and tell him that she was more than ready to give them another chance, but her mind wouldn't let her. Not yet.

"Ms. Kennedy?"

Danielle snapped out of her thoughts and focused on the young woman standing in front of her.

"Mr. Spencer will see you now."

Danielle stood and straightened out her skirt. Following the assistant to an office in the back of the bank, she said a silent affirmation that this would be the one. The "yes" she needed to begin making her dream a reality. With a confident smile, she entered the office and shook his hand.

Saturday night, Xavier unpacked his store-bought chicken and corn bread. It was almost eight o'clock; he was bone tired. Working twelve- and fifteen-hour days, he was securing more and more work for his studio, and the production of *The Fashion Design House* was set to begin next week. The long hours were needed to stay on top of his new business venture, but were also a way to hopefully keep her off his mind.

He'd gone to see Danielle at the store under the pretense of buying a present for Melinda. The three hundred dollars he spent were well worth it for the opportunity to talk to her again—to see her again. When she didn't budge on her decision, he made one more attempt. Not wanting to suffocate her, he put the choice firmly in her hands. If she wanted a relationship with him—personal or professional—then she'd have to come to him. She had yet to come, and that disappointment ran rampant through him.

The buzzing of security caught him by surprise. Not expecting anyone, he walked to the front door and pressed the button. "Hello."

"It's me."

The last person he would have expected to come by. Xavier pressed the button and held it long enough for the front door to open. A few minutes later, there was a knock at the door.

"I haven't heard from you in a while, thought I'd come by and check on you."

Shutting the door behind Reggie, Xavier led him into the kitchen. "I'm just fixing something to eat."

"Takeout?"

"Yep."

"Again?"

"So?"

Reggie looked around the kitchen at the various containers in the trash. Chinese, pizza, Italian. The entire United Nations was represented in his garbage can. "Still no word?"

"Yes, Reggie," Xavier said, feeling annoyed. "As a matter of fact, she stopped by here earlier, declared her undying love for me, accepted my offer to invest, and we're getting married next month."

The sarcastic comment only magnified how out of sorts Reggie's brother was. "You did everything you could. I know you may not want to hear this, but sometimes people just don't love you back."

The harsh words stung his heart, but he quickly recovered. "That's just it, Reg. After what we shared that night, I find it next to impossible to believe that she doesn't love me. Nobody can fake it that well."

Reggie laughed and hoped he was right. "How long are you going to do this to yourself?"

"What?"

Looking around the kitchen, Reggie was surprised that he had to clarify his statement. "Mope. Work yourself ragged. Eat takeout."

"What difference does is make to you?"

Caring about his brother had never been an issue for Reggie. "All I'm saying is that no one was hoping that you and Danielle could work this thing out more than me. But maybe it's time to move on."

Before Xavier could answer, the buzzer sounded again.

"You expecting company?"

"Nope."

Xavier walked to the front door and pushed the button. "Yes?"

"Xavier? It's Danielle. Can I come up?"

For a moment, time stood still. He couldn't believe that her voice was on the other end. Pressing the button, he heard his brother come up behind him.

"I guess that's my cue to go. Call me if you need me."

Just as his brother walked down the hall, she got off the elevator and headed his way. Stopping briefly to speak to Reggie, she was standing in Xavier's living room in the next few minutes.

The black-and-white peasant blouse and the ankle pants she wore showed off her height. Was there ever a time she didn't look completely put together? "Can I get you something to drink?"

"No, thank you. This isn't a social visit," she said, determined to stick to the point of her call.

Letting her have control of the night, he took a seat on the couch. "So what kind of visit is this?"

Danielle watched him casually take a seat on the sofa. The same sofa where she'd screamed his name a little over a week ago. He stretched his arms along the back of the sofa, and she worked overtime to avoid noticing the sculpted muscles that were being shown off by the shorts and tank top he wore. He looked good. Too good.

Taking a deep breath, she refocused her attention and stated her objective. "Business."

Xavier remained quiet, waiting for her to continue.

"How much of my pie do you want?"

The double meaning of her words weren't lost on either on them and Danielle quickly corrected her question. "The last time we talked about this . . ."

"The night we made love?" he said innocently.

Danielle stared at him and his expression didn't change. He wasn't going to make this easy on her. Clearing her throat, she said, "Yes, that night. You talked about your role as an investor. What would the terms of our deal be?"

Before answering, Xavier was curious about what brought her here, and asked.

Danielle took a seat in a chair on the other side of the coffee table. "I wanted to do this on my own, and even though I knew my chances of getting traditional financing would be slim, I owed it to myself to try."

"And nothing worked out?"

"The banks didn't like my lack of business experience or my credit score. And the SBA? Get a load of this. They told me to come back after I had been in business for a few years. Imagine that? You go to an organization that's supposed to help businesses get off the ground, and they want you to be off the ground before they'll give you the money."

She was rambling and Xavier could tell this conversation was making her extremely uncomfortable. He'd never known her to be in need. To have to depend on someone else. "That's the government for you."

"Yeah, well, they aren't doing a thing for me." Leaning forward, she said, "I'm interested in your offer to help."

It had been Xavier's original thought to let her take the money and have at it. According to the information in her plan, she'd carefully laid out each expenditure and time table for her goals. But his plans to be a silent partner had changed. This was the perfect opportunity to show her that she could have the boutique and a relationship with him. "I'd want not only to invest in Danielle's, but to help you with each stage of the process."

"How would you have time to do that?" Danielle asked, a little surprised that he wanted to be involved. "You've got your own business to worry about. I know you've got several projects in various stages of production. Not to mention *The Fashion Design House*."

"True," Xavier said. "I wouldn't be in on every little decision, just there to help you with your major issues."

Pacing the floor, Danielle thought through his offer. He was handing her store to her on a silver platter. All she had to do was accept it. *What other option do you have?*

Stretching her hand out, she nodded. "You have a deal."

Xavier stared at their interlocked hands and wanted to ask whether she'd changed her mind about the other offer he made. Instead, he removed his hand. "I was just about to eat. Do you want to join me?"

"I don't want to intrude."

"Don't be silly," he said. "It's nothing fancy."

Opting for juice instead of wine, they spent the remainder of the evening talking about plans for the store. Danielle kept the conversation going and couldn't hold back her excitement now that she'd agreed to take the money.

But throughout the evening, there was a sexual undercurrent that neither of them could deny, but both refused to acknowledge. When they moved their conversation from the kitchen to the living room, it didn't take much for Danielle to remember that passion-filled night that started out on the very couch she sat on. "I better get going. It's almost midnight."

She stood and he followed. As he walked her to the

door, the restraint to keep his hands off her was driving him insane, but he was determined to respect her wishes for a platonic, business partnership.

Opening the door, he stepped to the side to let her pass through.

Just inches from him, Danielle inhaled his scent and closed her eyes for a brief moment. When she opened them, Xavier leaned forward. Not wanting to go down that road again, she was helpless to stop her body from taking over. Before she realized it, she'd puckered her lips and leaned forward. When she felt the lips on her cheek, she stepped back, embarrassed by the fact that she appeared to want a more personal kiss.

Xavier tried to hide his smile, but failed miserably. That little incident told him all he needed to know. She still wanted him. That small piece of information gave him hope that one day she would declare it. "Good night, Danielle."

Xavier shut the door behind her, wondering how long it would take for her to come to her senses and admit that they deserved to be together.

# *Chapter Fourteen*

Danielle examined the two dummies standing in front of her. The mannequins, naked as the day their plastic parts were attached to each other, had been stripped of their business suits in favor of a more casual look. With summer looming, the vacation season was fast approaching. Many of their customers would begin putting together their warm-weather wardrobe. Dressing them in the latest resort wear would be a definite draw for the store to those walking past the display window. Flipping through the racks of new arrivals, Danielle began putting several looks together.

"I see you've come in on your day off . . . again," Elaine said, coming into the stockroom.

"I wasn't planning to, but when I called to see if a special order had arrived for Mrs. Carter, Patricia said we'd gotten a shipment. I couldn't wait to see what came in." Danielle put a light blue silk-thread sleeveless sweater on one of her mannequins.

Any other employee would have had Elaine balking at paying the overtime, but with Danielle, her enthusiasm and commitment reminded her of someone she used to know years ago—herself.

When she left the field of law almost twenty years ago, it was because her passion couldn't be fulfilled in the courtroom. Though she'd always pictured herself as an entrepreneur, her family wouldn't hear of it. She was the only child, and her father had put on her all of the goals and ambitions that he would have put on a son. A well-respected attorney who later went on to become a judge, he'd had high expectations for Elaine. He constantly reminded her how smart and intelligent she was. Her career options, in his eyes, were limited to jobs that required her to go to college, followed by an advanced degree. That was how, he told her, she would make something of her life.

After following her father's plans, Elaine graduated from Georgetown Law School armed with several job offers, compliments of her father. Having her pick of top law firms with salaries over a hundred thousand dollars, Elaine threw everyone for a loop when she chose to work as a district attorney.

Hoping to have a real impact on the community, she buried herself in her work. But the satisfaction never came. Between the deals that had to be cut with defendants and the victims that never seemed at peace, she came to the realization that she was just going through the motions as a lawyer. The idea of spending the next ten or twenty years as an attorney made her decide to get out.

Refusing to tell anyone, for fear of being talked out of her decision, she began looking for opportunities for a new career. That day came when she went shopping one day at Sara's Closet. Having just had a horrible day in court, she'd hoped that buying herself something new would lift her spirits. When she walked out an hour later with a new suit, she realized it wasn't just the new clothes that made her feel better, it was the owner who waited on her.

She remembered thinking that was the kind of job she was looking for. A way to treat someone that would make them have a better day. Continuing to shop at the store over the next year, Elaine overheard the owner talking

about selling the shop to another customer. Before she had time to think, she made an offer.

Once the price had been negotiated, Elaine felt a sense of peace and satisfaction that had been missing in her life. Sonya Dandridge, the previous owner, only had one request. The store had been named for her daughter who had died of leukemia—she wanted the name to remain the same. Elaine not only readily complied with that request, but every year, the store made a contribution to the Leukemia Research Foundation in honor of Sara for research. Elaine even met her husband at the store.

Roy walked in just two months after she'd taken over, looking for a gift for his sister. They flirted, but he left without asking her out. Shoving her disappointment aside, she continued with her work. One week later, he came in again, to buy a gift for his other sister. The following week he came in for a dress for yet another sister. Just as she was ringing up his purchase, he stopped her. Admitting that he only had one sister, he'd continued to come in, hoping to ask Elaine out, but getting cold feet every time. But he admitted his fear was costing him a fortune, so if Elaine didn't mind, she could cancel the sale and he could use that money to take her out to dinner. Twenty years later, the business still thrived, and so did her marriage to Roy.

Elaine viewed every day as an opportunity to make someone else feel good and look good—regardless of what was going on in their lives. Owning this store had given her pride, pleasure, and a sense of accomplishment. Financially, it had provided for her family and would enable her and her husband to enjoy a nice retirement. Even her father, who refused to speak to her for almost five years after she left the field of law, came around after realizing that he couldn't control his daughter's choices.

Danielle was just as she had been all those years ago.

Excited. Full of passion. Energized. She was just the jolt Elaine needed to remind of her of why she loved what she did.

There had been plenty of days in the beginning when she couldn't wait for a new line to arrive. There were times that creating displays, designing marketing materials, preparing for end-of-the-season sales used to wake her up early in the morning and keep her going late at night. That enthusiasm had died down over the years. Danielle was giving some of that back to her.

Picking up one of the scarves Danielle laid out, Elaine tossed it around the mannequin's neck. They both stepped back and studied the color it added, agreeing that it was just the right touch. Continuing her work, Danielle talked nonstop about trends and how Elaine should make sure her buyer got some of those items.

Normally, Elaine could talk about fashion for hours on end. But today, she only had one question on her mind—and it didn't have to do with displays, new summer wear, or mannequins. "How's the dating going?"

Without stopping her work, Danielle reacted nonchalantly. "Who said anything about dating?"

The attempt to appear cavalier had failed. That only piqued Elaine's interest more. Danielle rarely talked about her private life and hadn't mentioned a boyfriend, but Elaine couldn't squelch her curiosity. "Watching the time. Standing outside peering up and down the street. A young man—a very handsome young man—gets out of a nice car and opens the door for you. Then you get flowers. And he shows up again, looking handsome and debonair. Sounds like dating to me."

"It was business," Danielle insisted.

Elaine chuckled. "Is that what you young kids are calling it these days?"

"I'm almost thirty, you know," Danielle said, finally

starting to accept the fact that she was crossing the line into another decade of her life.

"And I'm still a generation older than you," Elaine reminded her.

Danielle smiled. "Like I said, it's business."

Leaning over to get a good look at her face, Elaine shook her head, not believing Danielle. "Then tell me why you have that silly grin on your face."

"I do not!" Danielle insisted.

"He looks familiar to me," Elaine said, already knowing the reason why.

Danielle didn't respond. Hoping she wouldn't connect the dots between the man who shopped in the store and the man who picked her up.

"Has he shopped in the store before?"

When Danielle didn't answer, she rephrased the question. "Is he a customer?"

"Which customer are you referring to?" Danielle said nonchalantly. "We have quite a few, you know."

"Patricia and I were paying close attention to not only the man but your reaction to the man. He seemed to have you flustered."

"You and your coconspirator have too much time on your hands," Danielle said. Seeing a disappointed expression on her face, Danielle inhaled deeply. "It's just that after you live a life in the spotlight, you begin to value your privacy."

After several seconds of silence, Elaine sat in one of the chairs. Clearing her throat, she said, "I have another confession to make."

Danielle didn't stop working. Jokingly she said, "What did you do this time? Did you actually go ahead and Google me?"

When Elaine didn't respond, Danielle set the clothes aside and gave Elaine her undivided attention.

"I was telling my daughter-in-law about you," Elaine started, trying to put the right words together. "She lives in Florida with my son. They have two great kids—twins."

"I hardly think that classifies as a confession," Danielle said, returning back to working on plastic model number two.

Elaine hesitated before continuing. "She actually did it. She Googled you."

It took a few moments for Danielle to understand what she was saying, but then the light finally went on. It was amazing how technology had changed the world. Not only was information readily available on any topic, it was also readily available on any person. Not knowing whether to be angry, offended, or indifferent, Danielle said, "And what did you find out?"

"That you really did make three million dollars the last year you worked," she answered incredulously.

That broke the tension and both women laughed.

"It's OK," Danielle said. And it was. There was nothing on the Internet that hadn't already been in print.

Elaine exhaled in relief. She'd felt guilty and wanted to let Danielle know what she had done. "Danielle Olivia?"

She hadn't heard that name in almost two years. The decision to drop her last name had not boded well with her parents. "I thought it sounded more exotic."

"Paula said you were something in your prime," Elaine said proudly, as if she had something to do with it. "Designers couldn't get enough of you."

Abandoning the display project, Danielle took a seat beside her and thought of her choice of words. "Well, they obviously did, because no one will hire me now."

"I understand you were, umm, a little . . . could be . . . some say . . . you were difficult to work with."

Danielle chuckled at her attempt to dress it up. "Difficult would not even begin to describe my behavior during that time."

"I find that hard to believe," Elaine said honestly. "In the time that I've known you, you've been none of those things."

"Thanks," Danielle said. Though she was never one to crave a pat on the back, those words meant a lot to her. "My 'difficult behavior' is how I ended up here."

"It's not such a bad place to be, is it?"

"A month ago, I couldn't have imagined that this is what my life would consist of," Danielle said sincerely. "But lately, I couldn't imagine having it any other way."

"And the guy who picked you up last night?" Elaine asked.

"Ahh, we're back to that," Danielle said, feeling more comfortable now that some of the details of her past life had been shared.

"It just seems like you have a little extra pep in your step."

That, Danielle could no longer deny. While she believed she'd made the right decision to focus on her career, she couldn't help but remember what a wonderful night they had. "Xavier Johnston."

"Oh," Elaine exclaimed, immediately covering her mouth when she realized how shocked she sounded.

"What is that supposed to mean?" Danielle said, eyeing her suspiciously.

Elaine glanced around the empty room, as if making sure no one would overhear her next words. Leaning forward, she lowered her voice as if she was about to spill the beans on a juicy piece of gossip. "According to my daughter-in-law, he's the one that you've publicly accused of ruining your career and he's countered with discussing your selfishness with anyone who would listen."

"You've just summed up our relationship," Danielle admitted.

"That had to be a while ago," Elaine reasoned. "From where I stand, it looks like you two have worked things out."

"Not exactly," Danielle said, not sure how much she should share with her boss. "He's interested in helping me with a business venture."

Elaine didn't have to wonder what type of business she was referring to. "A boutique of your own."

The statement had no hint of accusation, but Danielle got up and went back to work with the mannequin, acting as if she didn't hear her.

Placing a pair of shades on the mannequins, both now completed, Danielle said, "It's something I've been thinking about."

"It's OK, Danielle. No one would expect you to be a sales associate forever," Elaine said, hoping to put her at ease.

"I'm not interested in being a direct competitor," Danielle said. "I would cater to a different clientele. Younger, more chic."

"Don't worry about being my competition," Elaine answered. "You do what you have to do to make yourself happy. It's obvious to me, Patricia, and half the customers. You're hungry for all the knowledge you can get about the business. You've got your hands in just about everything around here, and you're doing a great job. You'd be a natural at something like this."

"Thanks for the vote of confidence." She'd been in this business a long time, and if she thought Danielle had what it took, then Danielle believed her.

"So when will I be losing my star employee?"

"Don't put an ad in the paper yet," Danielle said lightly. "Xavier and I didn't get into many details on our last date."

"I thought you said it was a business meeting?"

Having been tripped up by her own words, Danielle thought it best to end this conversation while she was ahead. "I better get these newly styled mannequins back in the front window."

Before Elaine could respond or ask any more questions, Danielle picked up one of her life-size dolls and headed out the door.

Xavier stood in the middle of the soundstage watching the crew make the final touches on the set. With all the major players in place, *The Fashion Design House* was right on schedule. The request for nine episodes would hopefully only be the beginning. The lineup of guests read like a who's who of the fashion world. Representatives from Sean John, Phat Farm, Versace, Roberto Cavalli, and stylists for the hottest pop stars and hip-hop groups had already been scheduled to be profiled.

Becoming one of the elite in Hollywood had been his original goal, but the closer he got to it, the more he realized he wanted more control than Hollywood would ever give. Taking a gamble, he decided to invest in himself. And that meant building this studio and producing work that he fully believed in and making it a commercial success. Things had started out well. His studio was producing commercials, public service announcements, and music videos.

"Things are coming together nicely."

Not hearing her approach, Xavier turned and smiled. "The set is going to be better than I imagined."

Placing her arm on his, she said, "You wanted to see me?"

As he stepped toward the exit, their contact was

disconnected. "Let's go to my office to discuss the shoot-ing schedule."

Layla followed Xavier, stepping over several wires, going through a couple of doors and down a long hall-way, finally entering the office suites.

Sitting down behind the large cherry-wood desk, Xavier motioned for Layla to take a seat in one of the leather chairs in front of him. "The raw footage from the promo spots we shot looks good. It's with editing now and should be ready by the end of the week."

Layla licked her lips and tossed back her hair. "That's great. Are they still slated to start running next week?"

"Yep," Xavier said, searching his desk for the schedule. Finding it underneath a stack of memos, he handed a copy to her.

Layla focused on his lips, but not on the words coming from them. She wondered how they would feel against her body. When her agent had gotten her this audition, she couldn't have been more excited. At twenty-five, her run-way days were about to end and it was time to prepare for her transition into another arena. She'd started working with an acting coach about six months ago, but jumped at the chance to host this show. The critics would be much more accepting of seeing her on television as herself, as opposed to playing someone else.

Having heard of Xavier Johnston through the grape-vine, she'd never had the pleasure of meeting him, but the moment she was in his presence, the attraction set in. Hedging her bets that he wouldn't appreciate her making a pass at him during the audition process, she held off on acting on her desires. Now that she'd gotten the job and signed the contracts, she considered him fair game.

Experience had taught her that the best way to get the ball rolling with a man was to point out something im-portant to him that they had in common. She'd come up with a surefire subject that would make them instant allies. "I understand you had a personal meeting with Danielle to tell her about your decision."

It was no secret there was no love lost between Xavier and Danielle. Rumors ran rampant that the only reason Danielle even had a shot at auditioning was so that he could turn her down. Layla figured the best way to start out building something personal with him was by showing him they had something in common: they both had issues with Danielle Kennedy.

"I did," he said, not offering any more information. After the progress he and Danielle had made over the past several weeks, the last thing he wanted to be reminded of was the cruel way he'd treated her that day he told her she didn't get the job.

"I can only imagine how much of a thrill that must have been for you," she said, unable to hide her disgust with Danielle.

Xavier set his papers to the side, interested in where Layla was taking this conversation.

"That woman was a witch," Layla continued, taking it as a good sign that she had his undivided attention. "I can't tell you how many times she caused havoc backstage at a show or delayed a shoot because of some diva-like request she had."

"I didn't know you worked that much with Danielle," Xavier said, attempting to hold his tongue. He might have taken this talk about Danielle in the past, but he refused to put up with it now.

Layla hesitated. "We actually only worked a couple of shows together, but you couldn't get away from the talk. Apparently no one wanted to work with her—models or designers."

"You really shouldn't believe everything you hear,"

Xavier pointed out, turning his attention back to the schedule.

"Come on, Xavier," Layla prodded, "you should know better than anyone how cruel that woman could be."

"Why is that?" he asked, his patience skating on thin ice.

"Everyone knows what she did to you the night of that live show." Adjusting her position, she leaned in closer and lowered her voice. "I even heard that you two had been a little item. But true to form, she treated you just as bad as she treated everyone else."

Xavier calmly folded his hands in front of him. "Is there a point to this conversation?"

Not exactly the response she'd hoped for, but she could work with it. Scooting closer to his desk, she lowered her eyes just slightly. "I just want you to know that I'm not like that. If I had a man like you, there would be no question where my loyalties lay."

Xavier watched her body language and picked up on her underlying message. What she was offering wasn't such a bad package. Hitting the modeling scene about eight years ago, she'd had a solid run in print work and commercials. She'd even snagged an endorsement from Clinique. She'd made smart business decisions and this job had been a major coup for her.

Tall, beautiful, and seemingly nice, Layla would be an asset to any man. Dressed in a gray pleated miniskirt, black cotton top, and high-heeled black boots, she carried off the sexy look without appearing trashy. She was the complete package: Ambitious. Successful. Gorgeous. That's what made her the perfect host for the show.

Although beautiful, she had an easygoing spirit and a sense of humor that came through to the audience. She was a supermodel with amazing looks. Their audience research showed that she didn't intimidate other women or come across like she was better than they were. All of these attributes added up to one great television personality. What it did not add up to for Xavier was a great personality.

He had his sights, and his heart, set on someone else. "It's good to know that you're dedicated to the success of this show. The first step toward that is making sure we're clear on the segments we're going to be taping in a few short weeks. So if you'll look at the sheet I gave you, we can go over the final details."

Layla sat back in her chair and redirected her attention to the papers in her hand. Not sure of what to make of his response, she contemplated her next move. On the one hand, this was supposed to be a business meeting. Maybe he was uncomfortable discussing non-business items in this setting. Perhaps she needed to get him away from the studio for him to fully relax. "It's almost five. Do you want to grab a drink? There's a great restaurant just a few blocks from here."

Without looking up from his papers, he answered in the negative. "No, thanks. I already have plans."

Missing the disappointed look on her face, Xavier continued with the meeting as if nothing had happened.

# Chapter Fifteen

Danielle completed two alteration order forms before deciding to call it a day. After putting the front display together, she'd stayed to help out Patricia and Elaine with customers. "I think I'll head out."

Patricia glanced out the window and nudged Elaine. "I think that's a great idea."

Danielle followed their gaze and didn't know whether to smile or be agitated. The black Benz with darkened windows was illegally parked across the street. The owner of the car leaned against the driver-side door looking in her direction.

Waving good-bye to her coworkers, she stepped out on the street and thought of ignoring him. Remembering he was an investor, she reluctantly changed her mind. What if he was here to discuss the boutique?

Trotting across the street, she berated herself for the flimsy excuse. There was probably nothing that would have stopped her from going to him. "How did you know where to find me?"

"When you weren't at Tanya's, I took a chance."

"Are unannounced visits going to become a habit with you?" Danielle asked, trying to scold him.

Feigning hurt at her, he said, "Aren't you glad to see me, partner?"

"I wouldn't toss that word around if I were you. We have yet to sign any papers."

"That's why I'm here."

Danielle immediately perked up. "Your lawyer has the papers ready?"

"Better," he said enthusiastically. "I have something I want you to see."

Walking around to the passenger side, he opened the door, waiting for her to follow.

Seeing her hesitation, he reached in and pulled out a dozen roses.

"Do you always give flowers to your business partners?"

"Only the ones who give amazing kisses."

Moving to stand in front of him, she took them out of his hand. "Am I supposed to be impressed?"

"Are you?"

Raising them to her nose, she inhaled the wonderful scent. "Maybe."

"Hey, that's better than a no." Pointing to the car, he said, "Now will you get in?"

She didn't move right away. "The last time I got in that car, we ended up at your place, drinking two bottles of wine and sharing a shower. I don't think I want to go there again—not now."

It was a subtle reminder that she intended to stick to her plan of a business-only relationship. To hear her say it again stung a little, but Xavier remembered his promise to his brother. He wanted to give her the space she needed. Then he intended to prove to her that she could have everything she wanted—including him. "You also got complete financing for your business the last time you got in this car."

Giving him a smile, she got in the car. "Touché."

The drive out of D.C. toward the Maryland state line took longer in the late afternoon traffic.

Noticing the direction they were headed, she relaxed. "At least I know we're not going to your place again."

"You sound disappointed," Xavier teased.

"Hardly," she said, hoping the disappointment in her voice wasn't audible. If she was being truthful with herself, she'd admit that she wouldn't mind it at all.

"Are you sure? Because the night's still young."

"Just drive."

Xavier smiled in satisfaction. She wasn't immune to what had happened between them that night, no matter what she tried to say. "I want you to know that I object to your philosophy that we can't continue what we started a couple of weeks ago."

"Are we going to have to talk about this every time we get together?"

Xavier had told her that he wouldn't put any pressure on her, and he was going to try to stick to that promise. "I just wanted to make sure my position was clear."

Turning into a parking garage, he pulled out the ticket from the entrance. "I respect your decision. Until you say otherwise, it's just business between us."

Danielle didn't know if she felt relief or disappointment.

The upscale shops at the Gallery Place were known for expensive high-end stores and great restaurants. Neiman Marcus and Saks Fifth Avenue anchored the shopping mall with other shops like Gianni Versace, Cartier, and Gucci located in the middle. Back in the day, malls like this used to be Danielle's old stomping ground, where she'd spend thousands of dollars in less than a few hours.

Riding the escalators to the second floor, she hoped Xavier hadn't dragged her out here to go shopping. The last thing she had in her bank account was anything that could be considered disposable income. She'd almost choked the first time she got her paycheck from the store. Even with her commissions, it was the smallest check, by far, that she'd ever received. Still, she couldn't have been more proud of it. She even offered Tanya some money for rent. But she wouldn't take it.

Maneuvering their way through the crowd, he reached back to hold her hand.

She stopped walking the second their fingers clasped.

Xavier felt a tug when he tried to keep moving. "What's wrong?"

Her eyes were locked on their entwined hands.

"So we don't get separated," he said to her unanswered question.

Figuring she'd appear silly if she made a big deal about it, she just nodded in agreement and held on.

Taking a few tentative steps, she put her reservations behind her and kept pace with him. After passing a couple more stores, he went left and entered one.

Danielle stopped as soon as they stepped over the threshold. To the right were the tiniest little dresses she'd ever seen. In a variety of styles and colors, they hung beside matching hats and socks. On the left were the shoes for the smallest feet. Timberland, Nike, and even what looked like Jimmy Choo shoes were displayed on the front rack. "Why in the world would you bring me to a baby store?"

When he didn't answer, she began thinking of her own possible solutions. Did he get someone else pregnant and this was his way of letting her know? No, that wasn't possible. Not after the night they'd shared. Maybe he wanted to have a baby, and since they were going to be business partners, he thought this might be another venture they could enter into together. Maybe . . .

"It won't be a baby store for long," he said, moving farther into the store without letting go of her hand.

"What are you talking about?" she said, shaking the silly thoughts she had out of her mind.

Pulling her closer, he leaned into her ear. "Word has it that the owner is not renewing her lease at the end of July."

Suddenly, it all began to make sense. Focusing on the space, and not the clothes, Danielle made a quick assessment. Guessing it to be between five or six thousand square feet, with many of the fixtures already in place, she could see this being an upscale women's store. There was only one problem, and she was surprised that Xavier didn't think of it first.

"That's great inside information, but it doesn't do us any good. I know for a fact that the waiting list on space in this mall is quite long. Even if we put our names on the list today, it could be a year, or more, before we actually got in here—and that's not guaranteeing this space."

"First things first," he said, as if what she said didn't have any impact. "What do you think about it? Can it work for Danielle's?"

"Can I help you look for something in particular?"

Engrossed in their conversation, neither noticed the salesperson who had been watching them ever since they arrived. No doubt, she wondered why they just stood in the front of the store without browsing.

"Um, no, thank you. We're just looking," Danielle said, feeling slightly embarrassed.

Giving them a strange look, the woman nodded. "Just let me know if you need anything."

Once she'd left them alone, Danielle smacked Xavier in the arm. "You got me acting like a crazy woman."

Grabbing her hand again, he led her to the section with the dresses. Picking up one, he showed it to her. "We can just pretend to be a happy couple shopping for the little bun in the oven."

Danielle took the dress from him and held it up. The soft blue cotton material was trimmed in yellow and had a flower in the corner. With the matching hat, it looked absolutely adorable. After staring at it for several seconds, she gave it back to him. "I think I've seen enough."

Xavier watched, dumbfounded, as she made her way out the store and headed back the way they came. Hanging the dress back on the rack, he caught the salesperson out of the corner of his eye, staring at them. Giving her a sweet smile, he said, "Have a nice day."

He found her sitting on a bench outside Ann Taylor. "What happened back there?"

"I just got a little frustrated seeing such a great location that we're not going to be able to get." The lie rolled off her tongue so easily she almost believed it.

Without responding right away, Xavier waited for her to say more. "Are you sure?"

She nodded and he decided not to push it. Sitting beside her, he said, "Under normal circumstances, your concerns would be valid. But this situation is far from normal."

"If you can get us to the top of the waiting list for a space that hasn't become available yet, I will be forever in your debt."

"Oohh, be careful what you say," Xavier warned. "I might decide to collect on that."

"I feel pretty safe making that claim," Danielle said. "I've started looking for locations in upscale areas. Even though the square-footage cost is quite pricey, there's still a long list of tenants waiting to get in."

"That's before you've heard my plan."

Intrigued, Danielle raised a curious eyebrow. "You've got a plan to get that space?"

"My investment was not just about your store," he said mysteriously.

"Now, this I gotta hear."

Standing, he reached out his hand to help her up.

"Come on. I'll buy you an ice cream cone and tell you all about it."

Danielle burst through the front door, barely able to contain her excitement. "Tanya! Tanya! Where are you?"

"I'm in the dining room."

Racing down the hall, Danielle stepped into the room, out of breath. "You won't believe what happened today when—"

She stopped in midsentence when she realized her sister wasn't alone. Christine and Natalie sat around the table with several material swatches and magazine pictures in front of them.

Standing, Tanya walked to Danielle and put her arm around her shoulder, guiding her to the table with her. "Perfect timing. We were just about to make the final selections and we need some real expert fashion advice."

Danielle stood beside the chair, but didn't take a seat. "Um, I didn't mean to interrupt. We can talk later."

"Don't be silly, Danielle," Tanya said, pulling a chair out for her. "The wedding is less than eight weeks away and we still haven't picked out bridesmaid gowns."

Danielle tried to send Tanya a silent signal with her eyes to please not make her do this, but Tanya either didn't pick up on it or chose to ignore it. Danielle had an inkling it was the latter.

"Have a seat, Danielle. We really could use your advice."

Danielle turned to Natalie, who patted the empty seat.

Cautiously sitting, Danielle took several of the pictures Tanya handed to her.

"The ceremony is going to be at noon, so I wanted something casual, but still appropriate for a wedding. We were looking at something tea length, but if we do that, I'd want a scarf and open-toe shoes."

Over the next half hour, they scanned magazine pictures and passed around the various swatches Tanya picked up from the fabric store. They applauded their success when they selected the fabrics and narrowed the dress selections down to two.

A cell phone rang and Natalie reached in her bag. As she checked the number, her eyes lit up. "Excuse me, ladies, I'll take this in the living room."

She left the room and Tanya gave Christine a knowing smile. "Must be Derrick."

"Has to be," Christine said to Tanya. "They've been going strong for quite a while now. I think it's serious."

Danielle kept looking at the dress options, ignoring the conversation. She had no idea who Derrick was and wasn't comfortable asking. These were Tanya's friends, not hers.

"Derrick is a doctor she met through BSI. She helped his parents get their dry-cleaning business back on track and they've been a hot item ever since."

Danielle looked up and realized Tanya was talking directly to her—making her feel a part of the group. As founder and president of Business Strategies Incorporated, Natalie spent her days helping small businesses in financial or tax trouble work their way through their problems. "I'm glad to hear that things are working out for her."

The buzzer on the oven went off and Tanya stood. "That means the cake is ready. You know I'm not much of a cook, so let's hope I got this right."

If Tanya left that room, that put her alone with Christine Ware, and that was the last place Danielle wanted to be. She scooted back in her chair. "Don't worry about it, Tanya. I'll take it out of the oven for you."

Before Danielle could get all her words out, Tanya was halfway out of the room. "I got it."

Christine set aside the fabrics and focused her attention on Danielle, who seemed to be enthralled with the latest issue of *Bride's* magazine. Her extremely short hair lay flat on her face, highlighting her facial features and light makeup. The jeans and corset blouse she wore made it hard to believe that she'd had a baby just four short months ago. "Awkward, isn't it?"

Danielle set the book aside and looked the other woman in the eye. She'd once heard that to make a future, you had to face your past. She didn't know how true that was for everything, but for this situation, it was right on the mark.

Her treatment of Christine on the few occasions that their paths crossed was nothing short of pure evil. Insulting her to her face, and trying to drive a wedge between her and Damian, should have guaranteed that they would never see each other again. But here they were, in her sister's house, about to have cake while picking out clothes for a wedding.

"I never had a chance to apologize to you for my behavior. What I did was selfish and uncalled for. There's no excuse for what I did and I want to say I'm sorry." Danielle had no idea whether Christine would think her words were sincere or accept her apology. She couldn't blame her if she didn't care at all. At least she'd gotten the words out—and she meant them.

Christine didn't speak for several moments. She'd spent a long time wondering how long this woman was going to wreak havoc in her life when she and Damian began dating, but as her love with Damian grew, Danielle had become more and more insignificant until it was as if she didn't exist at all.

When Tanya told Christine that Danielle was trying to change her ways, not only did she not believe her, but she couldn't have cared less.

Not getting a response from Christine, Danielle thought it best to move on. "I'm glad that Tanya asked me to be in her wedding. Growing up, we talked about how each of us would stand next to the other when we took our vows. I don't expect us to pretend to be something we're not, but for Tanya's sake, I'd like us to help her make this the best day of her life."

Christine listened and knew that she made perfect sense. "Danielle, I have to be honest with you, nothing irritated me more than to find out you were making your way back into Tanya's life. You caused her—everyone around her—so much pain. I just couldn't face the fact that you've changed.

"When I found out you were coming to stay with her, I personally thought that was the worst mistake she could make, but as we both know, Tanya has a mind of her own. Fortunately, it looks like she was right and I was wrong. I agree that we're a long ways from friends, but we're definitely able to be bridesmaids together."

Natalie came back into the room and paused when she saw the two of them. "Is, um, everything OK?"

"Everything's cool," Christine said. Picking up the pictures of the two final dresses, she held them up. "It's time to take a vote."

Later that evening, Tanya and Danielle sat in the living room with menus from at least ten catering companies spread out before them. Already on her second piece of cake, Danielle thought of the extra miles she'd have to run on the treadmill tomorrow to work it off.

"Good timing on getting that cake out of the oven."

"Come again?" Tanya said, feigning ignorance.

"Don't play with me, Tanya. You left me and Christine alone on purpose."

"How could I plan the timer on the oven to go off?"

she argued. "I didn't even know what time you would be home."

"OK, I'll give you that," Danielle conceded. "However, when I volunteered to get the cake, you knew exactly what you were doing."

Tanya started to deny it, and then changed her mind. "You got me. I wanted to give you and Christine a chance to talk."

"Or not talk," Danielle said pointedly. "You can't force two people to make nice if they don't want to."

"Well, which was it?" Tanya anxiously asked. When she'd returned from the kitchen, Natalie had also returned and the topic of conversation had been about the dress they selected. She had no idea what had happened between Christine and Danielle and didn't want to ask.

"Lucky for you, we talked."

"And?"

"And we won't be shopping or hanging out together any time soon, but we'll be able to help you make this the best wedding anyone has ever had."

"That's a start," Tanya said hopefully.

"That's probably all you're going to get," Danielle said, not wanting to get her sister's hopes up that they would ever be anything more. "Too much has happened between us."

"We'll see," Tanya said, not giving up hope that they could forge a friendship. "Tell me about this news you have. You came home anxious to share something, but got sidetracked by all this wedding stuff."

Thinking of the developments of earlier in the day, Danielle felt her excitement level starting to rise again. "I think I found a spot for my clothing boutique."

"Really, Danielle?" Tanya said. "Where?"

"The Gallery Place."

Tanya had spent the past fifteen years working in the

construction business. She understood real estate value, and how the leasing process worked for retail space. Not wanting to burst Danielle's bubble, she wondered how she thought she could pull that off. "Have you got a bid on a space there? If I remember correctly, they probably have a waiting list, not to mention that their square-footage pricing is probably off the charts. I thought you wanted to start small and then work your way up. This sounds like a big jump."

"That's exactly what I said, but Xavier said—"

"Xavier?" Tanya said, giving her a knowing smile. "Seems like you two are spending an awful lot of time together lately."

"Business," Danielle reminded her. "Just business."

Tanya rolled her eyes, indicating she didn't believe one word of that.

"Anyway, Xavier has put together a plan he thinks will take care of most of those issues."

Tanya stopped joking. There were some serious obstacles to overcome. "It must be magic, because I can't think of many ways to get around those issues."

Reaching across the coffee table, Danielle picked up the knife. "Let me get one more piece of cake and I'll tell you all about it.

Danielle stood on the set, thinking of how life never turns out like you plan it. Bittersweet was the only way to describe her feelings. She'd wanted that host job so badly that she would have done almost anything to get it. During the audition, she'd almost driven herself crazy focusing her entire life on this one job. The fact that she survived the disappointment could only be attributed to her decision to pursue the boutique. Things had a funny way of working out.

"Well, well, well. Look what the cat dragged in."

There was no need to face the person. Danielle knew exactly whom that voice belonged to. Refusing to acknowledge her, Danielle continued to face the other way.

"How in the world did you get through security?"

If it wasn't so pitiful, it would have been funny. Five years ago, Danielle had behaved the same way. Taking a deep breath, Danielle turned around and pasted on a sugary smile. "Good afternoon to you too, Layla."

The slow grin worked its way across her face, showing off white, perfectly capped teeth. "Did you suddenly get an itch to see the place where you *won't* be working?"

"Good thing I didn't expect more from you," Danielle said, glad to see that her words didn't have the sting she thought they would. "Otherwise, I would have been disappointed."

"As usual, you're your normal friendly self."

Danielle had met Layla six years ago during a shoot for Calvin Klein. Danielle at the time was writing her own ticket, and Layla was hot on her trail, ready to take over as soon as Danielle faded into the sunset.

Almost five years Danielle's junior, she was the obvious choice of the industry to take over Danielle's top spot when she moved on to other ventures. One would think that the two African-American women would have forged a bond, taking on a world that could oftentimes ignore them. But that was not to be for the two of them.

Danielle, used to getting top billing and the best opportunities, didn't have a problem with Layla waiting her turn. While she was beautiful and had already gotten several major covers, she still hadn't paid all her dues, and Danielle had every intention of making sure she understood that.

Layla, on the other hand, had different plans. Playing second fiddle had never been her forte and she wasn't about to start now. Pushing her agent to get her on every assignment that Danielle was going for only fueled the fight between them. In the end, Danielle's personality ruined her and Layla landed on top.

"What are you doing here, Danielle? Didn't you get the news? You're out. I'm in." Layla paused and snapped her finger. "Oh, that's right. It's been that way for quite some time."

Danielle thought of punching her in that loud mouth, but decided that she didn't want to wrinkle her designer suit. "Are you sure about this job you have? It is kind of odd that I would be on the set a few days before you start shooting."

For a moment, Layla panicked, but quickly recovered. Her contract was airtight. There was no way there would be a switch at this late date.

Danielle didn't miss her moment of fear. That gave her a tiny bit of satisfaction. Deciding to let her off the hook, Danielle said, "Layla, I'm not here to cause any trouble. I'm meeting Xavier and he's running late. I just thought I'd take a look around while I was waiting."

Layla didn't like the sound of that. Danielle and Xavier were supposedly adversaries. Casually picking an invisible piece of lint from her top, she asked, "Why are you meeting Xavier?"

A short chuckle escaped her lips and Danielle thought this woman must have mistaken her for a friend. "I believe you've just chartered yourself into territory classified as 'none of your business.'"

A little put out that they were meeting, Layla wondered if they were going to discuss business or something else. The entire crew buzzed with the news of Xavier's lunch with Danielle. Rumor had it that he treated her so badly that she left in tears. If that was the case, what was she doing here?

"Hi, Danielle, sorry I'm late."

Both women turned to him and Layla watched Xavier place a kiss on her cheek. She needed to get a handle on what was happening, and the only way she figured she could do that would be to get Xavier alone for a few minutes.

"Xavier, we've had some changes in the scheduling," Layla said, attempting to step in between the two. "A few conflicts with guests. If you have just a few minutes, we can discuss it before you have your meeting."

Xavier focused his attention on Layla and immediately dismissed her. "Not now, talk to Gina. She's the production assistant."

"We can't make final decisions without you," she reminded him.

Danielle watched the woman closely, paying particular attention to her tone of voice. She'd heard it many times over the years. It was the voice of someone interested—on a personal level. Did the two of them have something going on?

"Whatever you two work out I'm sure will be fine. Just have the revised schedule to me by the end of the week."

Layla was about to object when Xavier grabbed Danielle's hand. "Ready?"

The expression on Layla's face was priceless and Danielle got the answer to her unasked question. There wasn't anything going on between them—but not for lack of trying on Layla's part. If she hadn't made a move, she planned to. But this little display by Xavier had put a serious bump in her plan.

There had been many moments in Danielle's life when she ended up regretting her actions. When she cursed out the assistant stylist at a shoot in the Caribbean for *Glamour*—she regretted it. When she refused to wear the three outfits selected for her in a Caroline Herrera show, causing a twenty-minute delay—she regretted it.

Danielle had played the immature role more than once to get her way or to prove a point. The change in Danielle had eliminated all of that kind of behavior. But just like someone who kicks any habit, every now and then one will get the urge for just one more. This was one of those times.

What harm could one sarcastic remark do? One smug look? Surely someone like Layla was worth it. Starting with the snide remarks she'd made to Danielle when she first entered the studio about not getting the job, and up to her attempt to steer Xavier's attention away from her, Danielle had ample reason to stick it to her one last time. With a devilish comment on the tip of her tongue, Danielle started to speak when Xavier gave her hand a squeeze.

"I made reservations for lunch at one of your favorites— B. Smith's."

It was at that moment that Danielle remembered that she didn't have anything to prove to anyone. If Layla wanted to take the low road, that was her prerogative, but she wasn't going to take Danielle with her.

Danielle gave her a genuine smile. "It was nice seeing you again, Layla. Good luck with the show."

Layla stood still and watched them leave together. She was not sure if she'd heard her right, but it appeared as if Danielle was being nice. *That's impossible.* Shaking the thought from her mind, she went to search out Gina.

# Chapter Sixteen

After they'd sipped their iced teas and ordered lunch, Danielle set her menu aside. "And you thought you would have had PR problems with me."

"What's that supposed to mean?" Xavier said.

"Layla," Danielle explained. "That woman is a rattlesnake."

"That's not very nice," Xavier said.

"And she wants you."

Xavier laughed outright at the statement. Reaching across the table, he grabbed her hand. "Jealous?"

Thinking that Layla had a thing for Xavier was just a hunch—a stab in the dark—but he didn't deny it. "Should I be?"

"That depends," he said, removing his hand and sitting back in his chair.

"On?" she asked.

"You can only be jealous if you want me for yourself," he clarified. "The last time I checked, you weren't interested in anything beyond business."

Feigning a laugh, she reached down in her briefcase to pull out her portfolio to take notes. "Speaking of business, it's been almost a week since we looked at the space. Do you have any news yet?"

For a moment, Xavier thought Danielle would finally admit that what they had between them could no longer be ignored. That she was feeling for him what he was feeling for her. That they could quit playing games and give their relationship a chance. How could she have so much self-control when just being in her presence nearly drove him crazy with desire? Tossing those thoughts out of his mind, he put on his business hat. "Yes, as a matter of fact I do."

The waiter set their salads down in front of them and refilled their drinking glasses. When he left the table, Xavier started eating as if she didn't sit anxiously across from him waiting for an answer.

"Unless you want me to throw this glass of tea at you, you better start talking."

Raising his hands in defeat, he started to laugh. "OK, OK."

They had strategized on making Xavier's plan come together. Danielle had been put in charge of tweaking her proposal for the owners of the mall, the Orion Group. Painting the picture of how Danielle's would be a fabulous addition to their current line of retail stores had been the goal.

After talking with other tenants in the mall and reviewing the development plans for the surrounding community earlier in the week, she decided that having her store at the Gallery Place would put her in the best position for success. But her hard work would mean nothing if Xavier didn't come through on his part.

"Not a green light, but definite interest," Xavier said. "They'll get back to us in the next couple of weeks."

"What does that mean? Is that good?"

"In television talk?" Xavier said. "That's very good."

"So, now what?" Danielle said, anxious to keep the ball rolling.

"Now you keep doing what you're doing. Learning the business at Sara's Closet. Keep up with those conferences you've started attending on running retail businesses. However, I need you to stop contacting designers and wholesalers to see if they would be willing to help you out."

That was the core of her marketing plan. Danielle sat, puzzled. "Why would I want to do that? If this store is going to open as scheduled, I'll need to step it up a notch in that category."

"If this show goes through, that's going to be one of the strong selling points. To see if people still hate you, or if you, and they, will rise to the occasion."

"How ironic," Danielle said. "I don't even watch reality television shows, and here I am trying to become the star of one."

"If this thing goes as planned, you'll be the hottest thing on the market."

When Xavier showed her the space at the Gallery Place, Danielle had put her chances at slim to none of getting it. But Danielle hadn't known then about *The Grand Opening*. It was Xavier's ace in the hole. The idea would never have come to Danielle in a million years, but that would explain why he was a top producer and she wasn't.

*The Grand Opening* would track her quest to open her own clothing boutique, amid all the challenges that stood in her way. No business experience. Forging back into an industry that didn't want her. Could she handle it? Would others be willing to help her? Or would she fall flat on her face? That's what this show would answer.

The network loved it, not only because she was a toppled star—a has-been trying to reinvent herself—but it was likely that more than half of her audience would tune in just to see her fail. In this day and age, it was classic reality television.

With a guaranteed audience in the millions, there was

no doubt that the mall would be more than willing to do whatever finagling was necessary to secure that space. The free advertising alone would make it worth their while. The reshuffling of their waiting list to accommodate the show would magically happen for this kind of exposure.

After all the loan rejections and the seemingly impossible obstacles that she had to overcome, Danielle couldn't believe that she was so close to making it happen. "I want to thank you, Xavier. You've believed in this project from the start. Even if the television show doesn't work out, I'm going to stay the course until a space opens up in a location right for my boutique."

"You should really be proud of yourself. You're going to be a success with or without me."

It was a stroke of genius that Xavier had come up with the concept for the show before something similar had been pitched to a major network by someone else. With everyone scrambling for the next reality television hit, he was fairly sure they would OK a thirteen-episode season.

The meeting with the programming director at Fox went better than he expected. The idea for the show intrigued him, but it was the star of the show that thrilled him the most. The show wouldn't have a strong angle without Danielle in it. Without her, the sale would be much harder.

Danielle, thinking about all that had transpired in the last couple of months, wondered if she had made the right decision about Xavier. The night they shared together constantly played out in her mind, and many times it had been on her mind when she laid her head down at night and opened her eyes in the morning. Did she really only want to deal with him on a business level? "Xavier?"

Something in her tone caught his ear and he stopped eating. Staring into her eyes, he could have sworn that the distance she'd tried to keep between them was becoming shorter by the second.

"About a personal relationship between us . . ."

The shrill of his cell phone broke the spell, but he ignored it. "Yes?"

But it was too late. Whatever she had to say, she changed her mind. "You better get that. It could be important."

His annoyance was evident when he answered the call, but after a few seconds, his expression softened. Then, just as quickly, turned to panic. "OK, OK. Calm down. Where are you?"

Danielle waved to the waiter for the check. It didn't take much more information for her to know that this lunch was over.

As Xavier handed his credit card to the waiter without looking at the bill, Danielle didn't bother to argue about who would pay. He was too preoccupied with the caller on the other end. Writing down a few notes on his notepad, he talked a few more minutes and pushed End.

"I know everything's not OK."

"You're right about that. Melinda just went into labor, three weeks early, and Reggie is stuck in traffic coming from a client's site in Richmond. She wants me to meet her at the hospital and stay with her until he gets there."

Richmond was almost two hours away, so Danielle could understand why Melinda wanted someone with her.

Having met at his parents' anniversary party, they'd gotten together a few times after that. "You better get going."

"Oh no," he said, realizing that she intended for them to go their separate ways. "You have to go with me."

"What?" she said, surprised that he would even suggest it.

"Me?" he asked incredulously. "In a maternity ward? With a pregnant woman?"

Danielle couldn't suppress a giggle at the panic written

all over his face. Handling unexpected situations had never unnerved Xavier. "Xavier, she's your sister-in-law. I'm sure she'd rather be with you than a woman she barely knows when she delivers her baby."

Xavier's hand froze as he signed the receipt. The reality of the situation sank in and he clarified it for Danielle. "She will not be 'delivering her baby' with me anywhere near her. Reggie should be back in plenty enough time. Melinda is just looking for a little moral support."

Standing, they both grabbed their coats and Danielle returned her papers to her briefcase. "I don't know, Xavier." On the few occasions that Danielle had been around her, Melinda made it quite clear that Danielle could not count her as one of her fans.

Stepping around the table, he grabbed her hand and looked her straight in the eye. "Please, Danielle."

"OK, OK," she said, finally giving in. How could she deny someone who looked so desperate? "I'll go. But if she's not comfortable having me there, I'm out."

"Deal."

When they reached the maternity floor at George Washington University Hospital, they were immediately directed to Melinda's room. Xavier had spent most of the ride over yelling at his brother on his cell phone, chastising him for going to see a client so far away. What was he thinking? Reggie tried to explain that the baby's due date was still a couple of weeks away. Besides, he reasoned, this was to be his last out-of-town visit until after the baby was born.

Just outside the room, Xavier stopped. "You go ahead in."

"Are you crazy?" Danielle said. "Melinda probably doesn't even remember me. If she's been going through this alone, she probably needs to see a familiar face. Namely yours."

"What she would probably prefer is to see the face of a woman. Someone who can relate to her on an X-chromosome level," Xavier offered. "Or is it the Y chromosome?"

"What I need is for you two to stop bickering and get in here."

Xavier and Danielle stopped when they heard the voice from inside.

"See what you did?" he said. "You're making her upset."

"What *I* did?" Danielle said. "You're the one with some stupid theory on chromosomes."

"Will *somebody* get in here?"

Danielle pushed Xavier into the room, forcing him to walk behind the curtain.

"I hope we didn't disturb you," Danielle said, nudging Xavier to apologize.

"I'm sorry about that, Melinda," Xavier said, giving her a nervous smile. "I don't do well in hospitals."

Propped up on pillows, Melinda was hooked up to machines that tracked the baby's heartbeat and her contractions. "I should have known better than to call you, but you're the only family I have in town at this particular moment, so I had no choice."

Reaching for Danielle's hand, Xavier said, "You remember Danielle?"

Melinda half smiled at Danielle. How could she forget? The times that they spent together had been like whirlwind tornados. Danielle had a gift for taking any situation and making it about her.

Knowing that she and Xavier might be starting up again didn't sit well with her at all. When she voiced her objection, Reggie explained that Danielle was a different person now. Not quite sure if she believed him, she definitely didn't want to test his theory when she was about to give birth to her first child.

The first few times they got together, Melinda couldn't help but admire and feel a little jealous of Danielle and her success. Danielle's being beautiful, rich, and traveling to the most exotic places in the world made Melinda's life seem boring and uninteresting. Danielle exponentially increased those feelings by putting on airs and walking around as if she owned the world and everyone in it.

Melinda felt as if she had put forth every effort to build a friendship with her—to no avail. Danielle repeatedly made it known that she didn't have time to deal with people that didn't travel in her circles.

The day Melinda had heard about the breakup, she jumped for joy, grateful that Xavier was free from the woman she nicknamed "the tyrant." After that, no one was allowed to mention her name in front of Xavier, which suited Melinda just fine. Now it appeared that not only could they mention her name, they could share their most prized moment in life—birth.

"Oh," Melinda said with recognition. "Reggie said you were back in town."

Spending enough time around women with attitudes, Danielle could see that Melinda had harsh feelings toward her. Explaining to Melinda that the person she used to be now no longer existed wouldn't be a good idea right now. This was neither the place nor the time. This was Melinda's moment and if she was causing her any anxiety, she should go. "It's nice to see you again, Melinda. I just came with Xavier to make sure you were OK, but I'm going to be going now."

Xavier grabbed her hand. "You can't go now."

Danielle eyed Melinda and gave Xavier a confident squeeze. "You'll be just fine. Reggie will be here before you know it."

"How will you get home?"

"I'll take a cab to the studio and pick up my car."

With a quick hug, she kissed him on the cheek. "We'll talk later."

A few steps before she made it out the door, she heard her name.

Coming back around the curtain, she stared at Melinda. "Yes?"

"I could really use some more ice and water, but I hate being in this room alone. Can you stay a few minutes while Xavier gets it for me?"

Her tone had gone from rude to polite in the matter of a minute, and Danielle didn't have to figure out why. Xavier was uncomfortable, and Melinda couldn't bear to see him that way. The love she had for Xavier outweighed the dislike she had for Danielle.

The pardon was snatched up by Xavier and he was out the door in seconds.

The next few seconds were filled with silence. Until the machine started beeping.

Rushing to her side, Danielle held her hand as she rode out the next contraction. Once the pain subsided, Melinda took a few moments to catch her breath. "Thanks. Can you imagine if Xavier had to help me through that?"

Picturing that caused them both to laugh, breaking the ice from the discomfort they'd shared when Danielle first arrived. But the reprieve didn't last long.

"What are you doing, Danielle?"

The accusation in her voice indicated that their bonding moment was over. "I know we haven't gotten along in the past, and it's all my fault. You're about to experience one of the best moments in your life and I'm sure I'm the last person you want here. I promise, as soon as Xavier gets back, I'll go."

"I'm not talking about today," Melinda clarified. "I'm talking about Xavier. What are you doing to him?"

"I don't understand."

"When you two broke up, he was devastated," she explained. "He couldn't comprehend how you would treat him like all the rest."

"I know I hurt him—" Danielle started.

"Not hurt, Danielle. Destroyed. For months, he just went through the motions. If it wasn't for his work, none of us were sure that he would survive."

Danielle started to speak, but she wouldn't let her.

"Every day, for weeks, we had to put up with the tabloids and the entertainment news shows chronicling the breakup. All of them basically asking the question of how he could have been so stupid to think that he could change you. That you would be any different with him. All he had to do was look at your track record and he would have known.

"Wasn't there a pilot, Todd something or other, who gave up his job at the airlines to spend more time with you? And let's not forget about that defense attorney who almost lost his practice trying to cater to your every need. Richard Highland? The football player. I'm sure you remember him. He had the worst game of his career after you left him to go to Spain to work, planning not to return to him."

Danielle stood stoically, taking everything Melinda dished out. What choice did she have? Everything she said was true. No need to try to defend herself.

"But your public humiliation of Xavier took the cake. How could you do that to him?"

Her tirade ended with the onset of another contraction.

Without hesitation, Danielle went to her again, helping her breathe through it.

After the moment had passed, Danielle stood back and gathered up her belongings. It was the weirdest situation—being chastised after helping her breathe through a contraction. "You have every reason not to like me. During that time in my life, I wouldn't have liked me either. I've more than paid for what I did to Xavier—a hundred times over."

Melinda adjusted her position and listened attentively.

"I've given this speech more times than I can count, but it's worth repeating. I am not the same person. I've paid my dues for my behavior and will never treat people that way again. Xavier is a wonderful man, and the only thing I'm going to do to him is work with him on a professional level. So don't worry, his heart is safe."

"Here's the ice and water."

His timing couldn't have been better and Danielle said a quick good-bye and left the room.

Watching her go, Xavier turned his attention back to Melinda with questioning eyes. "What just happened here?"

Melinda rubbed her stomach and did some deep-breathing exercises. She couldn't believe how upset that woman had made her. Why was Xavier setting himself up for more heartache? "Why are you doing this?"

Putting the items on the tray beside the bed, Xavier looked confused. "Doing what?"

"Getting tangled up with her again."

"Give it a rest, Mel. You're in labor, for goodness' sake."

Her response was cut off by a nurse coming in to check on her progress.

Stepping into the hallway, he asked for directions to the waiting area, hoping to find Danielle.

He found her sitting in the corner with a cup of coffee in her hand and he sat beside her. "What did she say?"

Danielle found it refreshing that the blame for a bad situation didn't automatically come to her. She took a deep breath. This wasn't the time or the place to have this discussion. "Nothing I haven't heard before. But it's OK, really."

"No," Xavier said. "If anyone in this family has the right to hate you, it's me. And I've forgiven you. So whatever she said, just ignore."

In all of their trials and tribulations, and even through their night of passionate sex, she'd never heard him say the F word. "Do you mean that, Xavier? Can you honestly say that you've forgiven me?"

"Do you think I could have spent the night with you if I didn't?"

Relief crossed her face and Danielle stood. "Thanks for saying it, Xavier, because I truly am sorry for how things turned out for us."

"Does this mean you're ready to try again?" he asked hopefully.

"There you are. How could you leave your sister-in-law alone at a time like this?"

Catherine Johnston entered the room with authority. One look at Danielle and her face turned pale. "What in the world are you doing here?"

Her lack of approval was evident by her tight lips and stanch posture.

"Mom, you remember Danielle," he said, wrapping his arm around her waist.

Catherine noticed the gesture and didn't hide her disapproving expression. "How could I forget the woman who almost ruined your career?"

The "speech" came to mind about how she'd changed, how she wasn't the same person, and how she was sorry for what she'd done, but Danielle was just too tired to talk. Giving a worn-out smile, she headed for the exit. "It was nice to see you again, Mrs. Johnston."

When the double doors closed behind her, Xavier pulled his mother to the side. "How could you do that?"

"It was the truth, wasn't it?" she said, refusing to apologize for her comment.

"It was also two years ago."

"Don't take that tone with me."

Xavier took a deep breath and apologized to his mother for raising his voice. "Danielle and I—"

"Oh, Lord," Catherine said, taking a seat. "Please don't say it. Please don't tell me the two of you are back together. Are you a glutton for punishment? Did you not suffer enough the first time?"

This was what it must be like for Danielle, he thought, as she tried to convince those from her past that she'd turned over a new leaf. How many times had she tried to tell him that she wouldn't do the things she used to do? How many times did he laugh in her face, claiming not to believe her? No wonder Danielle didn't want to start a relationship with him again. It wasn't just about them. It was about his family. Convincing them that she was a different person would take a toll on her.

"Mom, Melinda is down the hall giving you your first grandchild. Is this discussion really important right now?"

"You're right," she said, "but this isn't the end of the conversation."

Xavier showed his mother to Melinda's room and left the two of them alone to go search out Danielle. Checking the cafeteria, gift shop, and other waiting rooms turned up nothing.

Stepping outside, he dialed her cell. Getting her voice mail, he left a message to contact him as soon as she got the message. With no clue of where she could be, he headed back upstairs to wait to meet his new niece or nephew.

# *Chapter Seventeen*

The next morning, Danielle arrived at the store earlier than usual. Unable to sleep, she decided to get a jump-start on taking inventory. At just a little before eight, she had almost two hours before the store would open and Patricia would arrive.

Standing at the front display table, she had just started sorting earrings when she heard a slight tap on the door. For some strange reason, she didn't need to peer out the window to know who it was. She'd let all his calls go to voice mail and she didn't bother to call him back. With the pending business venture, she couldn't avoid him for long, but she could make it at least one more day.

When they were together yesterday, she'd no longer denied that her feelings for him were still there and going strong. The idea that spending one night with him would be enough to satisfy her craving for him could only be described as ludicrous. He'd forgiven her and wanted to give them another chance. He even defended her to his family. But if they reunited, there would just be more questions, more insults, and more people to go up against who would wonder why he would give someone like her a second chance.

The knock on the door came again and she turned to face him.

"Open the door."

She couldn't hear the words but she could read his lips.

"Please, Danielle."

Going against her first instinct to put him off another day, she unlocked the door and let him in.

"How long did you plan on avoiding me?"

Danielle picked up a few empty boxes and headed toward the back of the store. "I'm not avoiding you. I'm working."

Following her, he wasn't going to let her off the hook that easily. "Were you working when you didn't answer your cell phone or return my calls?"

Opening the stockroom door, she put the boxes in the corner and looked around the small desk for more inventory tracking sheets. "You were busy with your family."

"Don't use that as an excuse," he said, watching her do everything but pay attention to him. "What's going on? Is this about my family?"

Thinking of his sister-in-law's comment and his mother's angry reception to her, Danielle tossed the papers back on the desk in frustration. Without warning, all the hurt feelings she'd experienced yesterday by the words thrown at her by his family game crashing forward. Her throat started to constrict and tears formed in the corners of her eyes.

Not sure what was happening, Xavier pulled her to him, wrapping his arms around her waist. "Talk to me."

"Your family hates me," she started. "As funny as it sounds, Melinda practically cursed me out in between contractions and your mother made it clear that I was the last person she wanted to see you with."

"They don't hate you," he said honestly. "They may hate what happened between us. I'm not going to lie, Danielle. For a time after we broke up, they saw how much it affected me. They just think they are looking out for my best interests."

"Same difference."

Stepping back, he grabbed a tissue off the desk and handed it to her. "My family is important to me, but they don't rule my life. What happened, and what happens, between us is just that—between us."

She heard the words but found them hard to believe. "How can we make a relationship work if it's going to cause friction with Melinda and your mom?"

Xavier heard the question, but focused on the meaning behind it. "Are you saying you want to give our relationship a second chance?"

The tears started to dry up and Danielle sniffled and wiped her nose. Was that what she just said? The words took her by surprise. Lowering her head, she tried to get her thoughts together. "I . . . I . . ."

"It's a yes-or-no question, Dee-Dee."

The nickname touched her heart and the answer became clear. Raising her head, she gazed into his eyes and released a slow smile. "Yes."

Without hesitation, he cupped her face and lowered his lips to hers.

The overwhelming sense of love took over and she couldn't get close enough. She wrapped her arms around his neck, slipping her tongue inside his mouth. Pressing into him, she felt all the frustration of the past twenty-four hours dissipating, and the only thing that mattered now was the two of them.

Without breaking contact, she reached down and unbuttoned his shirt and jerked it out of his pants in a matter of seconds. Running her fingers across his chest, she could feel his arousal growing.

"How long before someone comes?" he asked in between kisses.

"If I have my way, not long," she said seductively.

Xavier's laugh filled the room at the double meaning

of his question. "I'm talking about the store. When will Patricia or Elaine be here?"

Working the belt buckle on his pants, she answered when it was halfway off, "At least an hour."

Dropping to the floor, he pulled her with him. It didn't take long for her blue silk blouse to go over her head, joining his shirt on the floor beside them. He buried his head in her chest, the lacy bra serving as a thin barrier and her nipples responding immediately. He snapped the back of it, freeing her breasts, and he hungrily feasted on one, and then the other.

Danielle reached down and made quick work of un-buttoning his pants. Just as the zipper went down, the bell on the door buzzed.

They froze in place, and it took several seconds for it to register that someone else was in the store.

"I thought you said—"

"Believe me, Xavier," she said, her voice filled with panic, "this is not the time to argue about it."

Jumping to their feet, Danielle tossed Xavier his shirt while she scrambled to get her top over her head. Running her fingers through her hair, she slipped her shoes on just as he tucked his shirt back in his pants.

Buckling his belt, he pushed it through the hoop just as the stockroom door opened.

"Elaine, I didn't realize you were coming in early."

Elaine's eyes moved from Danielle to Xavier. "I thought I would come in and get a head start on inven-tory, but I noticed the earrings laid out and I guess you were thinking the same thing."

"Let me introduce you," Danielle said, hoping her voice sounded normal and she wasn't breathing too hard. "Xavier Johnston, Elaine Bartlett."

They shook hands and exchanged pleasantries before Xavier excused himself.

"I'll walk you to the door," Danielle volunteered.

When they were sure they were out of earshot, they both broke out in laughter. She playfully hit him in the arm. "You almost got us caught!"

"Me?" he said. "What happened to 'no one will be here for at least an hour'?"

"I feel like I'm in high school and I got caught by the principal."

"Oh," Xavier teased. "What kinda girl were you in high school?"

Punching him in the arm, she glanced back at the storeroom to make sure they were still alone on the selling floor. "This is not funny."

"I know," he said, with still a hint of laughter in his voice. "A few more minutes and your boss would have gotten one heck of a peep show."

"See you later?"

"Dinner. My place."

"I'll bring dessert."

Danielle watched Xavier drive off before heading back to the storeroom. With any luck, Elaine wouldn't have noticed anything and the only topic of conversation would be related to the store.

"Having business meetings in the morning?" Elaine said, with a knowing smile.

"He just came by to, umm, schedule a meeting for later."

"So you two are still just business associates?"

Danielle picked up the inventory form and began to fill it out. "Yep, that's it."

Elaine nodded and stacked up register tape, staples, and tape to restock the front counter. She walked through the door without so much as a backward glance.

Danielle exhaled a deep breath before chuckling softly at how close they came to getting caught.

"Danielle?"

Clearing her amused expression off her face, she answered Elaine, who had poked her head back in the stockroom door.

"Your shirt is on backward."

Thank God she already had color in her skin; otherwise, she would have turned a deep red.

Elaine's laughter lingered after she'd fixed her clothes and continued taking inventory.

Later that afternoon, Danielle made her way through the studio halls looking for Xavier. Not finding him in his office, she asked his assistant, who said he was probably on the set of *The Fashion Design House,* as they were scheduled to start shooting today.

Entering the staging area, she hung back as the crew was hard at work setting up the next segment. Xavier stood beside the director, plotting out angles and reviewing last-minute details.

Hearing "quiet on the set," Danielle hardly breathed when the director yelled, "Action!"

Layla did her spiel, predicting what would be the hottest fashion trends for the upcoming season. They must have spent a fortune on a coach because she was actually fairly good. When she heard the word "cut," Danielle stepped over a few wires and made her way to him.

"Hey you," he said.

"Hi," she said. "I don't mean to interrupt but I wanted to talk to you."

Layla watched the couple walk to the opposite side of the set, wondering what was going on between those two.

"I heard from the Orion Group today."

"And?"

"They bought it, Xavier," Danielle said, unable to contain her exuberance. "Hook, line, and sinker."

Picking her up, he swung her around, placing kisses

all around her face. "That's fantastic. All we have to do now is wait to hear from the network."

"I don't know how to thank you for all your help."

Leaning in closer, he gave a wicked smile. "You can give me a piece of that pie tonight."

"You got it," she said, remembering their interruption that morning and anticipating their evening.

"Xavier, we need you over here," one of the crew members yelled.

With a quick kiss on her lips, he headed back over to the set. "I'll see you tonight."

Danielle was making her way through the lobby when she heard her name being called.

Layla trotted toward her. "I'm glad I caught up with you."

"Why?" Danielle said, not even pretending to be friendly. "What could we possibly have to talk about?"

"Xavier."

Not falling into the trap of fighting over a man she already had, Danielle continued walking. "Again I ask, what could we possibly have to talk about?"

"Our shooting schedule is ramping up. We'll be on the road the next several weeks. Interviewing, visiting hot spots in the fashion world."

"And your point?" Danielle asked.

"I beat you once, I can beat you again."

"Has it only been once?" Danielle asked thoughtfully, as if she were trying to think back over their history. "And yet we've gone up against each other so many times."

"Cute, Danielle. Real cute," Layla said. "Keep that attitude when your man is spending his days, and nights, on location with me."

"Are you finished? Because I'm getting quite bored with this conversation."

Before she could answer, Danielle pushed through the front doors and headed across the parking lot.

Danielle congratulated herself on yet another mile-stone. She'd managed to get out of that situation without using words that would make her churchgoing mother drop to her knees.

Later that evening, Danielle lay in Xavier's lap as he fed her grapes. Deciding to go healthy, they dined on mineral water, baked fish, and brown rice. If she was going to be in front of the camera again, she'd have to lay off the lasagna and bread. "How's Melinda?"

"Thanks for asking—especially after how she treated you. She and son Jacob are doing just fine. I told her we'd come by this weekend."

Danielle sat up. "Why would you do that? Will your parents be there? Does she even want me in her house?"

"Don't worry," he said, hoping to calm her nerves. "They're going to have to accept you. You're going to be a part of my life for a long time—whether they like it or not."

"Do they have to accept me in person?" she asked, half joking. "Maybe we could just exchange e-mail."

"I've talked to them," Xavier reassured her. "There'll be no more mean words. I promise."

"Now that you've dealt with them, what are you going to do about that Layla chick?" Danielle said, remember-ing the run-in with her earlier that day.

"Layla? What about her?"

"Oh, come on, Xavier," Danielle said. "Don't tell me you haven't noticed that she wants you."

"She's made a few moves," he admitted. "But I've shot them all down."

"Well, she obviously doesn't see it that way. She threw in my face the fact that you two would be shooting on location over the next several weeks."

Leaning over, he kissed her lips. "You have nothing to worry about. The only thing I want from Layla is a number-one television show."

"Is that all you want from me too, a number-one television show?"

"Uh-uh," he said, sliding his hand down the front of her cargo pants. "That's the last thing I want from you."

Closing her eyes, Danielle caught her breath when he touched her most sensitive spot.

"You know what I want from you?"

Danielle could barely keep her senses about her, but she managed to get out one word. "What?"

"Your love."

Opening her eyes when she heard his request, she stared directly into his. His beautiful eyes had always been her measuring stick. There was never a need to guess where she stood with him, because the truth was always there. Over the years, there were many emotions she'd seen in them. Attraction. Lust. Caring. Anger. Regret. Tonight, there was no question what was in them, and his heart. Love.

"I love you, Xavier. I don't think I ever stopped loving you. One stupid mistake took you away from me. I don't intend to let that happen again."

Xavier softly kissed her. "I love you, too, Dee-Dee. Always have. Always will."

Following him to the bedroom, she watched as he turned on the CD, and Luther's voice filled the room. Lighting several candles placed strategically on the dresser and nightstand, he guided her to the bed. "Tell me about your dreams."

"What?" she said, feeling her face warm with embarrassment.

"You said you've been dreaming of me. I want to make those dreams a reality."

Danielle relayed her fantasies and Xavier followed her description to a tee. That's when Danielle confirmed that nothing could compare to the real thing.

# *Chapter Eighteen*

The following Sunday afternoon, Danielle nervously stood outside the home of Reginald and Melinda Johnston with a large gift bag filled with pacifiers, onesies, and little bibs that said "I love my mommy," which she hoped would act as a peace offering. Shifting nervously from one foot to other, she grabbed Xavier's hand to stop him from ringing the doorbell—again.

"We can't stand out here all day," he said.

"I know," Danielle said, realizing how ridiculous they must have looked. They'd been standing on the porch for almost ten minutes.

Hoping to put her at ease, he gave her a reassuring kiss on the lips. "I promise. We'll stay for as long as you want. Give the signal and we're out."

Nodding in agreement, Danielle reached up and pushed the button herself.

Catherine answered the door and gave Xavier a hug. "'Bout time you came over to see your nephew. He's grown since the last time you saw him."

"Good to see you, too, Mom," Xavier said, entering the foyer.

Danielle hesitated and stood on the porch.

Catherine's smile faltered when she noticed Danielle. Stepping to the side, she motioned for her to come in, but didn't say anything.

"Hello, Mrs. Johnston," Danielle said, moving to stand beside Xavier.

Catherine watched him place his arm around her waist, pulling her securely to him. "Danielle."

"Hey, you guys, come on in." Reggie's cheerful voice boomed through and everyone sighed in relief. The tension had been thick.

"Jacob's asleep, but he'll be up soon enough," he continued. "Why don't you guys make yourself comfortable? I'll get drinks. Dinner will be ready in just a bit."

Melinda relaxed in the recliner chair with a glass of lemonade and reached up to give Xavier a hug. Her only acknowledgment of Danielle was a slight nod in her direction.

After an uncomfortable silence, Xavier handed Melinda the gift. "Thanks to Danielle, I think there are things in that bag Jacob can actually use."

Accepting the gift, she turned her attention to Danielle, offering a polite smile that didn't reach any other part of her face. "What have you been up to since your career ended?"

"Melinda," Xavier said. The problems his family had with Danielle would not be solved in one visit, but they could at least try to be civil to her.

"It's OK," Danielle said, touching his arm. It was a conversation that was bound to take place sooner or later. Might as well be sooner. In fact, she kind of liked Melinda's straightforward approach. That meant she always knew where she stood with her.

"As I'm sure you all know, I'm no longer modeling."

"And you're not in television either," Melinda added.

Xavier started to speak, because she had more than crossed the line, but Danielle beat him to it. "That's right. I'm completely out of the entertainment business. I've shifted my focus."

"What are you doing now?" Catherine asked. Not too rude, but not quite friendly.

"I've been working at a boutique in D.C. as a sales associate in preparation for opening my own store."

"She's been doing a fantastic job. By the time her own boutique is up and running, she'll be able to handle all aspects of the business." Xavier's words were said with pride, and Danielle squeezed his hand in silent thanks for his vote of confidence.

She was not quite sure what they'd expected her to say, but working at a boutique definitely wasn't it. In a matter of seconds, she could see some of their distrust of her diminish. If they thought they were still dealing with a spoiled, rich prima donna, they were in for the shock of their lives.

After they'd asked her several more questions, it became quite clear that Danielle was committed to her business venture. The fact that she spoke with such passion about it had to impress his family enough to at least stop asking Danielle embarrassing questions.

When they sat down to dinner, Danielle was thankful that the conversation revolved around feeding schedules, diaper changes, and private schools instead of her. Mr. Johnston told wonderful childhood stories that kept them all laughing and embarrassed both Reggie and Xavier. By the time dessert was served, she actually found herself feeling relaxed.

Danielle and Xavier went up to the nursery to visit little Jacob. Painted in shades of blue, the room was dimly lit by soft light on a Noah's-ark lamp in the corner. Having been fed and changed an hour ago, he quietly slept in his light blue sleeper with a little elephant on it.

Staring down at the tiny body, Xavier held Danielle's hand and the words of his brother resurfaced.

"The woman that will make you think about focusing

on something other than work. The woman that will make you seriously contemplate signing on for another project that will keep you away from her for long periods of time. The woman that will have you running home for dinner, mowing the lawn, and jumping for joy when she steps out of the bathroom and shows you that the stick turned blue."

He'd found that person. In Danielle. "You want to tell me what happened when we were in the baby store?"

Danielle didn't look at him, but knew exactly what he was referring to. His picking up on her peculiar behavior that day shouldn't have surprised her. He knew her too well.

When she didn't answer right away, Xavier felt a little fear. "Do you not want to have children?"

"Oh no," Danielle quickly corrected. "That's not it. I definitely want to have children someday."

Xavier visibly relaxed. Now that he'd found someone he wanted to share his life with, he looked forward to fatherhood. "Then what is it? You ran out of that store for no apparent reason and your mood wasn't the same for the rest of the day."

Looking at the tiny, pretty dresses and pretending to have a bun in the oven had caught her by surprise that day. "I have done some pretty selfish things in my day, and I've been working hard over the past year to make things right."

Danielle hesitated before continuing. Conversations with her sisters, parents, Christine, and Xavier flashed in her mind, demonstrating how much progress she'd made in doing just that. "But there are some things that can't be fixed."

A lone tear fell down her cheek and he raised his hand to gently wipe it away. "What are you talking about, Dee-Dee? What is it?"

Gazing up into his eyes, she made a confession that she never shared with anyone. "You aren't the only person who I chose my career over."

Xavier hugged her close. She didn't have to explain any further. Her declaration, made in a nursery, said it all.

As she sobbed quietly in his arms, he offered her silent comfort. It became clear to him what choice she had made.

With no word from the network on whether they were interested in his television show, Xavier hit the road for *The Fashion Design House*. Danielle filled her days with the store and her nights helping Tanya put the finishing touches on her wedding plans. Missing him terribly, she was glad for the distraction to keep her busy. With Tanya scheduled for the final fitting that afternoon, Danielle didn't even mind being in the company of Christine and Natalie. They'd managed to find common ground and had actually enjoyed each other's company the last time they got together.

With the rehearsal dinner a few short weeks away, she was thrilled that Xavier promised to be her date. There would be quite a few people she hadn't seen in a while and who might not be aware that she was a changed person. He would be her support and boost her confidence to help her make it through the night.

Her cell phone rang just as she was getting dressed.

"I've got great news."

"I'm listening," Danielle said, putting on her shoes.

With the prospect of once again being in front of the camera, Danielle had thought it wise to get herself an agent, and of course, only one person came to mind.

"I just got a call from the head of programming at Fox," Michelle said.

When they worked together in the past, Danielle had learned to decipher Michelle's voice inflections. Regardless of whether it was good news, bad news, or something in between, Danielle could figure it out before she got halfway through delivering the information. Her fast talking and her high-pitched tone told Danielle this was not just good news—this was great news. "What did they say?"

"They want the show!"

"Yes!" Danielle screamed, twirling around in circles. "I can't believe this. Could you ever have imagined this a year ago, Michelle?"

"No way," Michelle said honestly. "You were looking pretty much like a trivia question."

"Ha, ha," Danielle said, knowing she wasn't too far from telling the truth. "But look at me now. I get my boutique and Xavier gets his show."

"Well . . ." Michelle said.

Danielle abruptly stopped her celebration. That tone said that there was more to the story and she might not like it.

"You're half right," Michelle finished.

Danielle's heart sank and she braced herself. "What does that mean?"

Michelle wasn't sure how Danielle would take to the next bit of news, but it was information she had to have. "It means you get your boutique."

"And Xavier's show?" Danielle said.

Michelle, as usual, decided it best not to beat around the bush. "Won't be his."

Sitting on the bed, Danielle reached for her watch. "I don't understand."

Michelle reviewed her notes from the conference call that had ended less than fifteen minutes ago. "They love the concept, but want to make a few changes before signing on the dotted line."

Something told Danielle she wasn't going to like where this conversation was headed. "Changes like what?"

"They want the show to be produced by someone else."

Shocked, Danielle needed a second to respond. "But it was Xavier's idea."

"And they'll pay him dearly for it," Michelle said, glancing down at the figure quoted to her.

"Why?"

Explaining it exactly as they told it to her, Michelle said, "The reality television show is getting tough. It seems like one is going in to production every day. They want to go with someone with a proven record. The executive producer is someone who has three reality shows in the top-ten Nielsen ratings."

"Negotiable?" Danielle asked, already assuming what the answer would be.

"No."

Danielle wasn't surprised, but it was worth a shot. "What else?"

"They want to film in New York—Manhattan. Fifth Avenue to be exact."

This was too much. "But my store is opening in D.C."

"Is this really about a store, Danielle?" Michelle asked, not getting the enthusiastic response she'd expected.

"What do you mean?"

"The boutique was a great idea when you didn't have any other options, but this reality show could be just what you need to put you back on the radar." Michelle had already started planning how she could leverage this new development to her client's advantage.

"I don't want to be on the radar," Danielle said, feeling her temper growing. "I want to open a boutique."

Michelle took a deep breath, hoping to get across the

bigger picture. "If you open a boutique today, you won't see a profit for at least three years, according to your business plan. You'll be living off the little bit of money you have left and the small pay, if any, you'll get from the store."

Danielle didn't have to guess where she was going next.

"You make the deal for this show, you'll get thirty-five thousand per episode. That's almost a half million for the half season. That doesn't even include the publicity your store will get. You'll turn a profit the day you open. Not to mention this is network television and Layla is on cable."

Everything Michelle just laid out for her made perfect sense. The only thing she'd have to do was cut Xavier out and move—away from him. "I'll have to let you know."

"Danielle, being resurrected from the grave doesn't happen that much in this business," Michelle warned.

"I know."

"What exactly are you thinking about?"

"This is just happening so fast."

"Of course it is," Michelle said. "You know the routine. It always happens this fast."

"I'll get back to you soon."

"Don't take too long to think about it."

"I won't," she promised.

There was no question that this was the best of both worlds. She got cash back in her bank account and she got the store. Maybe Michelle was right. What was there to think about? Flipping her phone open again, she dialed Xavier's cell. Voice mail. Not sure of his production schedule, she called his hotel room.

"Hello."

The female voice caught her off guard, but it didn't

take long to figure out whom it belonged to. Choosing to bypass the pleasantries, Danielle said, "Put Xavier on the phone, Layla."

"I'm sorry, Xavier's extremely occupied right now. Is there a message I can give?"

Her voice dripped in amusement and sarcasm and it grated on Danielle's nerves. Danielle wasn't up to this today. "I'm not playing games with you."

"No games," Layla replied innocently. "He's in the shower. And I'm about to join him."

As if to prove her point, Danielle heard what sounded like a door opening with running water in the background. "Like I said, is there a message?"

Danielle hung up the phone without saying another word. *What else could possibly go wrong today?*

"Ouch!" The pin stuck Danielle by mistake and she jumped to the side.

"I'm sorry you have to stand still so long," the seamstress said, working on the bodice of the dress. "I want to make sure the seam is done perfectly."

Danielle pasted on a smile and turned as the seamstress said, "You would think as a former model, you wouldn't have a problem with this. Must be an off day."

Danielle ignored her comment. The woman had no idea how much of an off day it had been.

After a few more pins, Danielle was ready to step out of the dress they picked out for the bridesmaids.

The four of them headed over to Tanya's favorite Indian restaurant for lunch. With her mind focused on the conversation with Michelle and her boutique, Danielle wanted to bail out, but her sister was so excited, she couldn't let her down. It was the last get-together before the rehearsal dinner.

Once the women were seated and the orders placed, the talk turned to weddings.

Tanya had her planner in front of her, checking off all that had already been accomplished.

"The flowers are scheduled to arrive at nine that morning and the decorator wll be there at ten to set up the pew bows and candles. The limos have been reserved and the cake has been selected."

Closing the binder that had been her lifeline for the past several months, Tanya put it back in her bag. "Now that we've gotten that out of the way, it's time to find out what's going on with my sister."

Danielle glanced around at all the women, who stared back at her. "There's nothing going on with me."

"A former model who couldn't keep still for a fitting? A fake smile to go along with that fake laugh you've been giving us all afternoon," Tanya pointed out. "What's the deal?"

Aside from her sister, Danielle never had girlfriends that she could confide in. The relationships she formed with other women always had an element of business to them. After everything that had transpired this morning, she desperately needed some advice. Maybe the three of them could actually help her figure out what to do.

"I got a call today from my agent," Danielle stated. "I got the television show."

Tanya clapped her hands in excitement. "That's wonderful. Everything is working out just like you planned."

The smile Tanya gave her couldn't be matched. This day should have been one filled with celebration. Instead, it was a day where the decisions she made would affect not only her business but what she had with Xavier. "Not everything."

At their confused looks, Danielle spent the next twenty minutes explaining everything that had happened with the networks and Layla. They didn't interrupt and it felt good to talk things out of her head.

"First things first," Natalie said, after she'd completed her monologue. "Who is this little witch Layla and where can we find her?"

In the short time that Danielle had known Natalie, she could guess that they could be great friends if they could get past Danielle's history. She was feisty and didn't take any stuff from anyone. Filled with spunk, she was the type of friend that would take off her earrings, kick off her heels, pull her hair back in a ponytail, and be ready to go to blows for you.

"Believe me," Danielle said, finding it hard to believe that Natalie actually would be ready to defend her. "I've watched enough soap operas to know that the last thing she was getting ready to do was get in the shower with my man. I know he wouldn't do that to me."

"That's mighty mature of you," Tanya said. "If it was me, I probably would have been on the first plane to wherever they are to find out exactly what was going on."

"Oh, don't get me wrong," Danielle clarified. "That man definitely has a helluva lot of explaining to do to justify why that little wench was answering his phone."

"I just can't believe that women are still playing games like that," Christine chimed in. "She needs to get a life."

The three women didn't respond right away, remembering what Danielle had done to Christine just a few short years ago.

Glancing around the table to each woman, Christine realized how serious the looks on their faces were. "Relax, guys. Me and Danielle are semicool. If Natalie wasn't going to kick this Layla person's butt, then I was."

All three burst into laughter and Danielle couldn't help but discover why these women meant so much to Tanya. They were the epitome of friendship. For most of her adult life, she always viewed other women as her competition—whether it be for a job or a man. Never allowing herself to experience anything beyond a superficial relationship. Finally, she was able to accept the emotional support that other women could give her. It was a wonderful feeling.

"What's your plan of action?" Tanya asked.

"Nothing," Danielle said. "I'm sure he'll have a plausible explanation next time he calls and he'll tell me all about it."

"That's one problem solved," Tanya said, pretending to take notes. "Now, on to problem number two. The television show."

Danielle could think of nothing else since she'd gotten the call. There was no denying the scenario that Michelle laid out for her. If she decided to accept the terms of the offer, her money problems would be over and she'd have her store. But would it be worth the price she would have to pay? "What would each of you do?"

"You can't go by that," Christine said. "You have to make your own decision on this one."

"I work with people every day who are trying to get their ducks in a row to either get their business started or keep it going. You have someone offering a way to make that road easier," Natalie said. At BSI, her non-profit company, she could probably name at least ten people right off the bat that would jump at this opportunity in a heartbeat.

"So you're saying you would take the deal?" Danielle said.

"Would it really be so bad to have your store in the middle of Manhattan in front of a national audience?" Natalie said.

"But what about after the cameras go off?" Tanya added. "Is that where you want to continue to run your business? The competition is still the competition. The rent on that location is still going to be the rent on that location. None of that will change."

Danielle faced her sister and considered her words. "You're saying that I should stick with my original plan?"

"What about Xavier?" Christine added. "You guys just got back on track. Do you want to move away from him? Have a long-distance relationship? Spend most of your time apart?"

"It's not like she's moving to the other side of the world," Natalie said. "It's New York. A one-hour plane ride. A three-hour train ride. You'd probably see him just as much as you would if you stayed here."

Natalie had a good point. With both of their hectic schedules, it wasn't likely they would have time to see each other every day, even if she stayed in D.C. All their advice was good, it just didn't help her get any closer to making a decision.

"The bottom line is," Tanya said, "what do you ultimately want?"

She could answer that question without a second thought. "I want the store and Xavier."

"Here or in New York?" Christine asked.

Tanya shook her head. "That's not the decision here."

"Then what is?" Natalie said.

Reaching for her sister's hand, Tanya thought Danielle was missing one major point in this entire scenario. "When you started this quest to open your boutique, you made a conscious choice that you wanted out of the entertainment business. If you take this deal, you're not a store owner who works to satisfy her clients and help new designers, you're a commodity. You'll be at the mercy of the network and will have to make a lot of concessions— regardless of whether they say you will or not. They're already asking you to give up your producer and location. Is that the life you want to go back to?"

Danielle hadn't thought about it that way. When she got the information from Michelle, all she could think about was whether she should accept. She didn't give a second thought to whether she wanted to accept the terms that would affect her the rest of her life.

The waiter set the food on the table and everyone started to eat, each woman deep in her own thoughts, wondering what she would do if faced with the same situation.

# Chapter Nineteen

The clock beside the bed told her it was just after three in the morning. This time, it wasn't erotic dreams that had her tossing and turning, it was the opportunity that Michelle had presented to her earlier today. When she lost out on the job to Layla, she would have taken anything to get some part of her old life back. But that was before Danielle's. Before Xavier.

He'd called her earlier in the evening but only had a few minutes to talk, which suited Danielle just fine. Not mentioning Layla kind of put her out, but she opted not to say anything. That was a conversation that needed to take place face-to-face. It was also a good delay tactic, because she was still trying to figure out how Xavier would respond to the news. Would he see this as a good opportunity or a situation where she chose her own goals over him?

According to Natalie, that was not a hard decision. Why shouldn't Danielle jump at the chance to have everything she wanted? Fame. Fortune. Her store. And her man. Natalie couldn't see how she would be giving up anything; she would be gaining it all.

Tanya's point of view was a different story, yet just as valid. The spotlight had the power to do some major damage to Danielle's personality. When she had it in the past, she didn't handle it too well. Would this be a repeat performance? Would the attention go to her head again, or would she really be able to deal with it, not alienating her friends, her family, or Xavier?

Xavier. That was the other factor to consider. He'd been there and believed in her when no one else did. Putting up his own money when he had his own business to run and making sure his investment paid off by pitching the idea for the television show. How would he feel about being cut out of the deal? Having been in television all of his adult life, he was not new to this situation. This type of maneuvering happened all the time in the business. But did Xavier consider the arrangements between them just business? Would he understand if Danielle decided to take Fox up on their offer?

At a complete loss as to what to do, Danielle had called her mother last night, hoping she could provide some of her infinite wisdom in this situation. Since she came to D.C., she'd talked to Mable several times, keeping her updated on what was going on in her life. When she told her mom that she and Tanya had finally worked out their differences, she could hear her tears through the phone.

As she told her mother about the boutique, Mable gave Danielle her full support, telling her she had the ability to accomplish anything she set her mind to. The day she told her about her relationship with Xavier, her mother couldn't have been happier. Just like everyone else, her mother had heard the stories surrounding their breakup, but unlike all the rest, she believed that Danielle could change her ways and find true happiness. She didn't predict it would be with Xavier, but she was happy that they were able to find their way back to each other.

The year with her parents had been rough, and the entire time she stayed there, she counted the days until she could get her life back together and succeed on her own. Now that she'd been gone, she realized how much she missed them. They were scheduled to arrive in town the night before the rehearsal dinner. She couldn't wait for their plane to touch down in D.C.

On Friday, Danielle finished up with the last customer and started to close up the shop. It had been busy being in the midst of graduation and wedding season. Xavier was coming back today and she had offered to cook dinner for him at his place. Continuing to put him off this week, she'd claimed to be either busy with customers when he called her at the store or running around with Tanya trying to finalize her wedding plans.

The excuses sounded weak even to her, but he didn't push her. When they'd gotten off the phone last night, she could tell that he probably suspected something was going on, but he didn't ask. All he said was that if their relationship was going to work, they should always be honest with each other. Feeling a little guilty, she almost lashed out and asked about Layla, but she held her tongue. She would deal with that when he returned.

Xavier wasn't the only one putting her in a guilty mode. Michelle was putting the pressure on her, big time. The network was getting anxious and they wanted an answer ASAP. With them wanting to put the show in their fall lineup, there wasn't much time for her to mull over the decision.

Her agent had a hard time trying to figure out what she was thinking about and told her so. Once this show hit the airwaves, Michelle could almost guarantee Danielle every morning show, a *Dateline* or *20/20* spot, and if the show made the top five, *Oprah*. Danielle could practically hear her salivating at the idea—and the commissions she'd make.

When they spoke yesterday and Danielle still didn't have an answer, she pulled out her trump card.

"Danielle, we've been through a lot together. We've

traveled the world. We have celebrated amazing highs and we've cried together through some of the toughest times of our lives. And through all of that, have I ever steered you wrong? I've always looked out for you, as if you were my own daughter. You've never questioned my advice and I've never given you a reason. Don't question it now. Take the job. Take the money. Take your rightful place as the star that you were born to be."

"What about Xavier?" Danielle asked.

"What about him? He's not going anywhere," Michelle said, as if he were a nonissue. "Come on, Danielle. Do you really think you would be happy running a little boutique for the rest of your life?"


"Danielle?"

So engrossed was she in her thoughts that she didn't hear Elaine calling her name. "I'm sorry. I must have spaced out."

"You've been doing that quite a bit these last few days."

Danielle couldn't deny that. She'd messed up two special orders and had forgotten to send a customer's dress out for alterations. If it wasn't for Patricia catching the mistake, the client would have had nothing to wear to her husband's retirement party.

"Anything you want to talk about?"

Being fairly tight-lipped about her plans for the store, she didn't want to share too much until she had all the details worked out, but Elaine had become a good friend and mentor. "Actually, there is."

After Danielle told her story, Elaine sat quiet. Finally, she said, "A half million for about three months' work. Not bad."

"I know," Danielle admitted, thinking about her last

paycheck. "Not to mention the amount of publicity the store would get."

Elaine hadn't known Danielle that long, but in the short time they'd been in each other's lives, she had seen her grow, mature, attempt to learn a business, and fall in love. With so many tough decisions ahead of her, she needed to decide what she wanted to place the most value on. "You're saying it's the money and the publicity that's most important to you?"

When it was phrased that way, Danielle didn't know how to answer. "It just seems like this is the chance to get everything I want."

"Let me tell you a story."

Danielle listened intently as Elaine relayed the story of how she came to own Sara's Closet. Never having pegged her as an attorney, Danielle was fascinated by her family history, her pursuing a career she really didn't want, and then finding joy and peace in buying this store.

"You see, Danielle, I was making everybody happy— instead of myself. Once I decided to focus on what I wanted, it made all of my other decisions easy."

Danielle nodded in understanding.

Elaine continued, ignoring the customer that walked into the store. "When you first walked through these store doors and handed me your application, I could not have imagined that you would be a fit."

Danielle cracked a smile, remembering that day she tried to explain what she had written on her application.

"A former rich model? It had disaster written all over it. However, these past few months have shown me that we are more alike than different.

"We each had our own careers, thinking we knew exactly what we wanted. But when the feeling of peace and joy leaves you, you start to wonder how you're going to spend the rest of your life doing something you're beginning to hate. That's when you know it's time for a change."

"What would you do?" Danielle asked.

"Just ask yourself two questions. Do you want what you put in that business plan? Or have you been fooling yourself all this time, trying to convince yourself that you didn't need the fame because, at that time, it wasn't available to you?"

"I've been asking myself those same questions."

"That's the person you want to get your answer from. Your friends and family mean well, but I advise you to discount everything they've said. Make this decision on your own. Remember, Michelle wants you to do the show because she thinks she's giving you what you want. Fox wants you to do the show for the ratings and the money. But what do you want? If you did the show on their terms—why would you be doing it? And can you live with those reasons?"

Before Danielle could respond, a customer came to the counter and Elaine gave her her full attention.

Later that evening, Danielle opened the oven door and tried to gauge whether the food was ready or not. The instructions said to bake for thirty minutes, but you could never be sure whether it would be enough time or too much time. Never one to feel at home in the kitchen, she thought of this attempt at cooking as her way of welcoming Xavier back. It was also a way to help her get up the nerve to have the conversation with him that could no longer be avoided.

Avoiding Michelle's calls had not been easy, but she couldn't give her her decision until she shared it with Xavier first. Michelle's last message said that the paperwork had arrived and she could either FedEx the documents or Danielle could come to New York and they could celebrate the occasion in style.

Setting the table in the dining room, she thought it would be nice if they ate by candlelight. She only hoped the effort she was putting into this evening would make the conversation that much easier to have.

Just as she was pulling the bread out of the oven, she heard the door open.

Excited to see him after being apart, she practically ran to him, arms wide open. "Hey, baby. I missed you so much. I even ventured into the kitchen to cook for you. I'm sure my lasagna won't be as good as yours, but at least I tried."

Giving him a playful kiss on the lips, Danielle stopped talking when she realized he wasn't responding to her. Taking a closer look in his eyes, she dropped her hands to her side. "What is it?"

Dropping his bags in the small foyer, he walked past her without so much as a hello.

Following him, she found him in the living room. Having just gotten off a four-hour plane ride, he obviously had opted for comfort by wearing a sweat suit and tennis shoes.

"What's the matter?"

"You tell me," he said, pacing in front of the fireplace.

"What are you talking about?"

Stopping briefly, he turned to her, staring her directly in the eyes. "I'm talking about being honest with each other. I'm talking about putting us first."

Danielle didn't respond, but instead tried to figure out what he was talking about. Had he heard something about the show?

When she didn't answer, that only incensed him more. "You were real busy this week while I was gone. No time to talk. Most times my calls went to your voice mail. Just couldn't quite find the time to get back with me."

Danielle opened her mouth to explain.

"Save the excuses, Danielle," he said, not giving her a chance to speak. "Did you think I wouldn't find out? Did you think no one would tell me? It's *my* show."

"I wanted to tell you, but I didn't know what to do," Danielle said.

"Oh, that's classic, Danielle," Xavier said sarcastically.

"What are you talking about?"

"Only thinking of herself. Only worrying about her little part of the world."

"That's not true," she argued.

"Isn't it?" he challenged. "Why didn't you tell me they offered to buy the show? Why didn't you tell me they wanted to push me out?"

"I couldn't decide."

"That's my point, Danielle. We're supposed to be in this thing together."

"Michelle said there was no negotiating on the production of the show."

Xavier laughed cynically at the situation. "You don't get it, do you?"

"What?"

"I'm not talking about business—I'm talking about us. We're supposed to be in this relationship together."

"Xavier, I—"

"If you weren't interested in talking to me about it when you found out, I'm not interested in talking about it with you now."

Danielle started to get angry at how he was treating her. All week, she had been racking her brain about what to do, contemplating giving up money, fame, and a television show for him, and this was how he wanted to act? "What the hell was Layla doing in your hotel room?"

The question caught Xavier off guard and he didn't respond right away.

"That's right. I called your room the day I found out to tell you about it, and that little trick answered your phone. I believe you were in the shower."

"Are you accusing me of something?" Xavier asked, feeling anger rise in him.

"I'm just asking a question," Danielle answered flippantly. "Don't try to turn this around. We are talking about the fact that you were faced with a major life decision and you didn't come to me. You left me out in the cold. What does that say about our relationship?"

"I warned you about Layla. I told you she was going to try to get her claws into you. Obviously you didn't heed my advice, since she's been all up in your room while you guys were out of town."

The look on his face was classic. He'd had no idea she knew.

He ignored her questions about Layla. "Are you going to take the show and go to New York?"

"Are you going to explain why the host of your show was answering your phone?"

They both stared each other with anger blazing in their eyes. Neither made a move or said a word.

Danielle walked past him and picked her purse up off the couch before heading to the front door. He didn't try to stop her.

"Enjoy your dinner," she yelled back at him before slamming the door.

Danielle sat in her car fuming with anger. How dare he question her commitment to this relationship? If anyone should have given her credit for all that she had accomplished this past year, it should have been him.

After putting up with being broke, out of work, and his family, he should have been more than understanding about the current plight she found herself in. Taking her cell phone out of her purse, she dialed Michelle's home number. If there was ever any doubt of what decision she was going to make, it had become abundantly clear to her in the last ten minutes.

Michelle answered on the second ring. The discussion was short and to the point. It didn't last more than two minutes.

Tanya was in the living room putting ribbons on minisize bottles of champagne inscribed with her and Brandon's names, along with their wedding date, when Danielle breezed in, cursing to the air.

Sitting across from her sister, she picked up one of the ribbons and started helping.

Tanya waited several seconds for her to calm down from whatever had her obviously in a tizzy. "Shouldn't you be sharing dinner with your man right about now?"

"There is no dinner and there's definitely no man."

Finishing another bottle, Tanya gently placed it in the cardboard box with the others. "Anything you want to talk about?"

"No," Danielle said, messing up the first ribbon, untying it, and starting over.

Tanya continued working without talking.

"You know how much I agonized over this decision about the show and going to New York?"

"I know," Tanya said, figuring she'd start talking when she was ready.

"It kept me up at night. It occupied my thoughts during the day. I didn't take this situation lightly."

"No, you didn't."

"Then why is he penalizing me for taking time to think about it?"

"By *he*, I guess you mean Xavier."

Danielle replayed the entire conversation word for word for her sister. "So tell me, why is he so mad?"

"Why didn't you talk to him about the show the day Michelle called you?"

"I told you, I was waiting for him to come back so we could talk about it in person."

Placing another bottle in the box, Tanya reached for another ribbon. "But you called him right after you talked to Michelle, to tell him."

Danielle's ribbon didn't cooperate again, and she decided to set hers to the side and watch Tanya. "Well, we know how that call ended up."

"Layla answered the phone," Tanya said.

"Is there a point you're trying to make?"

"All this time, you've tried to act like you weren't the least bit bothered by the fact that she answered your telephone call."

Picking up another ribbon to try again, Danielle declared, "Xavier is not cheating on me."

"Oh, I've seen you two together and I agree," Tanya said truthfully. "That man is completely in love with you. But that's not what I'm getting at."

Danielle gave up on the ribbons, and stopped trying. "What are you getting at?"

"It's OK, Danielle," Tanya said. "You've tried so hard this past year to show everyone that you're not the same person you used to be. But you know what? You can still be a little spiteful. A little petty every now and then. We all are at some point. You just can't let it ruin your truly important relationships.

"You didn't want to have it out with Xavier about Layla, because you trust him, but a part of you was really annoyed that somehow she had finagled herself into his room—you didn't do anything about it for fear of being seen as the bad guy, the petty one, the overreactor. Add to that to the fact that Xavier, for whatever reason, let her in his room and you decided not to tell him about the call from Michelle."

Danielle started to deny it, but Tanya cut her off.

"Why didn't you just call him back? Why didn't you leave a message on his cell? You had ample opportunity to tell him something you had already planned to tell him. The only thing that changed your mind was Layla."

"Well," Danielle said, finally admitting that the incident with Layla bothered her more than she let on, "he should have volunteered the information about why she was there."

"And you should have volunteered the information about the television show."

Tuesday morning, Patricia and Elaine were planning the final touches on Danielle's going-away party. Customers and vendors were coming out on Friday afternoon to wish their favorite sales clerk good luck with her new adventure. Later that night, she would attend Tanya's rehearsal dinner and watch her say her vows the next day before taking the train on Sunday to start a new part of her life.

Even though it was Danielle's day off, she was in the back of the store, arranging a section of summer casual wear. Elaine had offered to give her the rest of the week off to give her time to get ready to move, but Danielle declined the offer. With that much time on her hands, the only thing she would do would be to spend her time thinking about Xavier.

She hadn't heard from him since the night they'd argued. After her conversation with Tanya, she realized that in her effort to make sure that Layla wouldn't come between them, she allowed her to do just that. Looking back, she'd done exactly what Tanya said, and it cost her dearly.

"Danielle, can you come to the front for a minute?"

Putting the last set of blouses on hangers, she moved to the front to see what Elaine needed. She was staring out the front window, and Danielle followed her gaze. Across the street, illegally parked, was a black Benz with a very attractive man standing in front of it.

"I'll be right back," Danielle said, trying to sound casual.

"Take your time," Elaine said, unable to hide her smile.

Danielle hadn't been too forthcoming with what had happened between the two of them, but because she was leaving and hadn't stopped moping since she made that decision, Elaine knew that things weren't working out.

"What do you think?" Patricia asked Elaine as they watched her walk out the front door.

"I think they'll both be miserable without each other."

Going against the light, Danielle trotted across the street. As mad as she had been at him, she couldn't control the butterflies of excitement that swirled in her stomach at the idea of being with him again—even if it was in the middle of a major street. Obviously not going to any business meeting, he had on a pair of shorts and a polo shirt.

She stopped in front of him. With his shades, she couldn't see his eyes, so she had no idea what he was feeling or thinking.

"I wanted to stop by and give you this," he said, handing her an envelope.

Peeking inside, Danielle looked up in shock. "You're still going to give me the money?"

Xavier smiled at her choice of words. "Not *give.* Invest. I still want my piece of the pie." The double meaning of that statement didn't go unnoticed by either one of them, but both were too on edge to acknowledge it.

"I didn't think you would—"

"Hold up my end of the deal?" Xavier said, finishing the sentence for her.

"I just didn't think we'd be partners anymore."

"I offered this money to you because of the solid business plan you put together, not because I wanted something from you. Once those cameras go off and the show is off the air, you'll still have a business to run. That money will help keep you going until your profits come in. Of course, I'm back to being a silent partner."

"Thank you."

"No need to thank me. What happened between us doesn't change the fact that it's still a good business plan."

"And what happened between us?"

"You didn't trust me," he said.

"I know nothing happened between you and Layla."

"I'm not talking about me and Layla," he said, slightly frustrated that she still didn't understand his point of view. "You didn't trust me to support you."

"Xavier, I—"

"Good luck, Danielle."

She had no choice but to step back as he got in his car. Without saying another word, he drove down the street and out of her life.

Danielle walked back into the store and didn't say anything to either Patricia or Elaine. That told them all they needed to know: there was no reconciliation.

When the chimes buzzed, Danielle didn't even turn around. She suddenly didn't feel like working. Deciding to take Elaine up on her offer, she planned to take the rest of the week off. Grabbing her purse from the back, she took one last look around the stockroom. Smiling, she remembered all the memories that had been created in the short time that Sara's Closet had been a part of her life. The talks with Elaine, the lunch breaks with Patricia, and that one passionate moment that almost happened with Xavier. To this day, she blushed every time she thought about it.

Danielle was moving through the store when she felt a hand on her arm.

"Please say it isn't so. You're not really leaving us, are you?"

Danielle gave Mrs. Lucas a warm smile and a quick hug. "I'm afraid so."

"My husband is really going to miss you."

"Your husband?"

"He's loved every outfit you've picked out for me. Says I've been looking ten years younger lately."

Danielle remembered that first day when Elaine had all but written her off. If it wasn't for Mrs. Lucas and her willingness to let Danielle dress her, things might have turned out very differently. It was only fitting that the last customer she serve be her. "What are you shopping for today?"

"We're going on a dinner cruise—early evening."

Setting her purse to the side, Danielle linked arms with Mrs. Lucas. "Have I got the look for you!"

# Chapter Twenty

Xavier heard the buzzer on the security panel and glanced at the clock. Six thirty. Danielle was probably on her way to the church for Tanya's wedding rehearsal dinner. Couldn't be her at the door.

It had taken every piece of strength to drive away from her that day. He loved her with all his heart, but she couldn't relinquish complete control. She didn't know how. How could they have a future if she wouldn't allow him to be there for her? That had been her problem in the past, and it was her problem now.

He couldn't have cared less if he produced the show or not. What was important was her happiness and success. But she didn't give him a chance to show that to her. She took that away from him.

The buzzer sounded again and he pushed the button to open the door. A few moments later, Reggie entered his condo and took a seat on the sofa.

"What do you want?"

"Shouldn't you be somewhere?" Reggie asked, leaning back, making himself comfortable.

"If I should, then why did you come over?"

"Because I had the strange feeling that you would be sitting here, looking stupid."

Xavier wasn't in the mood to have this discussion.

"Don't try to defend her, Reggie. She was wrong and you know it."

Reggie didn't respond, but instead, stared at his brother as if he was in the wrong.

"She should have told me," Xavier said.

"Agreed."

Xavier narrowed his eyes. Agreement was the last thing he would have expected from Reggie.

"And is that the reason you refuse to see her anymore?"

"What more do I need?"

"What kind of expectations did you have for her once you started seeing her again?"

"What are you talking about?"

"Did you expect her to never make a mistake? To never do something wrong?"

"Nobody's perfect," Xavier said, a little annoyed.

"But you expected her to be?"

"No, I didn't."

Reggie leaned forward to get his full attention. "This isn't about the fact that she didn't tell you something. This is about the fact that you thought she was going to choose her career over you again."

"You're wrong. It didn't matter to me what decision she made."

"Are you sure?"

Xavier didn't say anything as he contemplated his brother's words. He'd heard through the grapevine how the deal was supposed to go down. Danielle was in—he was out. Instead of the network contacting him, they'd contacted Michelle, figuring if they could secure the talent for the show, it would be that much easier to buy him off.

For the next couple of days, he'd kept waiting for Danielle to say something—anything. But instead, he got the runaround. Always on the go. No time to talk. The more she blew him off, the angrier he got. If she didn't plan to do the show without him, why didn't she want to discuss it with him?

"You keep harping on the fact that she should have trusted you," Reggie said. "You need to take your own advice. Maybe you should have a little more trust in her."

The group of about twenty-five sat around banquet tables laughing and talking. The rehearsal at the church had gone smoothly and Tanya and Brandon's wedding party and guests were enjoying dinner hosted at a historic mansion. Danielle tried her best to be in a festive mood. The music was lively, the conversation was good, and the soon-to-be married couple looked extremely happy. But she couldn't get it together. Each passing day that brought her closer to leaving for New York caused her spirits to drop a little more.

As the meal winded down, Danielle grabbed a glass of champagne and headed out onto the terrace. The sun was just starting to set and the gardens were filled with colorful flowers.

"How's my baby girl?"

Danielle smiled before turning around. Her parents had arrived in town yesterday, and with all the activities, this was the first moment she'd had alone with either of them. "Fine, Mama."

Mable Kennedy watched her daughter's expression and knew that was a big fat lie. "I understand a lot has been going on since you got here."

"I've told you about my job, my store, and the opportunity in New York."

"Things seemed to have really worked out for you," Mable said.

"Yes," Danielle said quietly. "They have."

"Then why do you look so sad? This is what you wanted, isn't it?"

Danielle stared at her mother and gave what she hoped to be a convincing smile. "Exactly."

"Danielle, your father and I have always loved you. Not because you were a supermodel, not because you were a sales clerk, not because you were rich, and not because you lost your money. We loved you because you are our daughter and you have a beautiful spirit. We are proud of you. You don't have to prove anything to us—or anyone else for that matter. You only have to be true to yourself.

"Now, I'm not sure why that young man is not at your side tonight, but you don't look happy about it. If you want things to work out in your professional career or your personal life, all you have to do is follow your heart. If by doing so you get fame and fortune—great. If you don't—that's great too. Success is not found in your bank account or by the number of fans you have. Success is measured by the peace and joy that you have in your heart."

Danielle hugged her mother tight, holding back her tears.

"I came out here to tell you they're about to make the toast. Are you ready to go back inside?"

"You go ahead, Mom," Danielle said, needing a few minutes to get herself together. "I'll be right in."

Looking out over the grounds, Danielle reveled in the peacefulness of the scene. She wished she could bottle it up and take it with her. Lord knows there were few gardens in the concrete world they called New York.

Her mother's words ran through her mind again. She used the same words as Elaine had. Peace. Joy.

"I should be intimidated talking to someone as beautiful as you, but I figure, since I'm so handsome, we'd make a fabulous couple."

Danielle didn't turn around right away, for fear that she was hallucinating.

"It worked before. I was hoping it would work one last time."

This time, Danielle did look his way. "Xavier, what are you doing here?"

"Apologizing."

"Xavier, you don't have to."

"Hear me out." Taking a few steps toward her, he reached out and held her hands. "When I found out that you knew about the deal and didn't tell me, I felt like you were discounting me—much like I felt years ago. I know that wasn't the case now, and I hope that you'll forgive me."

"I want to apologize, too," Danielle said. "I should have told you about the offer, but when I tried to call you and Layla answered the phone, I got all bent out of shape."

Xavier decided to come clean. "We switched rooms."

"What?"

"You know how divas can be," Xavier told her, nudging her teasingly. "My suite was larger and had a view of the pool. She demanded it. I gave it to her. I didn't have a chance to call you. When you called the room, she must have been the one getting ready to take a shower, because I was nowhere near her."

Danielle set her glass down and wrapped her arms around him. "I love you, Xavier."

"I love you, too."

The next morning, Tanya's house buzzed with excitement as the women got ready for the big day. When the limos arrived to take them to the church, Tanya held Danielle back while the others went outside.

"You look beautiful, Tanya," Danielle said. The strapless A-line dress was handbeaded with a matching veil and train. The dress was fit for a queen.

"In all the excitement, I forgot to tell you that a FedEx package came for you while you were getting your hair done this morning. It's on the kitchen table."

"I'll get it later," Danielle said. "We've got a wedding to get to."

"It's from New York," Tanya said.

Michelle had promised to FedEx the contracts as soon as she got them. "It will be here when I get back."

Tanya wasn't sure she was hearing her sister correctly. It wasn't like her to be so cavalier about anything that had to do with her boutique.

Danielle headed for the front door. "Come on, girl. Let's go get you married."

As Danielle took her spot at the altar, she realized how blessed she was. A family who supported her. An employer who gave her a chance when no one else would. A man who loved her. That's what she had here.

What did she have in New York? She searched her mind for one thing that would give her comfort. Not even the idea of Danielle's in New York gave her that feeling.

The bridal march began and Tanya and her father started down the aisle. The congregation stood and Tanya started toward Brandon and her new life. After she'd spent an hour on her makeup, the tears streamed down, ruining it all. Funny thing, she still looked gorgeous.

Twenty minutes later, the guests were introduced to Mr. and Mrs. Brandon Ware.

After what seemed like hundreds of pictures, they all headed to the reception. After the receiving line had been completed and the food was being served, Danielle went in search of Xavier.

Finding him in deep conversation with her mother,

she interrupted and stepped out on the terrace. "I need to talk to you."

The seriousness of her tone sent warning bells off in his head. "What's going on?"

She leaned into his ear and Xavier couldn't believe what he was hearing.

Monday morning, the bell on the door at Sara's Closet sounded and Elaine looked up from her paperwork. "Danielle! What are you doing here?"

"I'm here to work," Danielle said, walking behind the counter.

"But you're supposed to be in New York."

"Changed my mind," Danielle said, as if it was no big deal.

"What about your television show?"

"There won't be any show. I want a boutique. Right here in D.C. Not in New York. Not on national television."

"Why did you turn them down?"

Danielle stopped moving and turned to stare her mentor in the eyes. "Because it didn't give me peace and joy."

"Danielle," Elaine said, heading back to the stockroom. "Let's talk."

*Three months later*

The flurry of activity inside the store was an organized panic. Tanya and Christine worked at breakneck speed to get the last bit of merchandise on the racks. Natalie was at the front counter making sure the credit card machines were hooked up properly to the register. Xavier was busy moving empty boxes to the back room, and Danielle finished making coffee and setting out pastries.

The countdown had begun. In ten minutes, Danielle's would be open for business. After all the hard work, the day had finally arrived. Elaine, Patricia, and even Michelle were all on hand for the ribbon cutting.

It had taken a lot of sweet-talking to finally get Michelle over her disbelief that she turned down the offer from Fox. In all her years, she'd never had anyone walk away from a half million dollars. But once Danielle really thought about what she wanted, the choice was easy.

"Everything looks great, Danielle."

Danielle turned to the voice and gave a gigantic smile. "Thanks, Elaine. I'm so glad you could make it."

"Are you kidding? I wouldn't miss this for the world."

"How's life in Florida?"

"I love it. Seeing my grandchildren every day has been great."

Elaine took a walk around the store, shaking her head in approval. "I can't believe how much you've done. How much you've changed. It looks great."

"I couldn't have done it without you. How can I ever thank you for selling your store to me?"

"The peace and joy I see in your eyes is thanks enough."

Danielle reached for her hand. "I never could have done this without you. Everything you taught me will help me make this venture a true success."

"Hey, baby," Xavier said. "Sorry to interrupt, but it's time."

Everyone gathered out front and at ten o'clock on the nose, Danielle's officially opened for business. Between the previous customers of Sara's Closet and the marketing Danielle had done, there were actually a few customers waiting to come in.

"I hope you have something for me to wear to my annual Labor Day barbecue."

Danielle turned to the voice and gave Mrs. Lucas a hug. "You bet. Just follow me."

Twelve hours later, the last customer had left and the last sale had been made. Sitting in the storeroom, she counted her first day's receipts. "Not bad."

"That's good to hear, because your investor wants a return on his money."

Xavier stood in the doorway, looking just as tired as she felt. "I never knew retail could be so exhausting."

"But it's a good feeling," Danielle said, ready to do it all again tomorrow. "I can't believe I finally have my own store."

"Come here," Xavier said, pulling her out of the chair and into her arms. "I have another investment I'd like to make."

"I'm listening."

"Let's get married."

Danielle looked at him, wondering if she heard him correctly. "Is that the best proposal you could come up with?"

Hearing the teasing in her voice, he stepped back and reached right outside the door. He produced a picnic basket and a bottle of wine. Sitting on the floor, he pulled her with him. Opening the basket, he pulled out lasagna, Caesar salad, and bread. He reached in one more time and retrieved a small velvet case.

"Now, that's more like it," she said, reaching for the box.

"Uh-uh," he said, setting it aside. Reaching for her blouse, he started to unbutton it. "Not until I get a piece of your pie."

With the doors locked and no chance of anyone walking in, they pushed the food aside and finished what they'd started in the stockroom all those months ago.

Dear Readers,

I want to thank all of you for your continued support. I hope you enjoyed the latest book in my *Love* series. Danielle definitely had some serious soul searching to do before she and Xavier could find their ways back to each other.

As always, I would love to hear from you. I can be reached at www.doreenrainey.com or doreenrainey @prodigy.net.

Until next time . . .

Doreen

## About the Author

Doreen Rainey started writing when she discovered the wonderful line of Arabesque books in the late 1990s. A graduate of Spelman College, she currently resides in the Washington, D.C., area with her husband, Reginald. Doreen's other works include *Just for You, The Perfect Date,* and *One True Thing*.

Her award-winning *Love* series include *Foundation for Love* and *Can't Deny Love. Foundation for Love* received the EMMA Award for Favorite New Author and *Can't Deny Love* received the EMMA Award for Favorite Sequel.